Lock Down Publications and Ca$h Presents

MONEY AND DEAD HOMIES

UNBROKEN

I0679389

Written By
DERRICK L. SUMMERS

DERRICK L. SUMMERS

Lock Down Publications
P.O. Box 944
Stockbridge, GA 30281
www.lockdownpublications.com

Like our page on Facebook: Lock Down Publications
www.facebook.com/lockdownpublications.ldp

Stay Connected with Us!

Text **LOCKDOWN** to 22828 to stay up-to-date with new releases, sneak peaks, contests and more...

Like our page on Facebook:
Lock Down Publications

Join Lock Down Publications/The New Era Reading Group

Visit our website:
www.lockdownpublications.com

Follow us on Instagram:
Lock Down Publications

Email Us: We want to hear from you!

Chapter 1

"Tunk mothafuckas!" Uzi screamed, slamming the cards on the table, then proceeded to scoop up the pile of money off the table.

"Not again!" Cold said in frustration and threw his cards in.

"I told y'all niggas, I'm the best that ever did this shit," Uzi boasted. "As a matter of fact, Trap, let me get a half ounce of that sand."

Trap sold him a half ounce and Uzi immediately began to make lines on the table. He rolled up a hundred-dollar bill and sniffed a line up each nostril.

"It's your deal nigga, hurry up!" Cold said.

"Nigga, don't rush me to take your money," Uzi said, now geeked up from the cocaine.

The night was vibrant and the winning continue. Uzi sniffed the cocaine and talked shit all night. The liquor house hosted a small crowd and many became entertained by the four men playing cards. Cold had lost a little over a grand, but the money was the least of his worries. Uzi was suspiciously lucky tonight. Cold began to pay close attention to Uzi's hands every time he dealt. He was convinced that Uzi was dealing his hand from the bottom of the deck but wanted to be sure.

"Eighteen! Now catch that!" Uzi yelled, slamming the cards on the table once again.

Cold waited until the deal was back on Uzi. "Let's raise the bet to fifty dollars and a hundred dollars for tunk."

"Nigga, you ain't saying shit. Bet it up, and the deal is on me." Uzi exclaimed arrogantly just as Cold anticipated.

Cold took a sip from his drink and subtly observed Uzi's deal. Indeed, Uzi was dealing his own hand from the bottom of the deck.

"You cheating motherfucka!" Cold yelled.

"What the fuck do you mean I'm cheating? Nigga, you're just made because I'm taking all your money." Uzi said defensively.

Cold jumped up from the table and pulled out a .9mm, aiming it at Uzi. The people standing around the table instantly departed from the house.

"So what? You're just going to rob me for your money back? You better put that gun up before you get yourself killed up in this motherfucka! You know who the fuck I am. They don't call me Uzi for nothing, you little ass nigga."

Cold fired, piercing Uzi with bullets. The effect from the cocaine gave Uzi miraculous adrenaline. He jumped up and ran, screaming. Cold chased and continued to fire shots, penetrating bullets in Uzi's back until the clip was emptied.

"This nigga is killing me!" Uzi cried. He made it into the kitchen and stood against the sink, gasping.

Cold walked into the kitchen, reloading the gun.

"Please stop shooting me, Cold, just take the money. I'm already dead," Uzi pleaded and pulled the money out of his pocket, throwing it on the floor.

"This ain't about the money," Cold said, and emptied another twelve rounds, watching Uzi's body slump over and drop.

Trap had stayed in the house and watched, paralyzed by the whole scene. Cold turned and glared at him.

"I promise you I won't say anything," Trap stuttered. Trap was the only person that Cold knew from that neighborhood.

"Good!" Cold ran out of the house. Outside, everyone was gone. He hopped in the stolen car, got rid of it immediately, and went to a friend's house.

5

Boom! Boom! Boom! . . . Boom! Boom! Boom!

"Who is it?" answered a deep voice.

"It's Cold. Open the door!"

"What the hell do you want knocking on my door at 3 o'clock in the morning? Gina's asleep," the man said.

"Slick, just open the door."

"I got to go to work this morning, so take your ass on somewhere, Cold."

"I got some crack for you!"

There was a momentary silence, immediately interrupted by the clinking sound of the locks being unlatched. The door was finally opened by a toothless Slick, smiling. He stepped aside and allowed Cold to enter the house.

"You should've said so!" Slick said.

Cold extracted the crack out of his pocket and, as promised, gave some to Slick, then went to Gina's room.

Gina was Slick's daughter. She was ten years Cold's senior, but that didn't affect their carnal relationship. Their relationship was convenient for sex and business. Gina had been taught by Slick how to cook up cocaine and had, by far, out-mastered Slick and anyone else Cold knew. That made Gina a perfect commodity.

Cold took off his pants and shirt and softly slid in the bed beside Gina to avoid awakening her, then dozed off.

Two hours later, Cold was awakened by the nudging of Slick.

"Ahh, Cold!" Slick whispered.

"What the fuck do you want?" Cold whispered back angrily.

"Let me get some credit."

"Nigga, you woke me up for some fucking credit?"

"I'm about to go to work and make a hundred dollars. I promise I'll pay you back when I get home."

Cold got up out of the bed, grabbed his pants, and gave Slick some crack.

"Thanks, I'll see you later!" Slick ran out the door.

Cold stayed up and went into the kitchen. He opened the refrigerator and found that the only thing there on the shelves was a half jar of mayonnaise, an emptied pickle jar, and a box of baking soda. Disgusted, he closed the door back, grabbed a chair, and walked back down the hallway. He looked in the room at Gina; she was still asleep. *Good*, he thought, and placed the chair in the middle of the hallway, where overhead was a door in the ceiling that led into the attic. He retrieved a backpack and closed the door back. He replaced the chair and went into the bathroom and hopped in the shower. It was convenient that Gina was asleep, because Cold wanted to have things prepared before waking her up.

Unbeknownst to Slick, Cold had been using Gina a lot lately to cook up cocaine. He preferred for Slick to be absent because Gina was not at the top of her game when he was present. So last night, and like many times before, Cold had given Mr. Eddie two hundred dollars to keep Slick busy doing work around his house. Mr. Eddie was to keep a hundred and pay Slick the other hundred, and keep Slick occupied from five in the morning to at least two in the afternoon.

After the shower, Cold got dressed, went into the kitchen, and pulled out two paper bags from the backpack. One contained money and the other contained nine ounces of cocaine. He began separating the money in tens, twenties, fifties, and hundreds. With the format that he learned long ago, Cold counted with efficiency, counting every fifty twenty-dollar bills to equate a thousand dollars, and every fifty hundreds equating five thousand dollars. It came to the sum of forty-seven thousand five hundred and seventy dollars. He further separated the money into bundles of ten thousand, with the exception of one in five thousand, and wrapped each bundle with ceramic wrap, then placed them back in the paper bag. He scribbled 45 on the paper bag for future reference and placed the paper bag back inside the backpack. He retrieved two envelopes and divided the four thousand dollars from his pants into the envelopes, sealed them up, and placed them in his pockets.

Cold stashed the nine ounces of cocaine inside one of the cabinets underneath some pots and pans, grabbed the backpack, and quietly slipped out the door and jumped in his car.

Chapter 2

Cold's first agenda was to drop off the money. Over the years, he had been secretly stashing money in the attic of his grandmother's house. He entered the house and went to his grandmother's room. She was peacefully sleeping, and he quietly closed the door.

After stashing the money, he went into the kitchen and grabbed his grandmother's medications. Every morning, he would stop by or call and make sure that his grandmother took her medications. He took pride in caring for his grandmother. He appreciated the unconditional love that she had given him growing up.

After helping his grandmother consume her medications, he kissed her back to sleep and left to proceed to his next errand.

It was 6:00 a.m., and Cold had two more stops to make. He drove from the Westchester houses through Bradford Drive and hopped on Freedom Drive to enter I-85 North. He exited the interstate on Beatties Ford Road, picked up his cell phone, and called his baby mother, Andreka.

"Hello?" Andreka answered in a soft, raspy voice.

"Hey, I'm about to pull up."

"Okay!"

Andreka was accustomed to Cold's early endeavors, being very much aware of the lifestyle that he was living, but she loved him nonetheless. Cold took damn good care of her and their two boys. Andreka still worked and tried not to be too dependent upon Cold because if something was to happen to him, she wanted to be able to maintain her lifestyle.

Cold pulled up to Andreka's house and got out of the car. He was walking up to the door when Andreka opened it, standing in a T-shirt and panties.

Cold admired Andreka lustfully while licking his lips.

"Damn, girl, you look good." He hugged and squeezed her ass cheeks.

"Is that you or your dick talking?" Andreka asked teasingly, rolling her eyes.

"Both. Good morning, beautiful!" Cold said, now fully inside the house.

"Good morning to you too!" Andreka sashayed to her room.

Cold followed and watched as Andreka purposely threw her ass cheeks from side to side.

"So how are the kids?" Cold handed Andreka one of the envelopes.

"They're okay," she answered dryly, knowing damn well he just talked to them last night and saw them two days ago.

Damn, two days ago, her mind reminisced when Cold came over and fucked her brains out. Her pussy was getting wet just thinking about it. She laid on the bed, not even bothering to cover herself.

Cold walked out of the room and checked in on his two sons—Peter Jr. and Adrian, who were—ages four and two. Cold fought the urge to wake them up because of the long day ahead, so he closed the door and went back to Andreka's room.

"You're even more beautiful in the morning," Cold said.

"You think so?" Andreka asked seductively, laying on her back and opening up her legs.

"You're damn right I think so."

"Prove it!"

Unable to resist, Cold walked over to the bed and pulled her panties off and planted soft kisses between her thighs.

Cold considered himself the master pussy eater. He sucked on her pussy lips and plunged his tongue in and out of her pussy. Her pussy was wet and throbbing. He used one hand to penetrate her with his fingers and the other hand to spread open her pussy lips and concentrated on her clitoris. She rotated her hips in a slow circular motion. Passionate moans and quiet screams of ecstasy escaped her lips. Andreka tensed up, then shivered and jolted, and her juices began to flow heavy into Cold's mouth. He continued to lick and suck until her body finally went limp.

Cold got up, freshened up in the bathroom, and left Andreka laying in a daze.

Cold looked at his watch when he stepped out the door. It was 7:00 a.m. He had one more stop to make at his other baby mother's house, Andrea.

It still amazed him that fate had allowed him to have two baby mothers with similar names and qualities. He had cheated on Andreka and gotten Andrea pregnant, which was the cause of him and Andreka's breakup.

Cold had taken Andrea out of the hood once their twin daughters were born and with a promise that she would get her life together. Cold taught Andrea how to manage and save money and set the foundation to the path for her to succeed. Andrea was still hood, but she was wise enough to take advantage of the opportunity and get her CNA license. Cold also offered to pay to further her career in nursing. She was currently working at *Carolina Medical Center* for the past two months, and to show his appreciation for her accomplishment, Cold had purchased her a three-bedroom house.

Cold took Beatties Ford Road down to West Trade Street and hopped on I-77 Southbound. Ten minutes later, he got on West Boulevard and called Andrea.

"Hello?" Andrea answered in a clear and sexy voice, softly spoken like Stacey Dash, a trait that attracted Cold.

"I know this is you, Cold," she yelled with an attitude after seconds of not getting a response.

"Oh, yea, what's up?" Cold said, coming out of his aroused thoughts.

"I'm about to leave for work."

"I thought you didn't have to work until 9:00 a.m.?"

"I switched shifts with this other girl this week, so I'll be going in at 8:00 a.m."

"Give me a minute before you leave, because I'm about to pull up and give you something."

"Well, hurry up, because I have to drop the kids off at daycare."

"Alright, I'll be there in five minutes."

When Cold arrived at Andrea's house, she was already waiting in the car. The twins, Jessica and Jelissa, were both asleep. Cold opened up the back door and kissed both of his baby girls, then closed the door back. He leaned in the window and handed Andrea the other envelope and kissed her on the cheek. He dropped his hand and massaged between her legs.

"We don't have time for that." She moved his hand.

"Hopefully later?"

"Maybe. I'll think about it."

"You better put on your seat belt," Cold demanded before Andrea pulled out of the driveway.

Chapter 3

Cold made a stop at Bojangles and ordered some breakfast biscuits, coffee, and orange juice and arrived back at Gina's house at 7:30 a.m. The time was perfect. He retrieved the package that was stashed in the kitchen cabinet. Gina was still asleep in the room. Cold woke her up and gave her some biscuits and orange juice.

"I got some work for you to do when you finish eating."

"Okay, but I want to take a shower first."

"That's cool."

Cold left the room and went into the kitchen. Gina got up and ate the biscuits, then went into the kitchen where Cold was sitting and eating.

"Give me about fifteen minutes."

Cold couldn't help but admire Gina's ass as it swayed away from. While Gina went to take a shower, Cold rolled up a blunt and pulled out everything Gina would need to cook up the cocaine. He walked towards the room when Gina emerged from the bathroom wrapped in a towel that covered her breasts and exposed half her ass cheeks. The kush was in full effect, and so were his hormones.

"Damn, Gina!" Cold mumbled with glassy eyes of lust.

Smiling, Gina grabbed Cold's hand and pulled him into the room. She let the towel drop, exposing her nakedness, then sat on the edge of the bed. Cold gave no resistance. Gina pulled down his pants and stuck his dick in her warm mouth.

"Damn, nigga, I love this big ass dick!" she said between slurps.

Cold smoked on the blunt and rolled his head slowly from side to side, enjoying the sensation. He grabbed the back of Gina's head and forced his dick deeper in her mouth with short, hard, and fast pumps, which caused her to choke a few times.

Ten minutes later, Cold took off his clothes and grabbed a condom from his pocket. He climbed between her legs and slowly inserted his dick inside her wet and pulpy pussy and went on to deliver long, hard, and fast strokes. He wasn't in the mood to make love to the pussy. He just wanted to fuck and beat the pussy up.

Gina screamed her lungs out. Cold fucked her in every position they could think of. Her pussy was wetter than a white-water river. She had so many orgasms she stopped counting after the seventh one. Gina's ass was perfectly shaped. Cold squeezed her hips tight while fucking her from the back, and when they switched to the backwards cowgirl position, she rode his ten-inch dick like a champ.

Gina had that bomb ass pussy, and she knew how to put it on Cold just right. They got finished and laid in the bed. They had fucked for about an hour. Cold knew he was behind schedule, but what did it matter? He was his own fucking boss.

Still a little exhausted, Cold got up out of the bed, went to the bathroom, and cleaned himself up. Gina followed upon his completion. Once dressed, they made their way into the kitchen to begin the task.

Cold pulled out the nine ounces of cocaine and poured the substance on the table and separated a few lines to the side. He rolled up a bill like a straw and passed it to Gina, who sniffed the lines up each nostril.

"Damn! This is some good shit!" Gina said, feeling the impact immediately from the drug.

After years of hustling, Cold had finally gotten the break that so many dope boys strive for—a connect with 90% or better of pure cocaine. He had driven all the way to Florida to pick up five kilos for ninety thousand, and the risk was worth it.

The move came when Cold's cousin Marco traveled from Riviera, Florida to visit him last month. Marco had brought a little recreational cocaine with him. The product was grade A, and Cold wanted it. Marco was connected with some Colombians, which piqued Cold's interest. Cold's intentions were to purchase a half kilo because he usually only copped nine ounces at a time from his plug in Charlotte. But when Marco spoke on prices, Cold's avarice burned, hearing kilos were going for eighteen thousand. Cold was tempted to tell Marco to get him ten. Hell, he was paying ten thousand eight hundred for nine ounces.

Cold listened attentively to Marco talk while concluding to no longer deal with his connect in Charlotte. He didn't expose to Marco the prices he was currently paying, nor did he act surprised when Marco mentioned the prices.

"Keep your composure and never expose your hand — a lesson Cold had learned early and mastered well."

"So will the cocaine always be high quality?" Cold had asked.

"I guarantee it 100%!" Marco replied like a salesman ready to close a deal.

"I want to do business only with you. The money is guaranteed. I trust you and only you. I don't want to meet anyone. I don't want people to know that you're dealing with your cousin. I don't want to talk on the phone about business. You will always know ahead of time what I want."

"I wouldn't want it any other way."

"Good! Let's start off with five kilos."

"Damn, Cold, you're moving that much work?"

"Look, I just want to try out these five kilos, and if or when I need more, you will be contacted. Now let me lay out some laws on how I want us to operate. First, the only words . . ."

15

At the age of twenty, Cold stood at five-nine and a hundred and ninety pounds. He was light brown-skinned with an athlete's physique. He was calculated, ambitious, and had a mind well beyond his years, which is what distinguished him from many others. He was born Peter Franklin and acquired the street name "Cold" because of his serious demeanor and penetrating eyes.

Cold had begun hustling at the age of thirteen. He figured out early what he wanted out of life and became attentive and self-disciplined. He saved money the day he picked up his first pack. He watched and learned from other drug dealers—from the older ones, the ones his age, and even the younger ones. He learned from the crackheads and the cops. He watched the cops to see what they looked for that caused them to run up on certain drug dealers. The streets were his classroom, and he was determined to graduate at the top of the class.

Cold never thought that he had made it to the age of twenty avoiding jail by luck. It was by calculated steps. He believed that a person created their own fate—from the crowd they hung around, to the person they were fucking, and the places they hung out. He wasn't naïve to the fact that fate can get twisted. He was prepared for that. That's why he took the initiative of paying a lawyer and a bondsman each a ten-thousand-dollar retainer fee.

For many years, Cold hustled hard and went to school after many sleepless nights. He had managed to save over two hundred and fifty thousand dollars just selling dimes and twenties in a seven-year span. He never sold any weight and dealt with loyal clientele. But now the game had changed. He was going to have to let a little more people in on his drug business. One thing for sure, he was going to have to make the wisest choices possible.

Chapter 4

It was about 1:30 in the afternoon when Cold and Gina finished cooking and bagging up the crack. Gina bought back thirteen ounces from the nine ounces, and they bagged up six ounces in dimes and twenties.

"Thank you, Gina," Cold said, preparing to leave.

"Oh, so you're just going to leave without giving me some more?" Gina asked.

"Just take some money out of the stash, and it's some coke right there on the table."

"I'm not talking about that." Gina walked over and grabbed his dick. "I'm talking about this."

Cold gave Gina what she wanted. He snatched her pants down, bent her over the kitchen table, and plunged inside of her. Gina threw that ass back at Cold as hard as he pounded his dick. She rotated and worked her ass in slow and fast motions, matching his every stroke.

Gina turned around, snatched the condom off, and wrapped her mouth around Cold's dick. She sucked and moved her head back and forth on his dick so fast, instantly he started cumming in her mouth. He nearly lost balance against the table from how hard she sucked the nut out of him. She swallowed every bit of his cum, not letting a single drop hit the ground.

"Now that's how a real bitch does it!" Gina wiped her mouth.

Cold cleaned himself up, grabbed everything, and drove to his Uncle Tim's apartment. Tim lived in South Side

Homes. He was partially disabled due to an amputated leg that was lost in a motorcycle accident many years back. Tim was twelve years older than Cold but taught Cold a lot about the streets. There was a time before the accident that Tim hustled and ran the streets hard. Even though Tim hadn't run the streets or picked up a pack in over a decade, his street IQ was still above average. He managed to give up the streets before falling victim to the prison system or the grave. Tim was a strong-willed man, but the amputation played a big part in his alcoholism. It covered the pain and self-pity he held inside.

Cold walked through the door. Tim was sitting in his wheelchair, pouring a glass of vodka. Tim's best friend, Jimmy, and his wife, Cheryl, were also there. Cold had known Jimmy and Cheryl for so long that he held them in the respect of an uncle and aunt.

"What's up, everyone?" Cold spoke.

"What's up, nephew?" they all responded back.

Jimmy immediately volunteered Cold into the conversation that had been interrupted by his entrance.

"Cold, can you please tell this woman that Prince is gay, because ain't no damn straight man going to be wearing heels, blouses, and cut-off booty pants!"

Not wanting to get involved in one of Jimmy and Cheryl's senseless debates, Cold submitted to keep quiet.

"You're just mad because your ass ain't Prince."

"That's a damn lie. Besides, if anybody wants to be Prince, all you have to do is dress up like a bitch, sing, and play a guitar."

"And Prince still gets more pussy than you, and more than what you ever had for that matter."

"You're crazy as hell if you think Prince done fucked more women than me. I don't care who he is or how much money he got."

"Well, damn, if you done fucked that many women, I may need to go and get my ass tested. They say HIV can live in you for ten years before you even know you got that shit."

"I don't have a mothafucking thing. I get tested every time I go to jail."

"Well, what about when your ass comes out?"

Cold couldn't help but shake his head at the two. This was how their everyday conversations went, and yet they were still together after fifteen years. Jimmy and Cheryl were good customers. They both had jobs, even though they did their dirt on the side.

Cold pulled out two twenty-pieces of crack and laid them on the table, bringing their conversation to a halt.

"I want y'all to tell me how this product is."

Jimmy and Cheryl got their stems out and went to work with the brillo and crack. The first hit was intensified. Their bodies became paralyzed, stuck in a wide-eyed daze, mouths twitching, words refusing to escape their lips. They finally came down off the high and were able to speak.

"Damn, Cold!" were the only words that could be spoken by the two.

Once Jimmy and Cheryl finished smoking, Cold got down to business.

"I asked that y'all meet me here because I want to offer y'all an opportunity to work for me bagging up my product. So are y'all willing to work for me?" Cold asked.

Each one agreed.

Cold pulled out seven ounces of the crack that Gina and he had not bagged up, along with a scale, and pushed it to Tim.

"I want you to weigh half in point twos and the other half in point fours," Cold told Tim.

He handed Jimmy and Cheryl a box of sandwich bags and pulled out a box of latex gloves.

"Don't get the sticky fingers," he immediately warned Jimmy and Cheryl. "I have some crack set aside for y'all for when anyone needs to take a break."

"Well, do you have a hit that'll last from the time we start to the time we finish? Hell, I'm jonesing and twitching just looking at all this crack," Cheryl said with her repartee.

But Cold was serious.

"If you feel that you can't handle the job, then walk away right now. I will respect your honesty before your disloyalty." Cold paused a moment before continuing. "If I can trust y'all with helping me with this, then I have big plans for the ones I can trust. I understand that y'all smoke, Jimmy and Cheryl. That's why I'm giving y'all the benefit of the doubt. I want us to work together as a team. I'm going to help y'all balance your habits. You won't have a reason to steal from me, so don't get greedy. You will be more than taken care of—not only with crack, but with money. Does everyone understand?"

Each one affirmed their understanding.

"And for you uncle Tim—your wages, we'll discuss amongst us two."

Tim just nodded.

Cold wanted to trust Jimmy and Cheryl. Each test would expose them to a life they couldn't have dreamed of.

They began working—cutting, weighing, and bagging up the crack. They kept all the point twos and point fours separated. After three hours and about four or five breaks, they completed their task.

"I have one more thing to do before I'm finished with y'all."

Cold poured out the bags of crack on the table and started counting, keeping the point twos and point fours separated.

"Do you need some help?" one of the three asked.

"No, I'm good," Cold responded without breaking count.

When he finished counting, he looked at each one of them.

"Welcome aboard."

"With my count—making all the point twos worth ten dollars and point fours twenty dollars—I have a perfect number that equals nine thousand and eight hundred dollars on the head. That's from exactly seven ounces, which was one hundred and ninety-six grams."

They all looked perplexed, like Cold had just spoken another language.

"Cold, all I heard was a bunch of numbers. Hell, you lost me after the first point. You're going to have to break that shit down. You know I smoke too much damn crack to be trying to work my brain like that," Cheryl proclaimed with an expression that showed she was dead ass serious.

Seeing that they all emulated the same expression, Cold responded, "Basically, we're going to be a very prosperous team."

They all smiled, but this showed them that Cold was very intelligent and thorough.

Cold reached in his pocket and pulled out five hundred dollars and split the money between Jimmy and Cheryl, and gave them each a hundred dollars' worth of crack.

"Uncle Tim, I'm going to get you straightened out later."

Tim just nodded.

Jimmy and Cheryl departed not too much longer after they finished bagging up. Cold wanted to talk to Tim privately because there were some things that weren't going to be discussed or involve Jimmy and Cheryl.

"Uncle Tim, I have a little more responsibility I want to give you if you're willing to accept it?"

"What is it?"

"I want you to hold the product here."

"That's not a problem, but that means no business will be conducted here."

"I agree with that, but what you saw today is only a small portion of what we're going to be dealing with. I don't want

Jimmy and Cheryl to know that you're keeping the product here."

"How much are we dealing with?"

Cold trusted Tim more than anybody, so he was completely honest.

"I'm going to bring what I can handle for the week, but right now I have five kilos—well, subtract nine ounces."

"Damn, nephew, who are you working for?"

"I'm not working for anyone. I just want to show you how serious my business is."

"Listen, nephew, it doesn't matter if you're selling five grams or five kilos, the game is always serious. Because just as there is a person that will kill you for five kilos, there's also one that will kill you for five grams. Let me explain something to you. This game is like a game of poker. The difference is that you're gambling with your life. Don't make this game a long-term career, because like poker, you have to know when to fold and walk away. You already have the street's biggest enemy against you—and that's the government. I'm telling you right now, nephew, I'm not staying for the long run. Now, if you want to cut ties with me right now, then go ahead and do it."

Tim paused for a few seconds, allowing Cold to take heed to his words, then continued.

"Also, you don't have room for any mistakes, so you better put one hundred percent into this and—through the grace of God—hope that you make it out alive. I've seen a lot of my homeboys I grew up with die or end up in prison for a very long time. I'm going to give you my one hundred percent while I'm in it. But when I'm out, I'm out. Do you understand me?"

"I understand you, Uncle Tim, and I won't do anything to stop you."

That's why Cold trusted and respected Tim so much. Because of Tim's wisdom, Cold was grounded. Tim was always honest and outspoken with people—whether they could handle the truth or not—with no exception for Cold.

"Well, let's get back to business. How are you planning on moving and operating this amount of product?"

"I have a few plans."

Cold didn't want to expose his plan just yet.

"Well, I'm here for you, nephew."

"Thanks, Unk. I'm about to go and make a few plays. I'll be back later."

Cold got up and left.

Chapter 5

Cold already had a plan devised, and the quicker it was put in motion, the quicker the profits could be reaped. He walked around the dilapidated brick apartments of South Side Homes that were in desperate need of renovation. He brought along two ounces and blessed each crackhead he ran into with a free piece.

Cold was preparing the customers. With the history of dealing with crackheads, Cold was going to begin from the angle of using crackheads for runners. He had a few names in mind to bring on board

Calculating his moves, Cold maneuvered around South Side Homes, never staying in one spot too long. He made sure that it took approximately an hour to hand out enough crack to market his product.

Finally, one of the potential runners walked up. It was Earl, a crackhead but a damn good hustler. Cold pulled out a twenty piece of crack and handed it to Earl.

"What's this for, Cold?" Earl quickly pulled out a stem right there in the open and put the crack on it.

"I want you to try this new product!"

Earl was already putting fire to the stem, sizzling the crack and inhaling the smoke. Cold waited a minute before trying to talk to Earl.

"Damn, Cold, where did you get this?" Earl asked, coming down off his high.

"I want you to work for me, and only me, Earl, and I guarantee you it will be more of that product for you to smoke, and even some cash to go with it."

"With this type of product, I will sell my ass for you, Cold!"

"Listen to me, Earl. I'm coming to you because I know you have potential. The most important thing I want you to know is, never fuck over me. You will not lack crack to smoke as long as you do your job, which is what you do every day."

"Don't worry, Cold, I got you."

"First, I need you to get a few people for me. Can you handle that?"

"Just tell me who, where, and when."

Cold pulled out a piece of paper with all the names of the people he wanted and gave it to Earl. Earl looked over the list and nodded.

"Okay, I think I can find all of them, but Catdaddy got locked up last night."

"Earl, I don't need you to think you can find them. I need you to find them. So can you find them or not? Because I can find someone else who can handle any task I give them."

"Yeah, I got this!"

Cold pulled out fifteen twenty pieces of crack and handed them to Earl.

"I want you to give each person on that list a twenty to smoke, and since Catdaddy is locked up, find E-Lo. You keep the other five pieces and tell them that I want to meet with them all in an hour, and it's going to be plenty more where that came from. And, Earl, if you got plans on shitting me, don't ever step foot back in South Side because I will kill you."

Cold gave Earl the destination where to meet him with the entourage and walked off.

Cold stopped at his car and retrieved a backpack out of the trunk before going inside Tim's apartment. Cold got the two separate bags of crack from Tim and placed them in the backpack.

While waiting for the meeting, Cold rolled up a blunt of kush and poured a shot of vodka in a glass. He sat there quietly replaying a plan in mind. He and Tim didn't say many words to each other the whole time they sat there. Cold had actually acquired that habit from Tim. Tim was never the one to talk a lot, but when spoken, his words were well thought out and powerful.

Nearing the time of the meeting, Cold went into the bathroom and changed clothes. He put on an all-black khaki suit and black Timberland boots and tucked a 9mm Beretta on his waistband. He threw the backpack over his shoulder and exited the apartment.

Arriving at the destination of where the meeting was to take place, everyone was there that was on the list, with the addition of one person that Cold disapproved of, and that was Big Perp.

"Who told you to bring him?" Cold asked.

Earl pointed at Big Perp.

Big Perp spoke up first. "I invited myself. Is that a problem with you, Cold?"

Big Perp was a character that used aggressive behavior, along with his size, to intimidate people, but Cold was unfazed by his tactics. Cold decided to look past the reason of how Big Perp found out about the meeting and thought of the possibility of using Big Perp for his aggressive potential.

Cold addressed Big Perp.

"Listen here, first you were not invited, but since you're here, I believe I can use you. But let me make one thing clear, Big Perp."

He paused and stared Big Perp in his eyes.

"I'm running this show, so I'm making the fucking rules. If you can't handle that, then get the fuck on."

"Little nigga, who the fuck do you think you're talking to?" Big Perp stepped toward Cold.

In the quickness of lightning, Cold pulled out the Beretta and fired twice past Big Perp's head. Big Perp jumped back, his heart pounding with a look of shock twisted with anger.

"What the fuck is wrong with you, nigga?" Big Perp exclaimed in anger.

Cold spoke slowly and ominously while still aiming the gun at Big Perp's head.

"Listen to me carefully. If you want to work for me, then understand right now that I'm the fucking boss. You can walk away right now, or you can shut the fuck up and listen."

Big Perp stared at Cold and then looked around at all the faces around him.

"Okay, Cold, I'm down, but if you ever shoot that gun at me again . . ."

"I will kill you!" Cold interrupted. "And I will kill anyone of you whoever tries to cross me. Now, if you want to walk away, then do so now."

Everyone stood in silence, and not one person walked away. The thought of getting plenty of crack and making money relinquished their fear of getting killed. Cold reached in the backpack and pulled out eleven cell phones and handed each one of the recruits a phone.

"This is how things are going to work. I have my code, which is seven, programmed under my number into all the phones. Now, what I want y'all to do, one at a time, is call my phone right now, starting with you, Earl."

Earl called the number, and Cold programmed the phone number under the number one and continued the process with each person he pointed to. Cold then had everyone exchange numbers with one another and program the exact same code as he had. Cold gave everyone time to program their phones before he began his speech.

"Y'all need to remember who is who because I don't want absolutely any names ever spoken on the phones. I picked you guys to work for me because I believe that you are some of the best hustlers in Charlotte I know. I believe in you.

That's why I chose y'all, and I know that you all have potential. I guarantee you we will have the best product on the market in South Side Homes. You will not lack crack for the customers nor yourselves as long as you do your job. A very important rule I want you to remember: *never fuck over me or anyone that's standing in this circle.* If you ever feel the need to test me, I will not hesitate to kill you. I want y'all to keep everyone in this circle alert of what's going on in this hood. The code for cops is 'grandma is getting off the bus,' and state what street the cops are on. Now, as far as pay, you will receive twenty percent of your sales and three hundred dollars every Sunday."

Cold reached into the backpack and pulled out one of the bags of crack and gave each person five twenties.

"This is for you to do whatever you want to do with it. Hopefully, you use it wisely, like to get customers. You will also deal directly with me until I tell you otherwise. I don't want to meet any customers. With that said, are there any questions?"

"Yeah, can I get an advancement on that three hundred dollars?" Big Perp asked, getting a few giggles.

"Listen to me, Big Perp. You have one fucking chance to fuck up, and I mean for something as simple as fucking over a customer. Do I make myself clear?" Cold said solemnly.

"Yeah, whatever." Big Perp brushed Cold's words off.

"Is there anything else? If not, this meeting is over," Cold said.

Chapter 6

Cold departed from the entourage and made a phone call to his homeboy, Pree. Pree had gotten released from prison a week ago after serving a five-year sentence for manslaughter. Cold didn't want to rush Pree into anything, but he really wanted Pree to be a part of his team. He needed someone that people in the hood feared and respected, and who was also loyal. Cold had only encountered Pree once since he's been out and had not discussed any of his plans with him. Cold had welcomed Pree home with the gifts of a thousand dollars, a cell phone, and some clothes. Tonight, Cold figured it was the time to run the idea to Pree.

"What up! Who is this?" Pree answered after the second ring.

"What up! This Cold. Are you in the hood?"

"Yeah, I'm at granny's. What's up?"

"I'm about to come through and pick you up, I need to holla at you."

"Okay, I'll be waiting in the parking lot."

Cold got in his car and drove around to Fairwood Street in South Side Homes and pulled into the parking lot where Pree was waiting. Pree saw Cold pull up and hopped in the passenger seat. They gave each other dap, and Cold drove around the block to Benjamin Street and parked in a parking lot.

Avoiding the small talk, Cold got straight down to business.

"It's like this, Pree. You know that I don't deal with or trust a lot of people, but I believe I can deal with you and trust you. I know that you just got out of prison, so I will understand if you decline my offer. So what I'm asking is for you to come and work for me."

Pree let out a light chuckle.

"So you want me to work for you?" Pree sarcastically repeated the question.

Cold, knowing that it was a rhetorical question, allowed the silence to proclaim his seriousness.

"First of all, I don't work for anyone but myself," Pree said, pointing his thumb at his chest. "Because when the pressure come, niggas sing like opera."

"Real recognize real. That's why I want you to fuck with me. I promise you that you're going to make more money dealing with me than working for yourself or any other legitimate corporation, and I promise you that I will never cross you."

Pree sat silent for a second, collecting his thoughts. It was obvious that Cold was not the same kid he knew five years ago. Cold had grown mentally and financially over the years of his absence, and Cold displayed an aura of confidence and sincerity.

Before Pree's five-year bid, he and Cold didn't hang out much. They knew each other for almost their entire lives. They were never enemies nor really close friends, but they always had a mutual respect for one another. Pree always looked at Cold as a typical person in the hood, but just a little more discreet than others. Cold always looked at Pree as a wild cannon, but Cold respected that Pree was a man of his word and never fucked over anybody.

"It's like this," Cold interrupted Pree's thoughts. "I want you to work for me because I'm taking full responsibility, and I need everything to be run my way. Maybe you should take a few days to think about it?"

Just as Pree was about to comment, Cold's cell phone rang. Cold looked at the caller ID. It was code one.

"What up? . . . Okay, meet me at the basketball court."

He disconnected the call and turned to Pree.

"Do you want to take a walk with me?"

"Yeah, let's go!"

They met up with Earl by the basketball court. Earl had a fifty-dollar sale waiting in the parking lot. Cold gave Earl the crack and waited for him to return with the money. Cold was going to use this process until the rest of his plan progressed.

While waiting for Earl to return, Cold's cell phone rang again. It was code three, in which Cold gave his whereabouts. The same process took place with code three as with Earl, and Cold's phone continued to ring. Pree stood back and watched as Cold was setting something off.

"You see what's happening? This is a new epidemic. Not only do I have the best product in Charlotte, but I have the best prices, and I'm not selling any weight. This is just the beginning, and it's going to get better, and I mean much better. I just need people that I can trust. I need loyalty and honor, which is already in your blood, Pree. You didn't have to learn how to be loyal and real. Everyone's not ready to be a part of this opportunity that I'm presenting to you. I know that if you come aboard, you will put in one hundred percent."

Pree continued to listen and watch Cold. After about three hours, Cold made a surprising amount of over five thousand dollars. At that rate, Cold was going to have to cook up some more work tonight.

Cold was about to leave the block when he was approached by a man wearing a blue khaki work suit with an angry countenance. Cold had seen this guy a few times and was pretty sure that he smoked crack.

"Have you seen Big Perp?" the guy asked.

"Why? What's the problem?"

"That motherfucka ran off with my money. I gave him a hundred dollars thirty minutes ago and he still hasn't returned with my shit," the guy answered angrily.

"Was that your first time sending him out to cop for you?"

"No, I've been sending him out all night for me and he's been coming back with some of the best shit that I have ever smoked. Maybe the person he was getting it from ran out? I don't know, but I want my money back. I knew that shit was just too damn good to last. That type of crack doesn't last long, but I should've never trusted Big Perp's ass anyway."

"Listen, what's your name?"

"Oh, just call me Blue." He extended his hand to Cold.

"Do you have a number, Blue?" Cold shook his hand.

"Sure!" Blue recited his number as Cold logged it in his phone.

"Check this out, Blue. I want you to go home and forget about Big Perp. I'm going to have someone give you a call, and I want you to deal with him and only him." Cold reached in his pocket and pulled out two hundred dollars and gave it to Blue.

Blue couldn't believe it. "Okay!" He hurried off.

Cold called Earl to come and see him. When Earl arrived, Cold gave him three hundred dollars' worth of crack and Blue's number.

"I want you to smoke with him to make sure he is not the police. I also gave him two hundred dollars, so make the sales too."

"Okay!" Earl walked off.

Cold and Pree walked to Cold's car, neither saying a word. Pree wanted to see how everything was going to play out, because the more he watched Cold, the more his curiosity was piqued. When they got to the car, Cold noticed the big, burly figure of Big Perp walking down Baltimore Street, fading in and out of the shadow of the streetlights.

Cold placed the backpack in the trunk and trotted toward Big Perp, and Pree briskly followed along. They caught up with Big Perp just in time to see him cross the street, about to head through the back of the park leading to Remount Road.

"Yo', Big Perp!" Cold yelled.

"What up, Cold?" Big Perp stopped and turned.

"I'm glad I caught up with you. I need you to take some work to Brook Hill."

"I was just heading over there. Who do you want me to take it to?"

Cold continued walking and talking while leading Big Perp further into the path that cut through the park.

"Let me give you their number. You got your phone on you?"

"Yeah!" Big Perp went to pull it out.

When Big Perp looked back up, his heart had filled with dread and hopelessness. For the first time in his life, he was afraid. Cold had a 9mm pointed directly at his head.

"I told you, Big Perp, do not test me," Cold said through clenched teeth.

"What the fuck are you talking about?" Big Perp's voice cracked with fear.

"You know what the fuck I'm talking about. I told you not to fuck over me, my workers, or my customers, and you couldn't honor that for one fucking day. I told you what the consequences were going to be, and I can't go back on my word. My name is about to be branded out here, and I have to make sure it's respected."

Before Big Perp could utter another word, three consecutive bullets entered his skull, taking his life instantly. Cold grabbed the cell phone out of Big Perp's hand and walked off with a stunned Pree trailing behind, speechless.

When they got back to the car, Cold drove off. Neither said a word about what just happened. Cold pulled out his phone and called Gina.

"Hello?" Gina answered on the first ring, anticipating this call all day.

"It's about to be a long night."

"I hope it's pleasure!"

"Work!"

"Well, can you bring me something to eat, baby?"

"I got you, but it's going to be about an hour or so. Is Slick there?"

"Yea, he's here."

"Okay, tell him I'm going to need him tonight, and I will bring y'all something to eat." Cold hung up.

"I can drop you off wherever you need me to, and you can just walk away. If you need more time to make a decision, I can respect that, but as of now, I can't expose you to any more than what you have already seen, which is already too much."

All doubts had left Pree's mind.

"When do I start, boss?"

Cold's face controlled a serious countenance.

"Now. But first, I have to go over a few rules, which I know I won't have a problem out of you. Don't ever fuck over me, my employees, and my clientele. I need one hundred percent loyalty and trust, and I will give you two hundred percent in return."

Stopped at a red light, Cold turned and looked at Pree.

"Look at me, Pree. If you break any of these rules, I will not hesitate to kill you. Do you understand?"

"I understand completely."

Pree may have killed someone before, but he had never murdered someone in cold blood like Cold had just done and acted so calm afterward. The look in Cold's eyes told a story of a cold-hearted person that wouldn't think twice about taking his life if he crossed him, but they also gleamed loyalty and sincerity. This gave Pree an adrenaline rush and a strong feeling that Cold was about to take them to another level.

"Welcome aboard. We have a lot of work to do tonight," Cold said.

"Let's go. I'm on duty twenty-four hours a day," Pree responded.

Chapter 7

Cold stopped at a drive-thru fast food restaurant and ordered about fifty dollars' worth of food. He ordered hamburgers, chicken, fries, and soft drinks, then drove to Gina's house in Clinton Park. Before Cold and Pree could step out of the car, Slick was coming out of the house toward the car.

"What's up, Cold?" Slick said with a toothless grin.

"What's up, Slick? This is Pree." Cold introduced the men once they were completely out of the car.

Cold had Slick grab all of the food from the back seat and take it into the house while he went to the trunk to retrieve the backpack.

"Come here for a second, Pree." Cold gave him another cell phone from the backpack and a 9mm, then went into the house.

Cold's stomach was growling from the neglect of daily nutrients. The last meal he had had long deserted his stomach. This was pleasure to his stomach and soul, and the way everyone else was devouring their meal said that their asses were guilty of neglecting gastric nutrients as well.

Upon completion of their meal, Cold gave Gina and Slick the recruitment speech, and they agreed to hop on board, which it was not a doubt they would. Cold authorized Pree with the authority over the operation Gina and Slick would be conducting at their house, which was cooking up the cocaine.

Cold gave Slick a few bags of crack and Gina some cocaine and handed a brown paper bag to Pree filled with the currency that was accumulated prior to their arrival.

"Count that," Cold told Pree while rolling up then sparking up a blunt.

Cold got up and walked to the other room to make a phone call. After several rings, a low, raspy voice proclaimed their presence.

"Hello?"

"I need you to pull out two for me, and I'll be there in about fifteen minutes."

"No problem." The call disconnected.

Cold walked back into the kitchen and announced that he had to take a ride. The drive was punctual. The back door had been left unlocked with the package waiting on the table. Small talk was irrelevant, but it was considerate to acknowledge the person of his arrival. Cold walked down the dark corridor to the room.

"Thanks, I'll lock up," Cold announced into the room and left.

When Cold arrived back at Gina's house, everyone was sitting around the table talking. Cold's cell phone began ringing repeatedly, but he'd anticipated these calls from the runners informing him of the recent murder of Big Perp and awaiting sales.

Cold used the event to his advantage. With cops gleaming for evidence and information around South Side Homes, he took the initiative to cook and bag up two more kilos. Before they began, Cold rolled up a blunt of kush and inhaled the smoke that instantly relaxed his mind.

"Damn, Cold, did you get any cigarettes?" Slick asked.

"You know damn well I don't smoke cigarettes," Cold retorted. "Do you mind taking Slick to the store?" Cold asked Pree.

"Nah, I don't mind. I need to get me some cigarettes and beer anyway."

"Well, get plenty!" Cold handed Pree a couple hundred dollars.

As soon as Pree and Slick walked out the door, Gina got on her knees in front of Cold and pulled out his dick and wrapped her warm mouth around it. She tried to put every inch down her throat. Her head moved back and forth faster and faster.

"Damn, Gina, that feels so good!" This was a moment of pure relaxation. Smoking a blunt while getting some super head. The sensation was an adrenaline rush. His toes curled and muscles tensed just before exploding in Gina's mouth.

They cleaned up just before Pree and Slick walked through the door. Everyone had their vices that would relax them during the task. They were ready to begin the long night and day ahead of them. Cold and Gina pulled out the pots and the big Pyrex that they were going to use to cook up the cocaine. They were going to cook up to a quarter kilo at a time. While they were preparing the water, Pree and Slick were at the kitchen table breaking the rocked-up cocaine down into powdery form.

They were amazed at seeing that much cocaine. Pree was thinking that he was now in the big league, fucking with a major player. Slick was in crack heaven and wished that it would last forever. Gina was alertfully fearful. She understood the enhanced danger that comes when dealing with this amount of drugs. Gina had dated quite a few drug dealers in her past, so she knew the odds and consequences that came with the game. But Gina saw something in Cold that she had never seen in any of the drug dealers she dated or been around. Behind Cold's baby face was a controlled coldness and a deep intellect. What altered her fear the most was when Cold told them that if they ever crossed him, he would not hesitate to kill them. She took serious heed, but it was Slick she was worried about. Slick always tried to get over on someone every chance he got. She felt a little relieved when Cold told them that they would be paid and that their drug habit would be taken care of. The two kilos of cocaine reassured her, but Slick's greed was still unsettling.

Cold was testing Slick by allowing him to break down the cocaine with Pree. Gina caught on to the trap immediately, and she hoped that Slick was aware of what was going on and didn't try anything stupid.

"Cold, I know it's not my business, but we're about to bag up two kilos of crack in dimes and twenties. Now where in the hell do you plan on getting rid of this much shit?" Slick asked.

"Why? Do you have some places in mind?" Cold asked.

"I have a nephew that lives in North Charlotte on Peagram Street, and he's a real dude to fuck with. He's respected over there and he won't try to shit you," Slick said.

"Do you think he will operate like I want him to?"

"All I can do is let you talk to him."

"That's cool. Try to get in contact with him as soon as possible so we can set up a meeting."

Gina had started cooking up the cocaine—scooping, measuring, mixing, and stirring. Perspiration was pouring down her face. She was working over the stove like she was preparing a Thanksgiving dinner.

"To help out, I know this guy on West Boulevard that might fit in. We were locked up together and bonded inside, and when he got released a few months before I did, he used to send me money and write. I know that may not mean shit to you because you have never been locked up, but it shows a lot about a man's character and his word. In prison, he showed me nothing but loyalty. He did a ten-year stretch for a body," Pree said.

"Okay, get in contact with him and explain to him how I work. If he can respect it, then we can talk."

"I'll hit him up as soon as possible."

"That goes for you too, Slick. When you talk to your nephew, let him know how I operate, and if he can't respect it, I don't need him."

"I'll do that, but you have to remember the lifestyle I live, so I may not be as convincing."

"You don't have to convince him of anything. Just put the cards on the table—whether he's with it or not. If he's interested in taking a step, I will handle him from there."

"Say no more!"

Chapter 8

Their bones ached and their bodies were exhausted from the passing hours of cutting, weighing, and bagging. By twelve the next afternoon, they had managed to cook up both kilos, bringing back fifty ounces apiece. They bagged up a majority of one kilo in dimes, twenties, fifties, and hundred pieces.

Cold came to a stopping point and decided to wait and finish bagging up the other kilo and the extras later. He wanted everyone to get some rest and go meet up with their people later.

Due to the fact that the cops were hot in South Side Homes, Cold wasn't going to open up business for a few days. He was going to use the opportunity to get things in order. He decided to take the next few days to cook and bag up all the cocaine that's including the other two and three-fourths of a kilo that was put up. It also gave him time to talk to the people he needed to talk to.

Cold was not about to leave all this crack in the house with Slick. He feared the risk of riding with it but decided to dare the chance. South Side Homes was too hot to take the product to Tim's apartment, so Cold dropped Pree off at the Motel 6 on Clinton Road with the product.

Cold's first errand after dropping Pree off at the room was to a car lot. He bought a used Honda and told the dealer that he would be back later that night to pick it up. He then went and purchased forty prepaid phones and put enough minutes on them to last a month.

Cold left the phone store and drove to his grandmother's house to check on her and pick up some cash. He was glad to see that she was taking a nap. He grabbed forty-five thousand dollars out of the attic as quietly as possible. Prior to departure, he made sure that his grandmother had not been disturbed.

Smookie was a guy from Bradford Drive. Cold had grown up with him doing juvenile delinquencies. Smookie was the misfortunate one who got apprehended a few times but always kept his mouth closed about Cold, who was always fortunate enough to escape apprehension. Smookie was dependable and loyal—that's why Cold wanted to recruit him.

"What up, who this?" Smookie answered the phone.

"What up! This Cold!"

"What's popping?" Smookie got excited.

"I need to holla at you. Where you at?" Cold asked.

"I'm on Rowan Street!" Smookie answered.

"I'll be there in about one minute. I'm leaving granny's house now."

"Alright, you'll see me. I'm on the block."

Cold picked up Smookie and got straight down to business first, giving the speech about loyalty, honor, and death.

"I'm also going to give you two grand for a starting bonus if you work for me."

Smookie couldn't resist. Besides, two grand up front just to sell someone else's drugs? Hell, he just made more in one day than he made all week and with that, a free phone.

"I'm all the way in."

"I need you to get ten of the best runners over here and call me when you do, so we can meet up."

"Okay, bet that up." Smookie exited the car.

Finally, after completing his errands, Cold called Andreka.

"Hello?" she answered.

"I'm about to go to your house and get some sleep."

"Well, you better not bring any bitches in my house."

"I wouldn't do any shit like that."

"Whatever. Are you going to be there when I get home?"

"What time are you getting home?"

"About five o'clock."

"Yea, I'll be here. Bye."

"I'll see you later."

After a few hours of rest, Cold was awakened by slaps and yells.

"Daddy! Daddy!" Pete Jr. and Adrian screamed, jumping him with excitement.

Cold playfully slammed them on the bed—he was acting like the ultimate wrestler of the world. Every time he slammed one on the bed, he'd raise his hands in victory as if posing for the world's strongest man.

"Y'all better stop jumping on my bed!" Andreka walked into the room.

"Aw, you're a party pooper!" Cold playfully whined.

"Yea, you're a party pooper, Mommie," both sons whined in unison.

Cold jumped up and tackled Andreka on the bed. While he was holding her down, both sons climbed on top of her, trying to help Cold. Cold slapped the bed each time he counted. When he got to two slaps, Andreka managed to wiggle out from Cold's grip and push the boys off her. She climbed on all three of them at the same time and slapped her hands on the bed, counting to three real fast.

"Ding! Ding! Ding! I win, I win!" Andreka jumped up and did a victory dance. Then she mimicked like a broadcaster. "The new heavyweight champion of the world is Andreka Miller!"

"Aw, you cheated," Cold said.

"Yeah, you cheated, Mommie," the boys mocked.

"Y'all are just mad because y'all got beat by a girl."

"Since you're the winner, how about you order and buy some pizza?" Cold emphasized the word *pizza* to get the boys excited.

"Yeah, we want pizza! We want pizza!" the boys shouted together.

"I'm the winner, so you should be buying the pizza." Andreka had her hand on her hip, snapping her neck and pointing her finger at Cold.

"Well, I guess you're right, but you have to order it."

"Okay." Andreka left the room.

The boys showed and told Cold all the things that they had done and learned at daycare. He congratulated them on their progress with their drawings, numbers, and words they had learned. They then ran off into their room to play video games.

Cold looked at the time. It was a quarter past six, so he decided to call Pree.

"Is everything good with you?"

"Yeah, I'm good. What up?"

"I need you to pay for the room for a few more nights, and I'm going to have my people—Jimmy and his wife— come by and pick you up. I want you to take them to Gina's house and start working on the other half of the project we didn't complete."

"I got you!"

Cold then called Jimmy and told him what he needed him to do.

"The pizza should be here in thirty minutes, so I'm about to hop in the shower," Andreka said when she walked back into the room, then began to strip out of her clothes.

"Let me shower first."

"Oh, so you don't want to take a shower with me?" Andreka seductively removed her panties.

"You know I do, so how about we wait until the pizza comes and let the boys eat and give them their baths first. Then you and I can take a bubble bath together."

"Umm, that sounds good." Andreka moaned and climbed on top of Cold and planted kisses on his neck and ear. "So, can I get a quickie until then?" she asked. She slid her hand down his pants and massaged him.

"I got a feeling that you're not going to accept no for an answer," he said.

"You know I'm not."

Cold laid back on the bed and let Andreka pull off his clothes. She put him in her warm mouth and bobbed greedily, putting every inch down her throat. Minutes after the enjoyment of Andreka's sloppy wet head game, Cold pulled her mouth off him.

Andreka laid back on the bed and Cold climbed between her thighs. Her pussy was wet and pulsating when he penetrated.

"Oh my God!" she screamed, her body erupting in ecstasy.

"Damn, your pussy is good!" Cold whispered in her ear as he pumped faster with long strokes, in circles, harder back and forth, and side to side.

Andreka kept up with every stroke and motion, arching her back and grinding her hips. Cold pulled out and turned Andreka over on her stomach and tooted her ass in the air. He penetrated doggy style with hard pumps, and she threw that ass back with the rhythm.

"Umm, you're so nasty!" she screamed while looking back at Cold pounding her ass out. "Yea, baby! Oh Yea! Umm yeah! Fuck this pussy!" she continued to scream.

"Throw that ass back at me! Yeah, that's what I'm talking about!" Cold hollered back while pumping hard strokes and slapping her ass.

Cold pumped hard as he could for fifteen minutes straight, slapping ass, pulling hair, and choking non-stop, not missing a beat. Andreka wanted to ride, so they switched positions. She grinded her hips in circular motions, hopped up and down, and pumped her hips.

"Oh yes, Cold!" she screamed and began to ride faster and faster.

"That's what I'm talking about. Ride this dick girl!" Cold screamed, rotating his hip under her.

Andreka's body convulsed and the juices began to flow heavy from her vagina. She moaned louder and louder from the pleasure of her orgasm. It was only moments later when Cold felt the sensation erupting out of him. The explosion left both of them in an exhausted state of ecstasy.

As soon as Andreka rolled off Cold, they heard the sound of the doorbell and the kids came banging on the door to let them know the pizza was there.

Cold ate with the kids and helped them with their showers and gave Andreka that promised bubble bath, then departed to begin his night.

Chapter 9

Cold departed at 9:00 p.m. He pulled out his cell phone and began making calls. The first was to Pree.

"What's good? How are things going?" Cold asked when Pree answered.

"Good, everything's under control."

Content with Pree's progress, Cold's next call was to Smookie.

"What up? Have you gotten that team together?"

"Yeah, I'm ready. What's the next move?"

"Bring the team and meet me behind the apartments on Rowan Street in an hour."

"Okay, I'll be there."

Cold drove to the Motel 6 where Pree stayed and retrieved twenty thousand dollars' worth of the bagged-up crack.

On the way to meet up with Smookie, Cold stopped at a convenience store to get some gas. He was about to begin pumping the gas when a cream EXT Escalade pulled up to the adjacent pump with dark tinted windows and twenty-six-inch rims. At first, Cold didn't really pay much attention to the driver, and he wasn't a materialistic individual to be impressed by the vehicle.

When the driver exited the vehicle, Cold's initial thought was that the girl was beautiful, but when she began to amble towards the store, he was hooked. She was about five foot even with a fat ass and slim waist. She had the body of a stripper with a gap between her legs the size of a pool ball, and she was bowlegged as hell. She wore black spandex pants and strap stiletto boots with a tight tee shirt exposing her pierced navel and the small of her back. Cold actually categorized her as a stripper, or that she was fucking with a hustler, but decided to relinquish the shallow thoughts. He waited until she came back out of the store and got to her pump.

"Excuse me, Miss, but can you pump my gas?"

"What do you mean, can I pump your gas?" she mocked with much attitude at Cold's lame-ass line. "Shouldn't you be asking me to pump *my* gas?"

"That's what the typical man would ask, and then he'll ask your name and number and can he take you out on a date. Not me. I want you to pump *my* gas and ask *me* for my name and number and when can *you* take *me* out on a date." Cold was feeling himself.

"Damn, you cocky! So what make you think I want your name, number, or even consider taking you out somewhere?"

"Why not? Look at me, I'm just your type."

"Now what make your arrogant ass think *you're* my type?" she smirked, eyebrow arched up and a hand on her hip.

"Because your walk changed from when you walked into the store and when you walked out and noticed me. And you're still here talking to me," Cold said confidently and started his pump, putting it on automatic. He then walked over to her tank and started the pump in the same manner. "Okay, I'll meet you halfway. Now it's your turn. My name is Cold, and I'd rather give you a hug because that's more gentleman-like." He grabbed her hand and pulled her into his arms.

"Nice to meet you, Cold." She allowed him to give her a friendly hug.

"And likewise. So what do you do?" Cold released their embrace.

"I own an exotic dance club called *Privileges.* And what do you do?"

"I'm getting the keys to the streets."

"Is that right? So you're a hustler?"

"We're all hustlers if we're getting money."

The knob on the gas pump on Cold's car popped, indicating the tank was full. Privilege walked over to Cold's tank, hung up the pump, screwed the gas cap back on, and walked back over to Cold.

"Thanks!"

When Privilege's pump popped, Cold emulated her process.

"Thank you!" Privilege climbed into her ride. "Well, I would ask you for your number, but I don't think my man will like that."

"Don't worry, gorgeous. When you want to be crowned a queen, you'll find me." Cold hopped in his car and pulled away.

Cold drove to meet Smookie, being about fifteen minutes early. When he got on Bradford Drive, Smookie was walking down the street. Cold picked him up and began breaking down his process.

"I want you to pay each runner three hundred dollars a week on Sundays. They will also get twenty percent of what they sell—in crack or money. That's their choice. It doesn't matter to me. You'll get twenty percent of each pack that you get from me. Listen to me, Smookie, don't be greedy. You're going to make plenty of money, so don't change anything. Leave it exactly the way I told you to sell it. Do you understand me?"

"Yeah, I got you!"

Cold grabbed the backpack from the back seat and handed it to Smookie.

"There's eleven cell phones inside. You keep one. And there's twenty thousand dollars' worth of crack already bagged up in dimes, twenties, fifties, and hundreds. Plus the two grand I promised you. With this pack, all I want back is nine grand. Use the rest to promote. When you get low, hit me up and be careful."

And with that, Smookie got out of the car and walked down Rowan Street to meet his entourage.

Cold made a phone call, and a voice picked up, more alive than last time.

"Hello?" the voice answered.

"What's up? I'm on my way to pick up the rest of that. I'll be there in about fifteen to twenty minutes."

"Okay." The voice hung up.

On the way to pick up the rest of the product, Cold called Pree.

"Have you talked to your people yet?"

"Yeah, I have. And Slick also talked to his people. We're just waiting on your next move."

"Call y'all's people back and tell them that I want to meet with them tonight. We'll give them a call back in an hour."

"A'ight, we got you!" Pree hung up.

Cold picked up the product and Tim, then went to Gina's house. When they arrived, everyone was at work cutting, weighing, and bagging up. Much to Cold's surprise, they had covered a lot of ground, nearly bagging up half a kilo.

"Our people are waiting on you, Cold," Pree said.

"Good! Now call your people back and tell them we're on our way." Cold gave Gina the bag with the product. "I want you to cook this up and bring back the same thing you brought back off the others."

After getting everything together, Cold, Pree, and Slick left, leaving Tim in charge. They met with Pree's homeboy Tricko first. Cold liked him immediately—he recognized the sincerity in Tricko. Cold gave Tricko the recruitment speech and filled him in on how things were operated with the runners and cell phones. Tricko was given a cell phone and welcomed on board, then told he'll be contacted.

Next, they drove to meet Slick's nephew Damont in North Charlotte. After going over everything with Damont, they drove to the car lot where Cold had purchased the Honda earlier. He gave Slick the keys and sent him back to help the others.

Cold and Pree went to the Walmart on Wilkinson Boulevard to shop for some items and discuss business privately. While waiting in line, Cold recognized an old classmate that he hadn't seen in years.

"What's been up, Chris?" Cold extended his fist out.

"Just trying to make it," Chris replied with a gold smile, extending his fist and knuckling Cold's. "So what have you been up to?"

Cold figured Chris was a hustler because of the gold teeth and jewelry on his neck, wrist, and fingers.

"Nothing much. Where are you living at?"

"I'm on Tuckaseegee."

When they got outside in the parking lot, Cold pried into Chris' way of life. They stood out there for about thirty minutes talking. By the time they were finished, Cold had recruited another soldier and another hood. Cold gave Chris a cell phone to use strictly for business.

"Hit me up when you get things together."

"Man, I can probably come up with twenty runners. That's not a problem," Chris said with confidence.

"Well, if you can, then get them."

They dapped up and rolled out.

Chapter 10

The following weeks, the product moved faster than what Cold had anticipated, and the supply was getting low. He called Marco and got on the plane the next day to Riviera, Florida. Marco picked up Cold at the airport, and with time being a lack of quantity, Cold immediately began to discuss business.

"I know this is short notice, but I need to double the load," Cold said.

"Damn, Cold! You're moving that shit like that?" Marco asked.

"Those streets have a major appetite. I'm just trying to feed them what I can," Cold said.

"Well, you're gonna have to stay another day so I can arrange things between my plug, but I can make it happen."

"That's cool, and I need you to take me to rent a car."

"So how are you planning on getting back with this amount of product?" Marco asked.

"I'm gonna drive back, how else?"

"Now what if your ass get pulled over and get caught, then what?"

"Then I'm gonna have to do the fucking time because I ain't a snitch." Cold got defensive.

"Do you know how much time you'll get for trafficking that much product through the interstate? Life! Unless you cooperate. But it's not about if you're a snitch. Why put yourself in that situation? What you need to do is get a mule, because you don't need to be riding with ten kilos from Florida to North Carolina. It doesn't make sense for you to risk your life when you can pay someone else to do that for you. Why risk your life, Cold? Think about it. You can always get drugs and money back, but once those people take your life in the system, you can't get that back."

"You're absolutely right. You know, I just got a problem with trusting people, especially when it comes to exposing my plug."

"Man, we're family. You can always trust me."

After renting a car, Cold went to rent a hotel room. He'd declined Marco's offer of staying the night at his house. Cold needed to apply Marco's advice, so the first step was to get the mules—and he knew just who to use.

"What's up, boss man?" Pree answered.

"I need you and Gina to catch a flight out here to Florida, like right now."

"Is everything okay?"

"Oh yeah, everything is good. I'll explain everything when y'all get here. Tell Tim he's in charge until I get back."

"Okay, we're on our way." Pree hung up.

Pree and Gina arrived early the next morning before daybreak, and Cold was there to pick them up. Later that day, they rented another car, preferably Crown Vics, considering the circumstances of the event. Then they met up with Marco. Introductions were made for future reference, and the product was loaded up in one of the cars. Gina drove the car with the product while Pree and Cold followed behind her.

They safely arrived back in Charlotte, and everyone immediately went to work—cooking, bagging, and trapping.

Each day and month that passed by, business gradually expanded for Cold. He had to open up traphouses to keep up with the traffic in all the neighborhoods he was set up in. He had two different houses where the product was cooked up and bagged. He used Pree, Gina, and Tim to transport the money and the product to and from Florida. He felt that with three people in three different cars, if things were to go wrong, one could be a distraction for Gina to elude.

Within a year, Cold was purchasing fifty kilos a month. He was grossing a little under a million dollars a week. After paying the workers and other operational expenses, his personal profit was about three hundred grand a week. Everybody on his team was getting paid, and everybody was happy.

But in the quiet distance on the east side of town, by far, there was a face smiling.

One sunny afternoon, Cold and Pree were riding the streets of Charlotte in Cold's new arctic white 550 Mercedes-Benz. Even though Cold wasn't much into materialistic things, there was a certain standard one had to follow when being a person in power—from the way one dressed, spoke, and conducted oneself.

While stopped at a red light, a burgundy LS 460 Lexus with twenty-two-inch rims pulled alongside them. A man was driving, having a heated discussion on the phone. He gave Cold and Pree no attention, but Pree recognized him.

"That's Primetime," Pree pointed the guy out to Cold. "He's the one I was telling you about that run the east side. Rumor has it that he's beginning to lose money and is trying to figure out who's behind it. We need to be careful and keep our ears and eyes open, because eventually he's gonna find out—and we don't know how he's gonna react."

"How much do you know about that guy?" Cold continued to drive along.

"All I know is that he got a lot of soldiers that will ride for him, and he's been supplying a lot of products in Charlotte. I heard he owns a few clubs, a record label, and a few restaurants."

"Do you think he's gonna become a problem?"

"I don't know, because no one has ever been able to compete with him. But I did hear that he had put out a few hits before over some territorial shit."

"Well, my territory is the west side. If he wants someone to respect his boundaries, he better respect mine."

"The dude may not know his boundaries."

"Well, the guy ain't too smart—or he thinks he's untouchable."

Cold observed that Primetime was driving alone. Cold retained all that information about Primetime. He was hoping that things wouldn't result in violence, but in this line of work, it was destined. Things had been going too well lately, and it was just a matter of time before something went wrong. One thing Cold did know was that when a person is looking for someone that is making their pockets short, usually it's not a friendly encounter.

"Do your man still have those guns?" Cold asked.

"Yeah. What are you looking for?" Pree asked.

"Weapons to go to war. I want everything he got."

"A'ight, I'll take care of it."

Chapter 11

Chris woke up in a state of tranquility. He took a look at the naked redbone asleep in his bed and smiled from the memories of last night. By far, she was the freakiest girl he ever had. She did things to him that took his sex game to the next level.

He rolled up a blunt, took a few pulls, and exhaled the smoke slowly, feeling the high instantly. Realizing he didn't have any cigarettes, he got dressed. Instead of driving, he decided to walk to Gate's corner store on Tuckaseegee Road, which was only a five-minute walk from his house on Avalon Street.

Coming out the door, he stood for a second to light a cigarette. A black Dodge Charger pulled up in front of the store.

"Damn," Chris mumbled under his breath, knowing who it was. He was caught slipping. He had left his gun at home, but he wasn't about to run or show any fear.

The altercation began about two weeks ago, when Trigger met this girl who stayed a few houses down from Chris' traphouse. The traphouse was doing numbers, and Trigger's greed got the best of him. He felt like Chris was soft and was an easy mark, so he decided to press Chris. But Chris wouldn't back down, so Trigger had only one solution to get Chris out of the way.

Chris never brought the situation to Cold's attention because he didn't want to look like he couldn't handle problems. He was going to take matters into his own hands when the time was right.

"What up, nigga?" Trigger asked aggressively, getting out of the car.

"What up?" Chris responded just as aggressively, standing his ground.

"Nigga, you know what's up. I told you what I was gonna do when I catch your bitch ass." Trigger pulled out a pistol and aimed it at Chris.

The blood drained out of Chris' face. Flustered, thoughts began racing—his life flashed before his eyes while frozen in time.

Trigger squeezed the trigger six times.

The bullets pierced Chris' flesh. Just like that, his soul left his body and faded into the darkness—gone, like he never existed.

Hours later, Cold was struck by the astonishing and devastating news of Chris' unexpected murder.

"Word on the street was that Primetime had put the hit out on Chris," Pree informed Cold over the phone.

"Do you know for sure?"

"My source is pretty strong."

Cold went silent for a moment before responding. "I want you to meet me at the spot in an hour."

Arriving at Gina's house, Cold was met by Pree and Tricko.

"I brought Tricko because he got some information about Chris' murder," Pree said.

"Tell me what you got, Tricko."

"There's this kid named Trigger that's known to do hits for Primetime. This chick I be kickin' it with stay a few houses down from Chris' traphouse recently and began fuckin' with that nigga Trigger. She told me that Chris and Trigger had words a couple of weeks ago. Later that night, she heard Trigger on the phone talkin' to Primetime about takin' over Tuckaseegee, but he had to get Chris out of the way. I can get this bitch to set that nigga Trigger up if you want."

"We're gonna get Trigger, but we got to touch Primetime's whole operation."

"What's the plan?" Pree asked.

"First, we need to learn what we're about to go up against. I want to find out everything about Primetime—from where he sleep, to who he's fuckin', to who he's workin' with. I want to know about his traphouses and his business."

"It won't be too hard to find out a lot of that information. I know a lot of his business is on the eastside."

"That mean we need to start on the eastside."

"I know about a few of his traphouses. He got one on Milton Road, one in Hampshire Hills, and one on Dinglewood. We can stick all three of them up."

"Nah, fuck the money and the drugs—I want blood for blood. How you think we can get inside?"

"That's easy. People on the eastside are so scared to fuck with Primetime, they damn near leave the door wide open. Anybody can come and go as long as you're spending money. Shit, half the people sittin' up in them are high as hell anyway."

"How you know all this?"

"I been to those myself with my cousin a while back."

"Can you get your cousin to give us a layout to those spots?"

"Yeah, I can do that."

"Good. That'll give us a picture of what we're up against and how to attack. Call your cousin now, because time is of the essence and I want the element of surprise. I also need you to go and pick up some weapons—but let's stick to handguns.

"Tricko, go pick up four bulletproof vests, then we'll meet back here in an hour."

Chapter 12

An hour later, they all arrived back at Gina's house, with the addition of Pree's cousin Antonio, who went by Ant. Ant laid out all the details of Primetime's traphouses. His details were so vivid and accurate that Cold had enough confidence to take their chances tonight. Ant also had information about some of Primetime's other traphouses. He was very informative and observant—someone Cold could use. So when Ant asked to be a part of the team, Cold accepted him.

With the information he received from Ant, Cold devised a plan with the present members.

"Listen up! I want us to hit one house at a time, beginning with the one on Milton Road. Tricko, I want you to park around the corner on the side street. We're going to use two cars, but three of us will arrive there in one car. Once we're out the house, we'll meet you around the corner, and Pree will hop in the car with you.

"I want us in and out. Fuck the money and the drugs. Once we're out, we'll burn the house down. We should be able to hit all three houses within five minutes of each other. Is everyone with me?" Cold asked.

"We're with you," everyone responded.

Cold finished going over the details of how all three traphouses would be hit in chronological order and the escape routes. They drove around in the stolen cars and traced all the cuts and paths they could use to escape out of each one of Primetime's traphouses if things went wrong.

"Any questions?" Cold asked before they began to implement the plan.

Their silence spoke louder than words.

Cold was very confident in the men—that they would accomplish this mission.

They pulled up to the traphouse on Milton Road and exited the car with an aura of belonging. There were two guys sitting on the porch, drinking and talking, not giving much attention to the trio that approached. They nodded in acknowledgment, not skipping a beat in their conversation.

Ant knocked on the door, and a guy answered with eyes of recognition. He turned around and left the door open for them to enter, not saying a word.

When they entered the traphouse, there were three other people sitting on two dingy couches, watching TV, now being joined by the doorman. They all looked as if they weren't far from their last hit. The house reeked of tobacco, urine, and alcohol, and besides the low volume on the TV, the house was pretty much quiet.

Ant led the way down the corridor and knocked on the first bedroom door they approached. A fat kid opened the door and looked them over for a few seconds before speaking.

"What y'all need?"

"My homie right here is trying to get some work," Ant spoke up, referring to Cold.

While they were talking, Pree had made his way down the hallway to check out the other rooms. The next room he came to had nothing but a table in it that was struggling to stand on three legs. The last room's door was closed. Pressing his ear against the door, he heard the sounds of grunts and moans. He slowly twisted the doorknob while pressing his shoulder against the door, slightly shifting his weight forward until the door cracked open.

His right hand was clutching the pistol tightly, itching to squeeze the trigger for the unexpected.

Inside the room, a guy was laying on his back, grunting and moaning as a naked woman with a big yellow ass gave him oral sex. The two were so caught up in the moment, neither noticed the pair of preying eyes peeping between the cracked door.

Down the hall, the fat kid had let Ant and Cold into the room. Sitting in the room was a half-naked girl staring blankly at the TV. From the spaced-out look, she probably wasn't even aware of their presence. The fat kid closed the door behind them and walked over to the night table. He opened the drawer and retrieved a scale and a ziplock bag.

"How much are you trying to get?" the fat kid asked, turning his back to retrieve the crack out of the bottom drawer.

"Let me get an ounce," Cold spoke up.

The fat kid turned back around and was abruptly facing the barrels of two 9mm Glocks. Aghast and astonished, he instantly became nauseated.

"You make one fucking move and your ass is dead," Cold said, aiming the pistols for a clear shot at the fat kid's head.

The girl didn't even blink or acknowledge the event that was taking place.

"Go see what's up with Pree and get the fire started. I'll handle these two."

Pree was still standing in the doorway, peeping into the room with his gun drawn when Ant approached him. Ant peeped in the room at what Pree was looking at and smiled.

"At least he'll die in pleasure. You got twenty seconds."

Ant walked off into the kitchen and doused gasoline everywhere with the soda bottles. He made a trail of gasoline from the kitchen back into the living room, where the four spaced-out individuals sat, oblivious to the events taking place.

Bang! Bang! Bang! Bang! Bang! Bang!

Shots echoed rapidly in the house from the two rooms.

Upon hearing the shots, Ant immediately pulled out his gun and pumped a single shot in each one of the four individuals sitting on the couches.

Cold and Pree came running down the hallway simultaneously toward Ant. On their way out the door, Ant ignited the fire.

The two guys who had been sitting on the porch when they arrived had now vanished.

They hopped in the car and drove around the corner to meet up with Tricko, where Pree joined him in the vehicle. Following the route according to the plan, they made their way to the second traphouse in Hampshire Hills in a matter of minutes.

Chapter 13

Upon arriving at the traphouse in Hampshire Hills, Tricko let Pree out of the car a block from the traphouse and positioned himself for the getaway route. Cold and Ant went to the traphouse and knocked on the door, which was answered by a guy familiar with Ant.

"What y'all need?" the guy asked, allowing them to enter.

"We need a pound of kush," Ant spoke up and pulled out the money.

While Ant was discussing business, Cold was sizing up the surroundings. There were four guys playing a video game, sitting on the couches, smoking a blunt, and talking shit to each other. This traphouse was nothing like the one on Milton Road, and the risk was much higher. These guys were a lot more coherent than the last victims, but the plan was already in motion, and there was no turning back now. The guys playing the video game might be easy targets as long as they stayed distracted by the game. There was also the possibility of more people being in the rooms.

After the dealer counted the money, he departed to one of the bedrooms, leaving Ant and Cold standing there.

Ding dong! Ding dong! The doorbell chimed, interrupting the guys' video game.

One of the guys got up and answered the door.

"What you need?" the kid asked Pree, who was standing in the doorway.

"I'm trying to get some kush," Pree said.

"Just wait here," the kid said, leaving Pree standing by Ant and Cold, then went back to playing the video game.

The dealer came back out of the room with a big Ziplock bag filled with kush and called Ant into the kitchen so they could weigh it on the scale.

Once Ant went into the kitchen with the dealer, Cold and Pree made their move. They both pulled out their pistols. Preoccupied by the video game, the four guys were oblivious to the danger approaching. Cold crept closer to the couch behind them, aiming two Glock 9mms at their heads.

"Any one of y'all niggas make one fucking move, I'm gonna blow your fucking brains out," Cold said, refocusing their attention on the two Glocks.

Pree had two .40 calibers. He began moving rapidly around the house, checking the rooms. All the rooms were empty. He finally made it into the kitchen, where Ant and the dealer—still oblivious to the situation—were wrapping up business. Pree walked straight up behind the dealer and shot him point-blank in the back of the head. His soul was seized by death before his body hit the ground.

Pree turned around and ran back to the living room. By the time he made it, Cold was firing all thirty-four rounds into the four guys, leaving none alive.

Ant had doused the kitchen with gasoline and made his way into the living room, laying a gasoline trail. He threw a match onto the gasoline, and they casually exited the house, closing the door behind them, then hopped in the car.

Leaving the crime scene, they heard sirens coming from everywhere in the distance. Cold had already anticipated the fire department and cops being en route to the house on Milton Road, so he used it to their advantage. With the cops preoccupied, it gave them the opportunity to conduct their next mission unseen—which was the last mission for tonight of their vicious crime spree.

Driving down Plaza Avenue, cop cars, ambulances, and fire trucks raced past them in the opposite direction.

"Do you think it's a good idea to continue with this?" Tricko asked Cold, feeling skeptical because of the heat from the cops.

"Of course, it's a good idea to continue. Look at the opportunity it presents with the cops being preoccupied. Yeah, I know we're pushing it close, but before they know what's happening, we'll be in and out."

Before pulling up at the traphouse on Dinglewood, Ant and Pree picked up Cold from around the corner.

"We already drove past the house, and nothing looks suspicious, but we need to hurry up before they begin getting phone calls," Cold told Pree and Ant.

The traphouse was ramshackle, a huff and a puff from the big bad wolf and the house would probably come tumbling down. Grass had long neglected the lawn. The cracked wooden exterior made the house look dilapidated and forlorn. They got out of the car and walked up to the house, and Ant gave the door a light knock.

A woman cracked the door—lookin' like a burnt-out stripper chewed up by drugs and the streets.

"Who y'all want?" she asked, holding a cigarette between her fingers.

"Is Mo here?" Ant asked.

"And who is you?" she asked with an attitude.

"Tell him it's Ant out here."

She looked at Ant, rolled her eyes, then closed the door. While they were waiting, Pree mumbled to them.

"Y'all know we have to kill that bitch, right?" he stated the obvious.

Pree was also skeptical about doing this last hit. Something kept eating at his gut, giving him butterflies. He wanted to tell Cold that they should walk away and count their blessings of getting away with the two clean hits, but he kept those thoughts to himself. He decided to be more cautious and alert and to anticipate something going wrong.

Moments later, a tall, skinny kid opened the door.

"What up, Ant?" Mo asked.

"What up, Mo! Me and my cousins are trying to get some weight. Are you straight?"

"Yeah, I'm straight, but why all three of y'all need to come?"

"I just wanted to introduce them to you so if they ever need to come without me, y'all can be acquainted with each other."

Turning, Ant introduced Cold and Pree as Tommy and JJ.

"Y'all niggas aren't the cops, are you?" Mo asked.

"Hell no, we ain't the fucking cops," Cold spoke up, feeling disgusted by even being asked that question.

"Damn, my nigga, you think I'm trying to set you up?" Ant retorted.

"I don't know what the fuck you'll do. Niggas getting set up every day," Mo shot back.

"Listen, we ain't the mothafucking cops. I have the money right here. All I want is an ounce of hard, so you can either serve me or I can leave," Cold said calmly.

"How about you give your money to Ant and he come in," Mo said.

Cold had run out of patience. The clock was ticking, so he decided to make a move.

"Okay."

He went to reach in his pocket to get the money but reached for the pistol on his waist instead. The motion was so fast that it caused Ant to jump back. Cold had the pistol pressed against Mo's face, with his other hand wrapped around Mo's neck, in a split second.

"Now listen to me, muthafucka, or I'm going to blow your fucking head off right here. How many people are in the house?"

"Fuck you!" Mo replied, then looked at Ant.

"Bitch, you dead."

"Nah, mothafucka, you're the dead man," Cold said.

By now, Ant and Pree had their guns brandished. Cold turned Mo toward the door and ordered him to open it. When they rushed into the house, there were about seven people standing and sitting around. Cold shot Mo straight in the back of the head, then aimed and fired at all moving targets. Ant and Pree followed, firing their guns rapidly.

Shots returned from the kitchen and bedrooms. There was so much gunfire that they had to retreat back to the front door. Bullets stung their vests but didn't penetrate.

The whole plan was going wrong.

Ant pulled out the bottles of gasoline and tossed them inside the house. He threw a match, causing the house to go up in flames. It gave them enough time to make it to the car and drive off, with bullets ricocheting off the vehicle.

They quickly made their way around the corner to the getaway cars. Cold jumped in the car with Tricko. Before Pree and Ant got in the other car they had parked, Ant set the car they had been using on fire, and with impetuous speed, they made their escape.

They hit Sugar Creek Road, then hopped on I-85 South. They weaved off and on different exits to make sure they weren't being followed. Once they felt they were clear of any tails, they headed to Gina's house.

Chapter 14

At Gina's house, they were all in pain from the impact of the gunshots to the bulletproof vests. Luckily, none of the bullets had penetrated anyone's vest but damn if it didn't feel like it. They had ice packs wrapped around their bodies and had taken pain pills, smoked weed, and drunk alcohol to relieve the pain.

Cold had Slick and a few young soldiers get rid of the cars and guns. After a few hours, Pree, Tricko, and Ant decided they were going to leave, and Cold decided to stay at Gina's house a little longer.

"Y'all be very careful driving out there, and don't have anything on you. Go straight to your destinations. The streets are hot, and the cops are looking for any Black man driving so they can shake them up. We came this far we don't need any bullshit mistakes," Cold told them before they all departed.

When everyone was gone, Gina and Cold were alone in the house. Gina got down on her knees and unbuckled Cold's pants. Cold's body was numbed from all the painkillers, weed, and alcohol, but that didn't prevent him from getting aroused. He stretched out on the couch and let Gina go to work on his dick.

Gina slid out of her pants and eased on top of Cold. She rode him slow and worked her hips in a steady motion. Clearing his mind, Cold went into a state of ecstasy, loving the feeling of Gina's wet pussy soaking his dick. The more aroused Cold got, the harder and faster Gina rode him, grinding and bouncing. The rhythm of her body and the sounds of her moans gave Cold a therapeutic relaxation. He closed his eyes and drifted into euphoria.

While Cold was fucking Gina, out on the eastside, Ant was on the way to a female's house for a late-night fuck. Ant had not listened to Cold about riding clean. He had kept the pound of kush they had purchased in Hampshire Hills, and no one was aware he'd kept it. He took advantage of the opportunity to make some extra money. Besides, Cold and Pree didn't need it the way they just threw money away, Ant thought, letting greed cloud his judgment.

Riding back to the eastside, Ant was talking on the phone to the female about some very intense sexual pleasures. He was caught up in the conversation and was unaware of the unmarked police car that pulled up behind him. Driving up North Tryon Street, Ant hit a pothole in the street, causing the phone to fall out of his hand. As he tried to catch the phone, the car swerved just enough to make the unmarked car light up with blue lights and sirens.

"Excuse me, sir, may I see your license and registration?" the officer asked upon approaching the car.

"Yes, sir," Ant complied.

"Sir, have you been drinking?"

"No, I haven't, officer."

Ant was expecting a ticket and to be on his way, but moments later, more cops pulled up to the scene, causing him to become a little uneasy about the situation.

The first officer came back to Ant's car while another took position on the passenger side.

"Excuse me, Mr. Jones, but will you step out of the car for a breathalyzer test?"

Ant wanted to refuse but knew that would only make the situation worse. Once Ant was out of the car, without asking for permission, the other cops began to search the car.

"Do you have any weapons or drugs inside the car?" one of the cops asked while searching.

"I didn't give any one of y'all permission to search my car, so I'd like it if y'all get out and stop violating my rights."

"Well, sir, you look like a suspect that was involved in a few homicides that occurred a few hours ago. Can you tell me where your whereabouts were within the last few hours?"

Ant's heart fell out of his chest upon hearing those words. His thoughts went to the girl from Dinglewood, but he was sure he had shot that bitch right in her chest.

Unbeknownst to Ant, the cop was only saying that to shake him up. The truth was, the cops didn't have any suspicion of Ant besides him being a Black man swerving at 2:00 a.m. The detectives hadn't interviewed anyone who'd given them any type of lead—but there was a girl in the hospital with a gunshot wound to the stomach who was looking to survive.

"I just came from my cousin's house, and I'm on my way to see my girl, if you don't mind, sir," Ant replied with composure.

Ignoring Ant's protest about the illegal search and violation of his rights, the officer continued to search and found the pound of kush under the passenger seat. With further searching, they also found an ounce of crack and a pistol in the trunk.

They escorted Ant to the interrogation office across the street from the Charlotte-Mecklenburg County Jail on 4th Street.

Detective Roundhouse came into the interrogation room and sat directly in front of Ant.

"I'm not about to sit here and bullshit with you. With your record, I can hand this case straight over to the Feds, and I guarantee you won't get less than twenty years. But . . . I'm willing to give you a chance to help yourself."

"There ain't shit I can help you with because I don't know shit."

"See, I don't give a shit about the drugs. I want information on those murders that's been going on. All you gotta do is give me one name, and I'll let you walk out of here right now."

Ant tapped his fingers on the table and looked around the room nervously as sweat trickled down his face.

"I have a name."

"Who?" the detective asked, lifting his posture in the seat.

"Norman Butter."

"So who is this guy?"

"He's my fucking lawyer."

Detective Roundhouse stood up, infuriated, and pointed his finger right in Ant's face.

"I'm gonna make sure you rot in this motherfucker."

And with that, the detective walked out of the interrogation room and slammed the door.

"Book his ass," he told one of the officers.

Ant had been booked and processed. One phone call to his child friend, Keisha immediately came and posted his bond.

Chapter 15

When Primetime received the news about what happened at the traphouse, he went ballistic. He couldn't believe someone actually had the audacity to do such a thing and think they were going to live. He called everyone that worked and dealt with him to try and figure out who did this. He wanted names, faces, and blood.

He paced around the house taking shot after shot of vodka, trying to make sense out of what happened.

"Trigger!"

The name popped into his head, and he knew it had something to do with that little wild-ass nigga. Trigger had been the one to convince him to try and set up shop on the west side once they got that kid Chris out the way.

Primetime picked up the phone and called Trigger.

"What's up?" Trigger answered.

"What the fuck do you know about that nigga that was gettin' too much money that was in our way?"

"It was just some bitch-ass nigga that was makin' too much money and was out the way," Trigger responded nonchalantly.

"Well, this bitch-ass nigga wasn't who you thought he was, and because of your ignorant ass, we're now in a fuckin' war. But do you know what the worst part about this is? We don't even know who we're in a fuckin' war with."

"So what happened?"

"What happened?" Primetime repeated with exasperation. "Let me tell you what happened. I have three

71

burnt-down traphouses with dead bodies everywhere. Now explain to me who is gonna pay for this?"

"Don't worry, I'll take care of it," Trigger said, not sounding convincing.

"Oh hell no! You done caused enough damage. You're not doin' this alone."

"So what's your plan?"

"I'ma call you back, but until then, stay your ass put. Don't do shit." Primetime hung up.

Primetime called four hit men and told them to come to the house. When they arrived, he laid out a plan.

"Right now, I'm waitin' on a source with some information on this kid Chris. In the meantime, Trigger is a loose cannon and a liability to my organization. I can't tolerate these types of mistakes from him or anyone else. We got almost ten dead bodies because of this stupid-ass nigga's ignorance."

Primetime was abruptly interrupted by the ring of his phone.

"What up?" he answered.

"Hey, I got that information for you on that kid Chris and who he was workin' for. Tell me where you at and I'll come to you," the caller said.

"I'm at the house."

The voice on the other end of the line was a guy named Fred from South Side Homes. He was a good associate of Primetime and a good customer for that kush. When Fred arrived at Primetime's house, he grabbed a seat at the kitchen table and got straight down to business.

"The kid Chris was workin' for Cold. Cold don't play any fuckin' games," Fred said.

"We figured that part out already," Primetime interrupted with sarcasm.

Fred continued, ignoring Primetime's comment.

"Anyway, he got the whole west side sewed up. He got traphouses on West Boulevard and South Side Homes that I know about, and the kid Chris ran his traphouse on Tuckaseegee."

"Do you know any of the addresses of his traphouses or any other place that he be at?"

Fred slid Primetime a piece of paper across the table.

"Those are the addresses that I know of, and I don't want this shit comin' back to me. Listen to me, Primetime . . ."

Fred became very serious, with a bit of nervousness.

"This guy Cold is a very dangerous mothafucka. He's not your average dope boy just tryin' to make a name for himself. He's probably gonna be anticipatin' you to hit his traphouses, so be careful. And remember,every move you thought of, or are thinkin' about, he already thought about it."

"Now you listen to me, Fred. I'm a very dangerous mothafucka too, and I'm by far not your average hustler. This punk can't think on my level."

Fred got up and walked to the door, then stopped and turned around to face Primetime.

"Okay . . . but never underestimate your enemy."

And with that, Fred left.

Primetime was the type of guy that let his pride and arrogance control him. He wanted both of Cold's traphouses ambushed just like his were—but he wanted to make his attack more brutal and devastating.

So when one of his hit men asked if the first plan was to be taking place, he told them that it was the first part to be taking place.

With Primetime being drunk and in a rage, his thoughts were careless and impulsive. The first part of his plan was to have Chris's funeral shot up, and he didn't care who got hit. He initially came up with that plan because he didn't have a clue who he was going to war against, but now it was all out of an act of tyranny.

Chapter 16

Trigger had been laying low since receiving word that Primetime had a hit on his head. He moved around town, avoiding the east side of Charlotte and the Tuckaseegee area where Primetime's hit men would most likely be looking for him. He'd also been informed that Cold had learned of his identity, so every move he made was a calculated step to escape death. He had to get out of Charlotte quick, fast, and in a hurry but the lack of money was holding him back. For the last three days, Trigger had been staying up all night hustling to get missing.

With limited places to go, tonight Trigger was in North Charlotte at a traphouse. His homeboy RaRa set him up to make some extra money and get some rest. The money was coming fast. Trigger anticipated staying there for two days and estimated he'd have enough to leave the state. Atlanta was where he wanted to go opportunities were in Atlanta.

With the past few days of sleepless nights, sleep began to get the best of Trigger. He wanted to go to a hotel, but decided he'd crash out in one of the rooms in the traphouse for a few hours. Besides, no one knew he was there anyway.

While Trigger was asleep, Damont came to the traphouse to check and see how things were going. For the last two months, Damont had been letting his young soldier RaRa run the traphouse. When he walked into the house, RaRa was on the couch asleep; he didn't even budge when Damont came in the door. This made Damont furious, because mistakes like that would get you dead or in prison.

Walking past RaRa, leaving him asleep, Damont made his way around the house, checking the rooms. He walked into the room where Trigger was stretched out across the bed and couldn't believe the fucking odds. He closed the door and walked back into the living room and woke RaRa up.

"Get up and be quiet," Damont demanded, jerking RaRa awake.

RaRa jumped up in a panic. "What's going on?"

"Just get out and shut up."

"But what about my homeboy in the back room?"

"Your homeboy is a dead man, so get the fuck out before your ass be one too," Damont said aggressively, shoving RaRa toward the door.

Following RaRa out the door, Damont went to the trunk of his car, grabbed a container filled with gasoline, and walked back into the house. He went straight to the room where Trigger was still asleep. He pulled out his pistol and hit Trigger hard across the head. Trigger jumped up, but before his mind even had time to register the pain, he was shot once in the stomach—causing a burning sensation to erupt through his body.

"Ahh, shit!" Trigger moaned, clutching his stomach.

"Yeah, mothafucka, this is a message from Chris," Damont screamed. Trigger's eyes widened, his mouth opening like he wanted to say something—then Damont emptied the last fifteen rounds into him.

Damont immediately grabbed the container of gasoline and doused it on Trigger's corpse and around the house. He collected all the money and drugs in a duffle bag, then set the fire ablaze as he calmly walked out of the house and closed the door.

He jumped in his car and called Cold while driving away.

Chapter 17

It was the morning of Chris' funeral. The dawn had given way to a full morning, exposing a pale, hard blue sky. The funeral was a sad beauty. Chris was in an oak casket dressed in an all-white Armani suit. Cold had paid for the entire funeral service and picked out the five-thousand-dollar suit for Chris to rest eternal in. Chris' mother and siblings picked out the casket and handled the rest of the funeral arrangements without worrying about the cost.

Cold did not attend the funeral, but he did go to the viewing of the body the day before. Cold wasn't fond of funerals ever since attending his mother's funeral at such a young age, who had died of AIDS. The mourning and emotions were something he did not want to bear because it brought back too many memories that he didn't want to relive.

All of Chris' friends and family were there to show their respect. Chris had three children by two women. His children's mothers and his mother were crying hysterically from the realization of Chris being gone forever. His two sisters, Christina and Crystal, were sitting there in a daze. Reality didn't hit them until they walked up to the casket and looked at Chris' lifeless body laying there idle. Christina fell out on the floor, and Crystal went hysterical trying to grab Chris out of the casket. It took six men to control the two women and get them back in their seats.

While everyone was in the church mourning, Primetime's hit men were loading up their guns. They were sitting in a black van parked down the street in view of the church, waiting for the ceremony service to exit.

Blow, one of the hit men, was actually apprehensive about shooting up a funeral. He respected the dead, but he feared Primetime's consequences more than walking away.

There were four hitmen in the van. They had AR-15 and AK-47 assault rifles with one-hundred-round clips for each, and a few handguns for backup. Primetime wanted them to use the assault rifles so his message would be delivered loud and clear.

In the church, the pastor was wrapping up the ceremonial eulogy.

"This is a case where the good have died young, but Chris is now in a better place with our Heavenly Father watching over us."

A cue was given to the choir, and they stood up and quietly began singing *Amazing Grace* as the pastor continued to say his final words.

"If Chris could speak to us now, he would tell us that his life was not taken to make anyone weak, but it was taken to make us stronger . . . and that he's in God's kingdom now," the pastor preached.

After the pastor's last words were spoken, the choir lifted their voices stronger into the air, preciously singing. The ushers got everyone to stand up and prepared them to exit the church. The six pallbearers began rolling the casket down the aisle toward the exit of the church.

Outside, the four hit men were sitting in complete silence in the van. Johnny, the driver of the van, sat up when he saw the church doors open and the pallbearers roll the casket out.

"Here we go, fellas," Johnny said, while cranking up the van and pulling the mask over his face.

Everyone in the van pulled the masks over their faces and cocked their guns. Johnny put the van in drive and slowly accelerated down the street toward the church. No one at the church was paying attention to the black van that was creeping toward them. People continued to exit the church, embracing each other with hugs and kisses before departing to their cars.

When the van got in front of the church, a havoc of gunfire erupted like a display of pyrotechnics. People ran and ducked for cover everywhere, trying to dodge bullets. Johnny revved the accelerator after three hundred rounds were fired at the people at the church.

The squad cars that were parked on the side of the church accelerated in high pursuit after the van. Johnny looked in the rearview mirror and pressed harder on the accelerator. Blow and the other two hit men were reloading their weapons. Mark, one of the hit men, was the first to reload. He stuck the AR-15 out the back window of the van and shot at the police cars. Bullets hit one squad car and caused it to veer off the road out of control and run straight into a telephone pole.

The officer in the second squad car returned fire, desperately trying to shoot out the van's tires. He zigzagged through the light traffic to avoid getting hit by the powerful arsenal and getting into a collision. He reloaded twice but still failed to dismantle the tires before running out of ammunition. He slowed down but continued to pursue the van from a distance while reporting the pursuit's whereabouts to the dispatcher.

Johnny looked in the rearview mirror and saw that the cop was still following them from a distance.

"Damn!" Johnny cursed under his breath, knowing they couldn't beat the cops' radios. They needed him close enough to shoot him out, but the cop wasn't allowing that. Johnny abruptly slap-dashed onto the interstate and smashed the gas pedal all the way to the floor. Two minutes on the interstate, he looked up in the sky and saw a helicopter in air pursuit. In the mirrors, there were more squad cars and state troopers racing up the highway. He needed to get off the interstate and get to a neighborhood, he thought, trying to improvise a maneuver.

"Damn!" Johnny cursed again in frustration, realizing how stupid they had been to use a fucking van. The van wouldn't even go past eighty miles per hour. He switched lanes, preparing to get off at the next exit to Sugar Creek Road. His plan was to make it to Hidden Valley housing development and jump out for it. He knew a few folks over there that wouldn't have a problem opening up their door—if only he could make it, maybe he'd get away.

Chapter 18

There was pandemonium at the church, with dead bodies and blood everywhere. People were hysterical from witnessing their loved ones be murdered in cold blood. Chris' casket was shot up, and his body had rolled out onto the ground when three of the pallbearers were shot, of which two died. Three kids ages five, seven, and eight who happened to be Chris' cousins, were shot and killed. In all, twelve people were pronounced dead, and over twenty others were hospitalized from gunshot wounds. Chris' sister, Crystal, was one of the wounded victims; she had been shot in the rib cage.

Fire trucks, ambulances, cops, and news reporters came from everywhere. The news reporters arrived and threw their cameras and microphones in people's faces, trying to get the first lead on the story. This mayhem was shown live on breaking news, and a majority of Charlotte was now tuned into the video coverage from the church to the high-speed pursuit.

Cold was sitting in Andrea's house, watching the news while holding Jessica and Jelissa in his arms. Andrea was sitting next to Cold, holding her mouth while tears fell down her cheeks. She couldn't believe what was happening, especially when they said that three kids were killed.

"How can someone be that evil and do something like that?" Andrea rhetorically asked.

Cold sat there with fire in his eyes because he knew who was behind this madness. In life, there were some lines you don't cross, and Primetime just crossed that line. He had misjudged Primetime. He would have never thought that Primetime was actually that reckless and coldhearted.

"Didn't you tell me that your friend's funeral was today?" Andrea asked, taking Cold out of his thoughts.

"That's it right there!"

"Oh my God! I'm so sorry!"

Cold didn't respond but continued to watch the news. His thoughts traveled back to Primetime. He was a reckless cannonball one Cold was going to use to his advantage. It was time to initiate a thorough surveillance on Primetime.

On the other side of town, Primetime was sitting in his living room, watching the news with a smirk on his face. He felt like he was on top of the world. He hated that those kids were killed, but hey . . . this was a cold world, he reasoned. To survive, you have to be just as cold or colder especially in the lifestyle he was living. One thing for sure, he reflected, a mothafucka will think twice before they fuck with him again, because this was surely going to put the fear of God in niggas now.

"I hope these mothafuckas burn in hell!" Privilege said, sitting beside Primetime.

Primetime didn't even acknowledge her statement because he was so in tune with his public mayhem. His behavior was impulsive, destructive, careless, and egotistical but he was proud of himself.

"Why would someone shoot innocent children, and not only that, shoot up a damn funeral?" Privilege continued to vent her anger.

Even though Privilege didn't know anyone at the funeral, she still cried her heart out for the families. But she was naïve to the fact that her man, the man she loved, was the mastermind behind the whole incident that was occurring. Privilege knew a lot about Primetime's operation but always minded her business when it came to his business on the streets. She understood what he did wasn't right by far, but the lifestyle he provided her compensated for the wrongs.

Chapter 19

Johnny veered off the interstate onto the exit to Sugar Creek Road.

"Y'all better get prepared to jump out and make a run for it," Johnny yelled to the three accomplices.

Blow was sitting in the back of the van, scared to death. The event was overwhelming; he never felt this close to death. Mark and PJ had their guns loaded and cocked. Mark had it in mind that he wasn't going back to prison. The AR-15 was his judge and jury. PJ was just young and dumb. This whole ordeal exhilarated him, and he felt like a character in a movie. The reality hadn't quite set in his mind yet.

Johnny was driving too fast up the exit ramp. He tried to slow down to make the turn off the ramp but ran straight into an eighteen-wheeler freight truck. The impact was vigorous. Johnny went flying out of the windshield, head first, smack into the freight truck, dying instantly.

The impact sent everyone flying to the front of the van. Blow was knocked out cold. Mark was the first one to begin moving. He immediately shook PJ and Blow. PJ slowly regained consciousness. Mark grabbed the AR-15 and looked out the window. Cops were approaching the van with their guns aimed.

"Get the fuck up, PJ," Mark yelled, and took aim out the window. He fired the AR-15 like it was the Vietnam War. The cops scrambled and returned gunfire.

PJ immediately grabbed the AK-47 upon hearing Mark shoot. He opened the side door of the van and jumped out in a full sprint down Sugar Creek Road, letting the AK-47 rip in any and all directions. Mark jumped out behind him but was unfortunate when multiple bullets pierced his body. He dropped to his knees; blood squirted out of his mouth before he landed face down on the ground. Another soul captured by death.

The cops had withdrawn from shooting at PJ to avoid hitting any innocent bystanders. The police helicopter was still on the trail, keeping the officers on the ground informed of PJ's whereabouts over radio frequency.

"This is chopper 147. We have the suspect in visual; he's running south on Snow White Street."

"Don't lose that motherfucker. I want y'all to corner his ass in," Detective Roundhouse yelled over the radio frequency.

Detective Roundhouse had just arrived on the scene on Sugar Creek. He'd been following the pursuit on the radio frequency since receiving the call ten minutes ago.

"Damn! Damn! Damn!" he repeated while hitting the steering wheel.

He was furious with himself.

"Out of all the days you chose to come to work late, this shit happens," he ridiculed himself out loud.

He wasn't even that upset about what was happening. What pissed him off was that he hadn't been the first one there. When the police dispatcher called his cell phone to inform him of what was happening and that the situation had already been in progress for about ten minutes, he went ballistic. He fiercely reprimanded the dispatcher for not contacting him sooner while running to the unmarked police car he drove home every night.

Now there, he was taking over, barking orders like a madman, and no one dared to question his judgment. Detective Roundhouse may be an egotistical and arrogant son of a bitch, but he was the best at what he did. He was a workaholic and a thinker under pressure. This was all engraved in him after being on the CMPD for over thirty years.

"This is chopper 147. The suspect just ran into a house. Do you copy?"

"I copy that, and I don't want anyone to do anything until I get there. Do you copy?" Detective Roundhouse radioed back.

"Copy," the radio repeatedly barked back from different squad cars.

"I want the SWAT team, and get me Detective Barnes."

"Roger that. Copy," someone radioed.

The SWAT team posted up all around the house. They had snipers set up on the tops of adjacent houses, behind cars, and in trees, trying to get a clear visual of PJ. The helicopter had been circling the house with an X-ray machine that detected any motion through a heat sensor, so they were aware that there were at least three hostages inside.

Detective Barnes had worked for the CMPD as a hostage negotiator for the past twenty-five years. He constantly called the house for the last five minutes, desperately trying to get in contact with the suspect or hostages.

PJ was in the house, pacing back and forth, contemplating his next move. He looked at the three ladies he held hostage at gunpoint and noticed the resemblance—they were mother and daughters. The two girls were no older than fourteen and sixteen years old and were sitting on the couch crying. With constricted tears, their mother tried her best to comfort them.

"It's all my fault. I'm sorry, I left the door open," one of the young girls said between sobs.

"No, it's not, baby. This is no one's fault, so don't you blame yourself for this, honey," the mother consoled her child.

PJ avoided peeping out of the window. He turned the TV on, and there, on breaking news, was the house he was in, holding a family hostage at gunpoint. The more he paced around, the more reality began to hit him. He had to come up with a plan . . . damn, he was between a rock and a hard place.

"Please don't hurt us!" the woman said, breaking PJ's train of thought.

The breaking news flashed back to where the incident first took place at the church, updating the conditions of the victims. The three females instantly became distraught, and their hope quickly diminished of making it out of this situation alive after seeing the actions of what this man was capable of doing. Even PJ stood there shocked, and right there he realized that his life was over. If he walked out that door, there were only two options that led to one result— death by bullets or the lethal injection.

PJ stopped pacing.

"Y'all stop crying. I'm not going to hurt y'all."

They complied and quieted down, but the young girls were still sniffling, with tears coming down their cheeks.

PJ began to talk out loud, continuing to ignore the ringing of the phone.

"I never met my father, and my mother died when I was ten years old."

The mother listened to PJ vent.

"I've been through so many different foster homes and group homes, I've lost count. I've been physically abused and molested."

PJ allowed the tears to fall down his cheeks.

"It's going to be okay. Life is not over for you. You still have a chance to make a difference," the mother said.

PJ shook his head.

"Nah, I don't have a chance. Hell, I never had a chance since I was born."

"Yes, you do. God put you on this earth for a purpose. No matter what you have done, He will forgive you. You just have to give Him your heart and repent."

"God don't forgive people like me. But can you do me a favor?"

"Just tell me what it is."

"Can you tell the families of the people I've hurt that I'm sorry?"

The mother placed her hand over her mouth and nodded. She allowed the tears to fall, knowing what was about to happen.

"You don't have to do that."

PJ picked up the phone and handed it to the mother, then turned and walked into the bathroom.

The mother's hands were trembling so bad she almost dropped the phone. She placed the phone to her ear and heard a man's voice repeatedly saying hello.

"Please don't hurt anyone," Detective Barnes said, hearing the heavy breathing over the phone.

"We . . . we . . . we're okay!" the mother stuttered while sniffling.

"Where is the suspect?"

Bang! It was a single shot to the head. PJ died instantly.

Blow had been rushed to the hospital and was now in ICU, in a coma. Detective Roundhouse made it clear that when Shawn Patterson, a.k.a. Blow, woke up out of his coma, he wanted to be the first person notified. He was furious and wanted some fucking answers for this mayhem, and this half-dead motherfucker was going to give them to him.

Chapter 20

Two weeks had passed since the catastrophe at the church. During that time, two of Cold's traphouses had been shot up. No one was killed or shot because everyone at the traphouses had been prepared for an ambush.

Cold had Primetime under surveillance 24/7 for the past two weeks. He'd acquired a lot of information about Primetime and was astonished that he had managed to stay alive this long. Primetime was not a street guy—his father was a pastor and his mother was a schoolteacher. He had inherited some money from his grandmother when she passed away, and he invested it into drugs.

Cold had the addresses of the two women Primetime had on the side, apart from his main girlfriend, Privilege. Cold remembered Privilege very well from the convenience store over a year ago. With all the information Cold had accumulated, he could've moved on Primetime at any time and taken him out. However, the more he watched Primetime's organization, the more he became intrigued by learning the inside of his operation. Cold gave credit to Primetime for having a well-established setup. Not once did he see Primetime's hands get dirty, but he still saw too many flaws.

Cold met up with Pree to get an update on the surveillance.

"This nigga is getting some major money. I followed some of his crew and learned about some of the other traphouses. One thing that's been bothering me is that not once did I see a drop-off or a pickup. Our surveillance on

Primetime—not once did I see a shipment. But maybe he get it by the month, so we'll just continue to keep a close eye on him."

Cold simply nodded.

"What about the traphouses? Do we still need to watch them?" Pree asked.

Cold pondered for a few seconds because there was no way in hell Primetime would keep all that shit sitting in those traphouses.

"When is it that you see someone come out the house with anything in their hands?"

"Man, I don't see anyone come out of that house with anything besides the garbage, and they keep plenty of it."

"Hold up—what did you say about the garbage?" Cold asked.

"They be having a shitload of garbage for a week—hell, they have at least two garbage cans full."

"That's it! I want you to follow the garbage trucks the next time they come."

"Man, are you sure about that?" Pree was thinking Cold was beginning to get desperate.

"You damn right I'm sure! That's got to be it, and I'm willing to bet that some of those bags are filled with cash."

"Well, if you say so." Pree was still pessimistic.

"Now I need you to think hard for me one more time, Pree. When is it that you ever see someone come to the house with bags or boxes—like delivery men, maintenance men, or anyone?"

Pree pondered for a moment, and then it hit him.

"You know what? The pizza man always delivers about five or more pizzas each week."

"Can you remember if it's the same delivery man?"

"Damn, I can't remember that, but I do remember that he delivers the same day the garbage is picked up."

Once Cold got confirmation from the other crew members who were on surveillance that the garbage pickups and pizza deliveries occurred on the exact same day, he immediately added some modifications by putting a surveillance team on the garbage trucks and pizza delivery man.

After a week of surveillance on the garbage trucks and pizza delivery men, Cold's suspicion was confirmed. The money and drugs were getting picked up and dropped off by them. Primetime was running his operation out of a pizza shop and was cleaning the money through the numerous businesses he owned.

Cold watched Primetime's operation in amazement. He couldn't believe that a guy like Primetime had built this operation by himself. This was a fucking empire, and it took brains to organize something like this.

Maybe I had misjudged Primetime.

One thing for sure—he was going to get inside Primetime's operation and find out who put this shit together.

Chapter 21

Meanwhile, during the following two weeks, Cold had his operation back together. He still had Primetime and his crew under surveillance around the clock.

Today, Cold followed Privilege to SouthPark Mall. He wanted to make it look like a mere coincidence for them to be running into each other. He watched as she ambled through the mall, accumulating bags from all the top designer stores.

Privilege was looking amazing. She was wearing a tight tan T-shirt that showed a little cleavage and exposed her belly piercing, but still classy with sex appeal. She had on a pair of cream tight jeans that wrapped around her voluptuous ass and gripped her bowlegged legs. Her feet were cozy in a pair of six-inch tan stiletto open-toe heels that boosted her five-foot stature. Her outfit complemented her well with sexual attraction.

She was still as gorgeous as Cold remembered her. He watched as guys couldn't keep their eyes off her. Some were even so bold as to look at her ass right in front of their girl, which brought about the envious glares from the women. Even some of the women couldn't help but admire Privilege's beauty. She sauntered through the mall with confidence in every step she took.

After an hour of shopping, Privilege made her way to the food department, and Cold made that his cue. He walked up behind Privilege in the Chick-fil-A line as she was struggling between holding her bags and reaching inside her purse.

"Can I give you a hand with that?" Cold asked.

"No, I'm okay," Privilege said, not looking up.

Losing the struggle, her purse fell out of her hand, and most of the contents went flying everywhere across the floor.

"Oh my God!" she said in frustration and immediately bent down and began picking up the contents that belonged in the purse.

Cold took advantage of the moment to admire her thong and tramp stamp that was right above the crack of her ass. The tattoo read *Slippery When Wet.* After restoring composure, Cold bent down and helped Privilege retrieve her personal items.

"Maybe just a little help won't hurt. What you think?" Cold said with a warm smile.

"Thank you!" Privilege looked up at Cold. "Hey, I remember you. Well, now I guess you're going to want me to buy you lunch?"

"You know me already." Cold was surprised that she remembered him and their conversation so well. "But first you have to let me grab a few bags out of your hands."

"Deal!" She handed Cold a few bags.

Once they ordered and found a table, they began with the small talk.

Acting naïve, Cold asked, "If I can remember correctly, don't you own a club or something?"

"Yes, I do, and it's called *Privileges*—in which you told me that you don't do clubs, if I remember correctly."

"You're right. It's just too much drama always happening at clubs."

"Well, not my club. I have a very professional establishment. It's for grown folks only," she said with a blushful smile.

"Oh yeah, it's a strip club, right?"

"Yes, but I like to refer to it as *exotic dancers.*"

"Do you dance?"

"I have danced occasionally for special events, but I concentrate more on the business and keeping the girls' heads above the water."

Cold nodded. "So you are smarter than a fifth grader?"

"Boy, you're crazy!" she giggled and playfully hit Cold on his arm.

"I'm just saying, after that episode in line you had me thinking."

"It's just that when a guy does something or gives a woman something, they always expect something in return."

"You're right, because I damn sure wanted something to eat—and thank you."

"Boy, you know what I'm talking about." She rolled her eyes. "You're welcome, though. So you still haven't told me what it is you do?" She became serious.

Talking with Privilege gave Cold a sense of relaxation and comfort that he never felt with anyone—and especially a woman. Looking into her eyes, he began to speak honestly—not only to get her reaction, but for her to know who he was.

"I consider myself an entrepreneur, but I'm looking for the right business to invest in."

"Basically, what you're saying is that you have the money, but you don't have a business plan or idea?"

"And there's also a legal issue," Cold tried to read her reaction.

Privilege kept Cold's stare.

"So you're trying to clean up your money?"

Cold just nodded.

"There's ways you can clean up your money without gaining any suspicion from the Feds or the IRS."

"Do you mind sharing a few ideas?"

"The best way to start cleaning your money is through a non-profit organization, and then you build from there."

Cold looked at Privilege with respect. The more she discussed business, the more he was willing to bet that Privilege was the business mind behind Primetime's operations.

"What is a good amount to start a non-profit organization without alerting the authorities?"

Their conversation was abruptly interrupted by the ringing of Privilege's cell phone. They were so caught up in their conversation that they both had lost track of time.

"Excuse me, but I have to answer this." Privilege answered the phone.

"Hey, baby!" she said and rolled her eyes at Cold, as if the guy on the phone meant nothing. "I'm about to leave the mall now and pick that up. Okay, baby, I'll see you in a little while. Bye, me too." With that, she ended the call.

"Well, I have to get going, but it was nice seeing you again." She paused to allow Cold to say his name.

"Just call me Cold. And if it's not a problem, I would like to discuss some more business with you, so may I leave you with my number?"

"Sure, and how about I leave you with my number also?"

They exchanged numbers, and Privilege got up and grabbed her bags and walked away. Halfway out of the food court, she looked back at Cold, who was admiring her ass. She blushed and winked flirtatiously, then completed her exit.

Privilege had found herself a little excited about meeting Cold. He was attractive, respectful, and he listens, she thought. She liked the way he asked questions instead of pretending that he knew all the answers. She liked how serious and attentive he became and how he showed a genuine interest in her knowledge about business. And he had an aura of confidence about himself that really attracted her.

Beep! Beep! A horn blew, knocking Privilege out of her reverie.

Chapter 22

Cold appointed Ant and a guy named Box to oversee the new traphouse on Tuckaseegee Road. Cold began to run his operation on a new level. He had people working in shifts in the traphouses and on the corners with phones. He switched up the drop-offs and pickups.

Cold had never been the person to overlook knowledge when it presented itself, no matter where it came from. He learned a lot from Primetime by watching his business operate. Watching Primetime's operation—and the conversation he had with Privilege—he now had a different perspective about business. He enrolled at Central Piedmont Community College for Business Management. He was determined to learn everything about business, including the non-profit organization.

For the following months, Cold gave Pree and Tricko more responsibilities over the operation. He assigned Pree as captain and Tricko as top lieutenant. Cold utilized his time going to school, and after school, he spent time avidly reading true organized crime books. He read about the Italian Mafia, the French Connection, the Cuban, Colombian, and Mexican cartels.He read up on criminology, forensic science, and law enforcement strategies so he could have an idea of how the police operate their investigations—and he learned his constitutional rights.

To defeat the enemy, you have to know the enemy! Cold's grandmother advised him whenever he had to face a confrontation.

What gave Cold his drive, determination, and ambition was his competitiveness. That was also the reason why he hadn't executed Primetime yet. Cold felt that Primetime was too incompetent to be ahead of him in the game.

The violent events had deceased between Cold and Primetime over the past months, but Cold still kept a minor surveillance on Primetime and his crew. He felt that one day the surveillance on Primetime would pay off, so he didn't mind spending the money and using the manpower— especially after acquiring the knowledge of criminology.

Cold wanted his establishment to be legendary, and this was the beginning of his legacy.

Chapter 23

Primetime was at home, pacing back and forth in the bar. He was patiently waiting on Tiffany, who JoJo was sent to pick up. Tiffany was the girl who survived the night his traphouse got shot up and burnt down. She had some valuable information—if he was willing to pay for it.

"Damn, it's been almost a half hour. Where in the fuck are they?" Primetime thought, looking at his watch for the hundredth time.

There was a knock at the door, and JoJo stuck his head in.

"Where is that bitch?" Primetime scolded before JoJo had a chance to utter a word.

JoJo stepped aside, and Tiffany entered with a defensive attitude.

"First of all, I'm not about to be too many more of your bitches. Second, you need me, so I suggest that you get your mothafucking attitude adjusted!" Tiffany angrily rebuked, approaching Primetime.

"Who the fuck do you think you're talking to, coming up in my shit giving demands? Bitch, you better stay in your lane!"

"Well, since I'm a bitch, this bitch want fifty thousand dollars for this information, or you can kiss my ass, nigga. Now how about that, bitch!.,"

"I'm not about to pay you fifty thousand dollars for shit. What you're about to do is cough up that information or end up in a pine box."

"How about you tell my brothers that." Tiffany put on a devilish grin, then continued. "You may know them or have heard of them. They go by the name Blood Brothers. Maybe I should be a little more specific—Drape, Nut Box, and Body Bag—and those are my biological brothers, if you're not aware of that. I've already informed them of our little meeting, so if I have any conflict with you or anything happens to me, believe that they will come for your ass, Mr. Primetime." She emphasized his name.

Primetime knew of her brothers very well. Hell, everybody knew the Blood Brothers. They were three dudes you didn't want to get on their bad side. They were ruthless and dangerous. They ran the biggest Blood gang in Charlotte and showed no mercy to adversaries. Primetime knew he was going to have to play this one real cool. The consequences would be brutal if he did anything to their sister.

Tiffany had Primetime just where she wanted. The fear flickered in his eyes when she mentioned her brothers.

For a second, they stood there and stared at each other, until Tiffany broke the silent tension in a composed manner.

"So may we start over? My name is Tiffany, not bitch."

Primetime continued to stare.

"Are we going to discuss business or what? Because I didn't come here to get into a war."

"Yeah, let's discuss business. Do you care for a drink?"

"No, thank you."

"About this fifty thousand dollars. There's no way I'm paying you that much."

"What are you willing to pay?"

"First of all, what do you have that's worth me taking into consideration to pay for?"

"I have names and an address of a person that I know was part of that shit that happened to your traphouse on Dinglewood, because I literally talked to him when I answered the door that night."

"Did you give the police this information?"

"Hell no!"

"Give me the names and address."

"Give me a price."

"I'll give you ten thousand dollars."

"You got to be kidding." Tiffany looked at Primetime like he just spit in her face.

"I saw you in a club with no problem making it rain hundreds of dollar bills, which was at least twenty-five grand or better. So I suggest that you quit being cheap, because I feel insulted."

Tiffany was right, even though Primetime hated to admit it. Tiffany was just another bitch looking for a come-up. Realizing that she wasn't going to let up, he decided to give in—just to get this greedy bitch out of his face.

"I'll give you twenty-five grand. Ten now, and if the information checks out, I'll give you the other fifteen grand later. Is that a deal?"

"We have a deal." Tiffany reached in her purse and pulled out a folded sheet of paper. She abruptly snatched her hand back before placing it in Primetime's hand.

"Money, please."

Primetime walked to his desk and pulled out ten grand and handed it to her.

"The guy I talked to the night I answered the door name is Antonio Jones, a.k.a. Ant. He had two other guys with him that I don't know, but he can lead you to them. I hear Ant is staying on the west side—I believe it's somewhere on Tuckaseegee. Anyway, his mother stays off Idlewild Road. As you can see, her address is written on the paper. He has a younger brother that's seventeen years old and attends East Mecklenburg High School. I also heard that Ant is working for a dude named Cold, and I hear Cold is a cold mothafucka," Tiffany added for a thrill.

Disregarding her last comment, Primetime was actually impressed by the detailed information Tiffany had gathered.

He walked back to the desk and retrieved the other fifteen grand and handed it to her.

"I'm going to take your word on this. I believe you, and if you can get this type of detailed information on people, then we may be able to do future business. What do you say?"

"Of course we can do more business." Tiffany smiled and shook Primetime's hand.

"And maybe pleasure," Primetime added flirtatiously, taking in Tiffany's light brown skin complexion, cute face, and fat ass. She was too rough around the edges to be his type, but she could be a valuable asset, he thought.

"Maybe," Tiffany flirted back. "Well, you have my number."

And with that, she walked out the door with JoJo to escort her back.

Upon their departure, Primetime immediately picked up the phone and began dialing.

Chapter 24

Things had worked out much better than what Tiffany had expected. She only had the intention of walking out with at least fifteen grand. She underhanded ten grand and the fifteen grand she agreed to divide amongst her and her brothers. The four siblings had contrived a plan to hustle Primetime and have him take care of their dirty work.

Tiffany was exhilarated; she had just acquired a partnership for business and pleasure with the one and only Primetime. Her pussy was getting wet just thinking about how her future was about to change.

After getting dropped off, Tiffany decided to call up a friend because right now, she needed her pussy ate and fucked real good, and Mellow-T was that nigga to do it.

"What up baby girl?" Mellow-T answered.

"You and that dick."

"Where are you at?" he asked.

"I'm at my new apartment in CitySide, do you know where that is?"

"Yeah, text me your address," Mellow-T said before he hung up.

Tiffany wanted her pussy to be nice and fresh for Mellow-T. He was the only man that she knew who was great at eating pussy and fucking her brains out. She popped some Molly, rolled up a blunt of Kush, and hopped in a bubble bath with Victoria's Secret fragrance.

Mellow-T was a thug nigga, so he arrived about a half hour later than what was promised. Tiffany didn't mind because the wait was worth it. When he walked through the door, Tiffany was waiting ass naked. She dropped straight on her knees and pulled out Mellow-T's dick and slurped on it like it was the last dick left on earth. Mellow-T just leaned back against the door and let her work.

Feeling himself about to cum, Mellow-T roughly snatched Tiffany up by her hair and pulled her forcefully over to the couch and bent her over. He quickly stripped his clothes and eased inside her pussy. He grabbed a handful of her hair with one hand and pulled, and squeezed her neck with his other hand, and began to deliver hard and rough strokes like a jackrabbit.

Tiffany loved getting fucked rough, and Mellow-T fucked her rough just the way she liked it, but this time, Mellow-T was a little too rough. He pushed her head into the couch and continued to pound inside her with deep, hard strokes. She wanted to tell him to take it easy a little bit, but the words failed to escape her mouth with her head buried into the couch. He was too powerful for her to get out of the awkward position. Her lungs burned from a lack of oxygen; she was on the verge of passing out, but somewhere in her wicked mind, desire came upon her like an earthquake, rumbling deep in every fiber of her body. Her resistance drowned in tidal waves of passion from each stroke he delivered until her body convulsed from a very intense, rapturous, and shuddering orgasm.

Moments later, she felt him shuddering and releasing the death grip on her head, allowing oxygen back into her lungs. They both sat on the couch breathless and sweating for about ten minutes until Mellow-T broke the silence.

"Ah, roll up a fucking blunt!" he ordered.

Tiffany rolled her eyes and sucked her teeth, but got her ass up and sashayed into the room to get the weed. She came back into the living room and rolled up. Halfway through the blunt, Tiffany had some inquiries.

"Do you know a guy named Cold that's supposed to run the West Side?" she asked.

"I don't know him personally, but I've heard of him. Why, what's up?" he asked.

"Do you know how to find him?"

"No. Why? Are you trying to get at him or something?" he asked.

"Well, if we can find out where he stay or be at, we may be able to get a lot of money."

"If I find out where that nigga stay, I won't need money because I'm going to kill that nigga myself," he stated.

"What did he do to you?" she asked.

"He killed my uncle Uzi in a liquor house over a card game a while back."

"We can work together and get him."

"I'll come up with a plan, but right now, I need to taste that pussy," Mellow-T said.

He got on his knees and pulled Tiffany to the edge of the couch and dove headfirst back into the pussy.

Chapter 25

During the past few months, being caught up in his studies, Cold had purposely failed to reach out to Privilege. On their next encounter, he wanted to be able to speak intellectually about business. Today, he decided to check in on Privilege.

After a few rings, Privilege's soft, beautiful voice answered with a polite, "Hello?"

"With a voice that beautiful, this got to be the hotline service."

Immediately, Privilege picked up on the baritone voice that was embedded in her head. She began to speak seductively, imitating a hotline operator.

"Daddy, you're right, and I'm all hot and ready to do anything you want. Just tell me what you want, Daddy."

"Well, tell Daddy what you're wearing?"

"I have on a pink edible thong, and I'm all oiled up, waiting on you, Big Daddy, to give it to me nice and slow with long strides."

Cold's dick was harder than a steel beam listening to Privilege—especially with the fact that he hadn't had sex in the past few months.

"Can you handle a long tongue giving you one of the wettest and most sensual orgasms you ever had?" Cold spoke in a dulcet whisper.

"Yes! . . . Okay, okay, that's enough." Privilege fanned herself and crossed her legs to stop the sensation that had begun to tingle between her legs. "Boy, you are crazy."

"You almost had me trying to jump through the phone talking to me like that."

"Yeah, I bet you would if you could." Privilege blushed, wishing he could really jump through the phone.

"So how have you been?" Cold leveled the conversation.

"I've been good, but I should be asking you how you been."

"Why haven't you called me?" Privilege immediately regretted her words, thinking she sounded desperate.

"My apologies. I've been a little busy."

"You must have found a lucky lady." Privilege immediately regretted her words again. *Damn, get it together, he's just a friend,* she reminded herself.

"No, I haven't. Actually, I've been attending school for Business Management."

Privilege was impressed. "I see you really mean business."

"In life, if you're going to do something, why not try to be the best at it? I don't like half-stepping in anything I do. Now, what I really want to do is give thanks to you for your encouragement."

"I don't know what I did to encourage you to get that much determination."

"You did so much from that one conversation we had in the mall. When you were discussing business, your intellect and potential encouraged and inspired me. I may not be on your level, but I hope that one day we can become business partners."

"I don't know what to say . . . You're welcome, and thanks. I didn't know I had that much of an effect on you. I would love to form a partnership with you."

Privilege really felt appreciated that someone noticed her true potential—besides just looking at her as a sex symbol or object.

"How about I take you out to lunch so we can discuss some future business ventures and have a toast to our new partnership?"

"That sounds great—only if you allow me to pick up the tab, and you can pick the restaurant."

"How about we meet at Rock Bottom uptown at 11 o'clock? That'll give us both enough time to get ready. What do you think?"

"That's perfect. Great minds think alike. I'll see you then."

After hanging up, Privilege was feeling exuberant. She felt like a teenage girl going out on a first date. Cold brought out a side in her that she hadn't felt in years. It was wrong, and she felt guilty about the way she thought about Cold. The desire was overwhelming, but she tried desperately to convince herself that it was only going to be a partnership for business and nothing else. Besides, there's no harm in fantasizing.

She had even fantasized about Cold a few times while having sex with Primetime—and it caused her to have multiple orgasms.

"Guilty pleasures!" she giggled out loud, while getting ready for her rendezvous with Cold.

Chapter 26

Being punctual was a principle Cold and Privilege both honored and took very seriously. If the opposing party didn't treat punctuality as a priority—whether in personal or business life—the relationship wouldn't last long. They both arrived at Rock Bottom at 11 o'clock sharp.

Privilege looked stunning. She had on a gold Prada knee-length dress with an open back that hugged her bodacious body, enticing every eye captured by her presence. On her feet were a pair of gold open-toe stiletto heels with straps that wrapped around her calves. The men's hormones in the restaurant pumped, and their temperatures reached four hundred degrees.

Cold was looking dapper himself—creased up in a pair of beige Ralph Lauren khakis and a beige and brown Ralph Lauren shirt that matched a pair of brown Polo boots. His waves were so rippled you'd get seasick if you stared too long.

The waitress ushered them through the restaurant to their reserved table. She gave them menus and took their drink orders, in which Cold ordered a bottle of chilled *Joseph Phelps Cabernet Sauvignon.*

"Very impressive!" Privilege recognized the fine wine.

"First, I would like to say that you look gorgeous, and it's a pleasure to be acquainted with you, Ms. Privilege . . ." Cold paused to allow her to complete her full name.

"Thank you, and it's Privilege Cai. And it's my pleasure to be acquainted with you as well, Mr. . . . ?"

"My real name is Peter Franklin. So tell me about Privilege Cai."

"Well, my mother is Asian and Black, which is where I get my chinky qualities, and my father was Haitian. He and my mother were never married, and my father passed away when I was eleven years old. I have an older brother."

"I'm sorry to hear about your father."

"It's okay. I've outgrown the depression and sadness."

Cold still caught a flicker of sadness cross her face. Changing the subject, Cold asked the question that Privilege was hoping to avoid.

"Do you mind telling me about your relationship—if it's not too personal?"

"Well, his name is Primetime. I've known him for many years, but we've been together for five now."

"So, any plans on getting married and having kids with this Primetime?"

"We never discuss those topics, and quite frankly, I don't know if I want to marry or have his kids." Privilege looked in Cold's eyes with a burning desire.

Their stare was interrupted when the waitress came back to the table with the wine and glasses. She poured their drinks and asked if they were ready to order.

Opening their menus for the first time, Cold allowed Privilege to order first.

"Yes, I would like to have the caviar for the appetizer, a chicken Caesar salad, and for the entrée, I'd like a sirloin steak well done, a baked potato with butter, cheese, and a sprinkle of bacon bits. Thank you."

"And you, sir?" the waitress turned to Cold.

"That sounded so delicious, I'll try the same thing."

"Your food should be ready in about forty-five minutes." The waitress collected their menus and departed.

"Now it's your turn to tell me about you, Mr. Peter Franklin, a.k.a. Cold."

Cold grabbed the glass of wine. "First, let's make a toast." He raised his glass.

Privilege picked up her glass, and Cold began making his toast.

"I would like to make a toast to a new beginning of friendship and partnership, to happiness and joy, to strength and growth, to business and success, and to you, Ms. Privilege Cai, for opening my mind up."

"Toast to that." Privilege touched glasses, then took a sip.

"So tell me the story." She got back to her interest in learning who Peter Franklin really was.

Taking another sip, then clearing his throat, Cold began. "My father is Jamaican, and my mother is Dominican and Black. My father resides in Jamaica—we don't communicate too often. My mother died of AIDS while I was young. I don't have any siblings that I know of. I take care of my grandmother. I have one uncle that's here in Charlotte. I have four kids with two women—two boys and twin girls."

The mention of two baby mothers and four children made Privilege a little disappointed. *Damn, I knew it was too good to be true. Keep cool. You're only his business partner anyway, so why does it matter*, she reminded herself.

Cold noticed the disappointed look on Privilege's face when he mentioned his four children and two baby mothers.

"I'm sorry about your mother."

"It's all right." Cold noticed Privilege still looked a little perplexed. "Are you all right?"

"Oh, yes, I'm fine. I just didn't picture you with any kids."

"My kids or their mothers won't ever come between us or our business." The look in Cold's eyes said, *Believe me, I got this shit under control.*

"I believe you, Cold." And Privilege sincerely believed him.

After finishing their meal and getting the table cleaned off, Cold opened up the small binder he'd brought along.

"Now that we're together, I would like to discuss my progress, a few business plans, and the type of money I'm trying to clean up."

"Okay, I'm listening."

"Well, the first thing I want to say is I'm not your average—let's use the term *street entrepreneur*. I'm playing with some very large numbers. I know it's going to take time and patience. I want to be thorough and have every dollar accounted for. As I told you over the phone, I've been doing a lot of studying in different fields—yet I'm still in my first semester, so I have a while to go.

"Now, where you come into play is educating me and putting your potential into use. Basically, what that means is I'm going to follow your lead. But for a beginner, I've taken the initiative in writing to the Small Business Administration Office to learn how to write a business plan. I've also gotten on my grandfather's payroll at the graveyard, and I've opened up a checking and savings account. My grandfather and I have been discussing signing the graveyard over in my name so I can use it as an asset to acquire loans. I'm also in the process of writing a book between my studies—which I can use in opening up a publishing company. I have many more ideas, but those are a few I wanted to brief you on so you won't feel like I'm trying to put everything on your plate. So what do you think?"

Privilege was amazed—she couldn't believe it. She had never met a drug dealer—or rather, a street entrepreneur—so intellectually business-minded with the potential Cold had. She was almost at a loss for words.

"Well, it seems to me that you really don't need me the way you have things so well thought out and put together."

"Don't kid yourself—I need you more than anyone right now, because you're going to be my better half. And without you, I don't think business will grow to its full potential."

"I'm overwhelmed that you feel that way about me, and I'm going to do my best. So how much are you trying to clean up?"

"*We* are going to clean up," Cold emphasized the *we*. "There is no *I* in *team*. But right now, between three to five million dollars—with a rapidly increasing number by the month."

Damn . . . and she thought Primetime was ballin' playing with a million dollars.

"Well, it's going to take a lot of time and patience to clean up that amount of money."

"Now you see why I need you?"

Privilege acknowledged Cold with a new, fond respect. Now convinced by his words—of not being the average street entrepreneur—she was reconsidering her destiny. She was going to make it a priority to be a part of Cold's dynasty.

Cold was confident that Privilege played a big financial role in Primetime's operation, but he was still convinced someone else was behind it. With time and patience, he would get that information out of Privilege. But right now, he wanted to pick her brain.

"Enough about business . . . didn't you say that your boyfriend's name is Primetime?"

"Yes, that's him," Privilege said, unenthused.

"Excuse me if I'm stepping over my boundaries, but is he the same Primetime that had something to do with that church getting shot up?"

Privilege was flabbergasted. "You mean Primetime had something to do with those kids getting killed?"

"I don't know for sure, but after you mentioned his name, I've been wondering where I heard that name before—and then it dawned on me. It was only a rumor I heard on the streets. It wasn't anything concrete or factual. Hell, it could be another Primetime." Cold scrutinized Privilege's body language for any tells of deception. He was confident she was being genuine.

Privilege sat there quietly, staring at her drink, lost in thought.

"I apologize if I discouraged you. I didn't mean to spoil the moment. Sometimes I'm aggressively blunt about things."

"Oh no, it's okay. But what if he *did* have something to do with those people getting killed . . . especially those innocent children?" Privilege became very emotional. "I don't think I can live with a man like that."

"What I said was just a rumor. So don't go off accusing him without facts. You know people will say anything out their mouths these days."

Privilege wiped the tear, looked at Cold, and forced a smile.

"You're right. I'm sorry for breaking down like that. It's just that I don't understand how someone can be that evil to do such a horrific thing."

"How about I take you to the spa so you can relax and clear your mind?"

"That's okay, maybe another time. I need to be heading home. I have a few errands I need to take care of."

After paying the tab, they went their separate ways—promising to schedule another meeting soon.

Chapter 27

Detective Roundhouse stood in a conference room in front of a team of police officers, looking over the unsolved murders from the last several months, trying to connect the dots.

"I'm going to start off with the murder of Chris that happened at Gates Convenience Store on Tuckaseegee Road. I believe his murder is a big key to solving a lot of the murders and arsons, and I'm going to explain to you why I've come to this theory." He placed a photo of Chris at the top of the bulletin board and continued.

"The reason why I'm starting our investigation here is because when someone goes through the length of shooting up your funeral, that means you have done something very terrible to someone, and they are taking it personal. I've reviewed the security camera at Gates Convenience Store, and we identified this guy—Jarvis Nelson, a.k.a. Trigger—as Chris' murderer." He placed a mugshot of Trigger underneath Chris'.

Then he placed a photo of a burnt corpse under Trigger's mugshot. "This is Trigger now, found shot and burned in a drug house in North Charlotte. Now, I'm going to skip to the four men who shot up Chris' funeral. Three of them are dead, and one is sitting in the Mecklenburg County Jail refusing to cooperate. I've done background checks on all of these guys and found out some interesting connections." He pinned another photo under Trigger's.

"Trigger and this guy, Perry Johnson, a.k.a. PJ—the guy that committed suicide after shooting up Chris' funeral— were arrested together about a year ago on a breaking and entering charge. Furthermore, I've learned that the address PJ used when he was arrested is also the same address of the house in Hampshire Hills that is part of a murder and arson investigation, along with two other houses on Milton Road and Dinglewood." He placed three pictures of the aftermath on the bulletin board.

"I believe there is a street war going on between some very dangerous individuals. We need to figure out the parties that are involved before more people get murdered. We need to hit the streets hard. That means we have to start putting a lot of pressure on our informants. We need to get names with faces of who is involved. We're also going to be teaming up with the drug unit, and maybe we'll be able to connect a few pieces. Any questions?"

"Yes, I have a question," a young cop said. "Do you really think the murders and arsons from the three neighborhoods are connected with Chris' murder? I mean, it could all be just a coincidence. Criminals do tend to cross paths."

"If you ever make it to be a detective—which I highly doubt with that mentality—you'll learn that we do not believe in coincidence. You investigate every angle thoroughly. Now, if there aren't any more questions, this meeting is adjourned."

Chapter 28

Antwan Jones was a gifted athlete in high school, standing at six foot six and weighing two hundred and ten pounds. He dominated the football field and the basketball court, but his love was on the basketball court. He had recruiters from many universities interested in acquiring his athletic abilities. He achieved well past the academic level that was required by the school's sports policy.

When Antwan acquired his driver's license, his older brother Ant had congratulated him with a Chrysler 300 with twenty-four-inch rims that enhanced his popularity amongst his peers. Ant did everything in his power to keep Antwan from the streets by spoiling him with money and materialistic things.

Antwan took his girlfriend Britney home every day after practice. She was a cheerleader, so their schedules were convenient with each other, and some days they would go to each other's house and study. Today had been an exception because Britney had some family affairs that she went to attend.

Going about a carefree life, Antwan was oblivious to the van that had been following him since leaving school. After dropping Britney off, he decided to go to the YMCA and work out for a couple of hours. At the gym, he lifted weights, ran the treadmill, and swam for about thirty minutes. Sitting in the locker room preparing to leave, he received a call from Britney.

Britney was ecstatic.

"Baby, do you remember my cousin I told you that played college basketball?"

"Yeah, I remember. Doesn't he play for Duke?"

"He did, because he just signed a contract to play in the NBA for the Charlotte Hornets! Can you believe it? Maybe this can give me a chance to be a cheerleader in the NBA." Britney was unable to control her enthusiasm.

Antwan was walking to his car, hearing the good news that had Britney exuberant.

"You know, I can even throw in a word for you, baby, and see if he can get some NBA scouts to come and look at you!"

"That's great, but I don't want you to feel obligated to do anything, because I want to complete college first."

Antwan gave no attention to the van that was parked right beside his car. He hit the button on the keychain to unlock the doors. He was about to open the door when the side door of the van opened up and three masked men jumped out. His cell phone fell to the ground as the men tussled to obtain him into the van. The struggle was brief and exhausting, but the men overpowered the strong and athletic Antwan into the van and drove away.

Britney was in a panic. She called Antwan's name repeatedly. She had heard the commotion and voices when the phone abruptly dropped. She didn't know what was going on, but she had a dreadful feeling that something terrible was happening to Antwan. Thinking rapidly, she grabbed her mother's cell phone and called the police, reporting the situation for them to go and check out the YMCA.

When the police arrived at the YMCA, they reviewed the surveillance cameras and verified that Antwan had indeed been abducted. The detectives went to Britney's house and bombarded her with questions. They asked about what had occurred that day, or any other day that could help give them a lead, but the emotionally distraught Britney was of no help to the investigation.

Antwan's mother was also bombarded with questions by the detectives, but she was also of no help. She did inform the detectives that she had another son that may be of some help. She had tried to contact Ant for hours, but to no avail, and that had put her in a more unsettling, distressful state.

The only thing she was left to do was pray that both of her sons were all right.

Chapter 29

Ant had been so busy trapping, time had slipped past. It was after 1:00 a.m. when he finally realized that he had left his phone in his car. He had a date set up when his shift was over at 2:00 a.m., and the girl was by far one of the baddest bitches he had ever met. He went outside to get the phone to call the girl Peaches to make sure that their date was still on.

He retrieved the phone, and his heart was immediately filled with apprehension — there were forty-seven missed calls from his mother. The butterflies caused his hands to shake nervously as he called his mother.

The phone was answered on the first ring. His mother was weeping hysterically and speaking incomprehensible words. Ant had to calm his mother down to fully comprehend what she was saying.

"They got Antwan," his mother was finally able to sputter.

"What do you mean they got Antwan? Who are you talking about?" Ant's anxiety kicked in.

"I don't know. Somebody kidnapped him from the YMCA earlier today and I've been trying to reach you."

"Are you sure about that? Maybe it's been a mistake. Just let me call him."

"The detectives have his phone and his car, Ant. They even have surveillance from the YMCA showing the whole abduction. He's gone, Ant. My baby is gone . . ." Her cries escaped again.

"It's going to be okay. I swear I'm going to find him. You just have to be strong, Ma." Ant was choked with emotions and fought back the tears that were trying to surface.

After hanging up, Ant made a silent prayer asking God to bring Antwan home alive. He sat in the car and cried, no longer able to hold his emotions in. Even though he prayed, he felt that Antwan was already dead.

He collected himself from the emotional breakdown and called Cold. After catching the voicemail once and five rings on the second call, Ant was finally greeted.

"Hello?" Cold answered in a raspy voice.

"They got my little brother, man!" Ant was still choked with emotions.

"Who got your brother?" Cold became fully awake.

"There's only one mothafucka that'll do some shit like this," Ant declared angrily.

"Slow down, Ant, and tell me what's going on."

"I just got off the phone with my mom and she said that Antwan got kidnapped leaving out the YMCA, and it's all on camera. He's gone, man . . . I know he's dead."

There was a short pause, leaving each man to collect his thoughts and figure out the next move.

"Listen, Ant, what we need to do is find that girl from the house that night. She was the only one who could've identified you."

"That bitch is dead, and that nigga Primetime is dead — I promise you, Cold."

"He may be using Antwan for collateral to bring us out," Cold reasoned.

"You know that nigga don't play like that, Cold."

"Can you give it until the morning? If we don't hear anything, we'll act accordingly and rationally. I know you're angry, Ant, but impulsiveness can cause big mistakes. I have his crew under surveillance, so let me make some phone calls and see if anyone's seen anything."

"All right, Cold. In the morning. And I'm going to see if I can find out some information about that girl."

"Thank you, Ant."

"Yeah."

"Please don't go and do something without thinking it through." The call ended.

Cold knew that if Primetime had anything to do with Ant's brother getting kidnapped, he was a dead man. One thing for sure — Ant was damn sure going to find out, because he had a lot of sources and street alliances on the Eastside. Word was destined to come to him about Antwan's abduction.

Cold began making calls, and after an hour of disappointments, he was perplexed. Shit didn't add up. If Primetime had something to do with the abduction, how did he slip past the surveillance team? Cold hoped to talk Ant into waiting and see if Antwan showed up or a ransom call came through before doing something he may regret later.

That was a desperate wish.

Chapter 30

Yellow crime scene tape was put up to shut the road off on Glenwood Road by the railroad tracks. Cops, forensic techs, the coroner, and news reporters were at the scene.

"The body was discovered by a pedestrian. It's the body of a young Black male with multiple gunshot wounds. The body cannot yet be identified due to the head shot wounds. The physical appearance and clothes match the description of Antwan Jones who was abducted yesterday evening," the forensic tech Allison said to Detective Roundhouse, who had just arrived at the scene.

Detective Roundhouse turned to his partner, Detective Wilson.

"Get in touch with Antwan's mother and tell her that we need his medical and dental records released to the morgue. And I want to find out more about the brother Antonio. I did a background check last night, and I see that he has a lengthy record, and he has pending charges. Maybe Antonio's lifestyle had something to do with this?"

"Or maybe it was an act of jealousy from a girl's boyfriend. From the report we have from his friends and girlfriend, Antwan was a very popular kid in high school. He had plenty of money, and the ladies loved him," Detective Wilson said.

"The problem with that is that there were four men involved — one driver and three to snatch him into the van. And not only that, the brutality of this murder suggests that this is a message. The M.O. of a jealous boyfriend won't go through the trouble of kidnapping a man with three other men, beat and kill him, then dump the body off on a railroad track. In my experience, that doesn't fit the profile of a jealous boyfriend.

"We need to locate Antonio and question him. I bet he has a lot of answers."

"That's if he'll talk to us."

"Well, criminals have, let's say, disputable reasoning when to cooperate with the cops when the crime hits home," Detective Roundhouse said, lighting up a cigarette.

"Let's just hope that we get to Antonio's before the other guys do if he's connected. Do you want me to put out an APB on him?"

"That won't be necessary."

Detective Roundhouse walked away to his patrol car. He was immediately swarmed by news reporters with microphones and cameras in his face. He politely stopped and commented.

"Sorry, we don't know the identity of the victim, but we're going to investigate this matter very thoroughly and bring someone to justice. So if anyone has any helpful information, please call Crime Stoppers or contact the Homicide Division and ask for Detective Roundhouse. Thank you."

And with that, he hopped in the car and drove away.

Hours later, once the body was taken to the morgue, through dental records, it was confirmed that the body was indeed seventeen-year-old Antwan Jones. Detective Roundhouse and Detective Wilson drove to Antwan's mother's house to inform her about the death.

"Ms. Jones, you don't have to go down to the morgue to identify the body of your son due to the gruesome and severe gunshot wounds to his face. But it's very imperative that we speak with Antonio," Detective Roundhouse said after Ms. Jones calmed down and got control of herself from the devastating news.

"I've already told him that the police wanted to speak with him, but I don't understand what he has to do with this."

"It's just that we're trying to find out if maybe someone was after him. The perps may have gotten Antwan because they couldn't get to Antonio. Ms. Jones, he's not in any trouble or anything — we're just trying to find a lead to solve your son's murder, and maybe Antonio can help us. We've contacted and questioned most of Antwan's friends, and he doesn't seem to have any enemies. Now on the other hand, and I'm not trying to prejudge, but Antonio has a pretty lengthy record, and if someone is after him, we need to find him before the perps do and Antonio ends up like Antwan. We're just trying to help, that's all, Ms. Jones. Help us save your other son."

Ms. Jones was back in tears. She couldn't even think about the thought of losing her other son. She got up from the couch, grabbed the phone, and called Ant.

Ant picked up on the second ring.

"What's up, Ma?"

"Antwan is dead," were the only words she managed to mutter before she began crying uncontrollably.

Detective Roundhouse walked up to Ms. Jones and rubbed his hand across her back in a consoling manner and grabbed the phone from her hand.

"Hello, Antonio, this is Detective Roundhouse from Homicide. I know that this is an inconvenient time due to your family's loss, but do you mind coming to the station so I can ask you a few questions?"

There was a long pause before Detective Roundhouse broke the silence.

"Listen, Antonio, you're not in any trouble. We just want to solve your brother's murder, and any information will be helpful — but we're going to need your help on this."

"I don't see how I can help. I'm just as lost as you guys are. And if I'm not in any trouble, then I don't have to come down to the station, so if you want to ask me any questions, feel free to do so while we're on the phone."

Detective Roundhouse wanted to question Ant in person, but right now he had no other choice because this was probably going to be his only chance.

"Okay, Antonio. Do you have any enemies or know your brother to have any enemies that would do something like this?"

"Far as I know, my brother didn't have any enemies, and I don't have any enemies."

"When was the last time you spoke to or seen Antwan?"

"The night before he got kidnapped."

"Did he seem paranoid or was he acting strange? Or did he mention anything about receiving threats from someone, such as a jealous boyfriend? Even if he said it in a joking manner?"

"No, there was nothing out of the ordinary. He was fine."

"Have you received any threats, Antonio?"

"No!"

Detective Roundhouse was getting nowhere with this, and he knew that Ant was not being completely honest. That's why he wanted to question Ant in person — to read his body language and apply more pressure.

"Antonio, it's very imperative that you come forward with any information that you think will be helpful to us. Right now, we're on the same team, and I want this person taken down just as bad as you do. I'm asking you to let us take this murderer down together — but in the right way, with the law on our side. I believe you know something that you're not sharing with me, and I don't want you to take matters into your own hands. Think about your mother, Antonio. Don't let her lose two sons — either to the grave or to the penitentiary."

"I'm sorry, I can't help, detective. But if you don't have any more questions, I would like for you to put my mother back on the phone."

"If I have any further questions, may I contact you?"

"I believe if you have any more questions, you're going to contact me anyway."

"Here's your mother, Antonio."

"Hey, baby," Ms. Jones received the phone with a little more composure.

"Ma, when those detectives leave, I'll be over there, okay."

"Yes, baby, I understand. I'll talk to you later."

Detective Roundhouse and Detective Wilson thanked Ms. Jones for her cooperation and gave her their final condolences, then left. When they got back in the car, Detective Wilson was curious.

"Why did you question Antonio over the phone?" he asked.

"That may have been our only opportunity to talk to him — if he's not dead by the end of the day."

"So what did he have to say?"

"Nothing helpful. But I believe he knows something," Detective Roundhouse said as he drove away.

Chapter 31

Privilege had been watching Primetime all day since he came in that morning. He had come in the house about 7:00 a.m. and jumped straight in the shower. He had been pacing around the house nervously, not saying a word — it was like he was in another world.

Privilege had asked him a few times if everything was alright.

The first time she got a response, he replied a quick "Yeah," with no further comments. The other times she asked, he just stared at her as if just realizing that she was in the house and didn't give a response.

Privilege knew something was terribly wrong — that something had happened. She had never seen Primetime act like that, and it made her nervous.

The uneasiness was replaced by fear when the 5 o'clock news came on, and the breaking story was about a young Black male found dead on the railroad tracks.

"That's it right there," Primetime mumbled under his breath while tuned deep into the thirty-second news clip.

After watching the news, Primetime got dressed and left the house without saying a word to Privilege.

Once Primetime left, Privilege needed someone to talk to, and the only person she could think of was Cold. She grabbed the phone and called him up.

"Hello!" Cold answered.

"Hey, Cold, I need to talk to you about something very important, but I don't want to talk over the phone. When you have the time, can we meet up somewhere?"

126

"Sure, where you at? Is everything okay with you?"

"Yes, I'm alright. It may be nothing really. Can you meet me at Showmars on Freedom Drive in thirty minutes?"

"I'm already on my way."

Upon both of them arriving at the restaurant, they ordered some food and found seats in the back. Neither touched their food, and they skipped past the small talk.

Privilege relayed everything that she had witnessed about Primetime's behavior — including watching the news and his abrupt departure. Cold listened attentively to every word without interruption.

"I swear, I think he had something to do with that kid getting killed," Privilege said.

"Why didn't you ask him?"

"Because he was so far gone I don't think he would've acknowledged me anyway. I just feel so terrible, Cold. What if he killed that boy and those people at the funeral? Do you think I should go to the police?"

"No! Don't go to the police, Privilege. If he did all of those things, trust me — his time is coming. In this game, you have to let the streets be the judge and jury. You have to take the good with the bad. You knew the type of lifestyle he was living before you started dealing with him. He's a drug dealer. And from what I hear, he is not a small-time drug dealer. In the streets, to be able to stand strong, you have to get respect — and killing people is a strong enforcement for getting respect. Now, I'm not saying what he did — or rather what we think he did — is right or is approved of, because that was innocent people and children, and there's a boundary that shouldn't be crossed."

"Can I ask you a question, Cold?"

"Sure, ask me."

"Have you ever killed someone?" Privilege stared straight in his eyes.

"Does it matter?"

"As long as it wasn't innocent people or kids."

"Then it doesn't matter." Cold took a sip from the watered-down soda.

Chapter 32

Primetime had been driving around town going nowhere, trying to escape the images from last night.

Last night, his men had brought the kid Antwan to an abandoned warehouse. Primetime had been drunk, and things got out of control. It was actually more of an ego thing, but he had killed Antwan.

Primetime had never killed anyone before — hell, he had never even shot a gun until last night. He had ordered many hits to get people killed, but not once did he ever partake in one until last night. His whole intentions were to beat the kid around a little and get him to call Ant — the one he really wanted — but the kid was stubborn. The kid had insulted him in front of his crew members and even had the audacity to spit in his face.

Primetime let his emotions take over and shot the kid seventeen times in the face and chest. Now the event kept vividly replaying over and over in his mind. It was like the kid was haunting him.

After hours of aimless driving, Primetime eventually made it back home. He was finally able to ease his mind of the haunting images of Antwan's dead body. Now he was filled with an adrenaline that made him feel powerful. He had a sinister smile as he thought about taking another human's life.

All fear and guilt was completely vanquished, and he was energetic.

When he walked into the room, Privilege was sound asleep. He knew he was blessed to have a woman like Privilege and had even thought about proposing a few times. Even though he didn't discuss his true feelings with Privilege, he knew that she loved him. Lately, though, he had been neglecting her and promised himself to make up for that.

He hopped in the shower, singing and dancing, thinking about the more fear and respect that he would gain from the streets. His ego was so big right now you couldn't knock it down with a cannonball. He felt invigorated getting out of the shower, and what would make this night end right was some pussy.

He climbed in bed behind Privilege and planted kisses on her neck and massaged her breasts. He slowly worked his hand down past her stomach to her panties.

"I wouldn't do that if I was you," Privilege said, stopping him as soon as his fingers went inside her panties. "I'm on my period."

She was actually glad that her period was on.

"Damn. Well, that don't have to stop you from making your man feel good with that pretty little mouth." He rubbed his fingers across her lips.

"I'm not in the mood for that, honey, but you can hold me."

"That's alright, because I got some business I need to go and take care of anyway."

Primetime kissed her on the forehead, got up, got dressed, and left without saying another word.

Privilege would've been furious, but ever since meeting Cold, she no longer cared about his neglect or sudden departures. She knew about both of Primetime's side chicks but didn't care anymore, because their relationship wasn't going to last too much longer.

She still had love for Primetime, but she wasn't in love with him anymore, and she no longer saw a future between them.

After he left, she just curled back up under the covers and fantasized about another man.

Cold.

Chapter 33

After leaving his mother's house, Ant ran around the Eastside of Charlotte for the rest of the day gathering information. He finally got Tiffany's name and learned that she was also the sister of Drape, Nut Box, and Body Bag — three crazy mothafuckas that ran the Eastside Bloods. But Ant was fearless at heart, and he was ready to deal with them after what he was going to do with their sister Tiffany.

By now, everybody on the Eastside knew about Ant's brother's murder, and everybody that knew or heard of Ant knew that it was going to be a bloodbath once he found out who was involved. The ones that it was essential to didn't take heed to the matter — pride and arrogance obscured their senses.

About 11 o'clock that night, Ant received a phone call from a source informing him that Tiffany and her brothers were on Dinglewood, and gave him the address. Ant took this matter personal, and he didn't want anyone to interfere with his plan, so he decided to take matters into his own hands. He drove around the block a few times, observing the house. The lights were on, and the music was playing loud — just as the source described.

Ant parked around the corner at the park located behind the houses on Dinglewood. He was ready — bulletproof vest on, AR-15, two .40 calibers, and his "Rambo knife," as he liked to call it. He was dressed in all-black with a ski mask on. He ran through the shadows in the park like a trained assassin until he arrived at the fence of the targeted house and hopped over.

The music grew louder the closer he got to the rear of the house. He went to the windows in the back of the house, trying to get a sight of any human figures. The bedrooms were dark, but he could see clear enough in them to know they were empty. He moved to the back door and peeped inside the windows, and could see Tiffany and her brothers laughing and joking around, trying to overtalk the loud music.

Ant pulled out the knife and walked back over to one of the bedroom windows that he had a better view in and felt more confident was empty. He cut the screen off and tried to lift the window — and to his surprise, the window went straight up with a light cracking sound. He climbed through the window real slow, trying not to make any noise by knocking something over, even though the music was blasting.

Once completely inside the room, Ant stood still to allow his eyes to adjust to the darkness, so as not to trip or run into anything. He then walked to the door and slowly turned the doorknob, with the AR-15 clutched tight in his other hand, ready to fire.

Tiffany and her brothers were getting wasted at Tiffany's friend Cynthia's house. They were sniffing cocaine, smoking blunts of kush, purple haze, diesel, and drinking on Grey Goose and Cîroc. They were having the time of their lives with the money they had gotten from Primetime. Not one of them noticed the bedroom door cracked open with two preying eyes focused on all of them.

"I'm going to work that nigga Primetime like an ATM machine," Tiffany said.

"Just make sure you put the word in for us, sis," Drape said.

"Don't worry, because by the time I get finished with that nigga, I'm going to have him make y'all his personal bodyguards. Hell, y'all are my brothers. That's why he gave me fifteen grand." Tiffany still hadn't disclosed the other ten grand from the twenty-five grand she really got.

"Instead of waiting on that nigga to call you, you call him and set something up," Nut Box said.

"Set something up, like what? Because I don't want to look thirsty and run him away," Tiffany said.

"How about we set up a business proposition? Tell him that we will personally bring that nigga Ant to him," Nut Box said.

"And how are we supposed to find that nigga Ant?" Tiffany was curious.

"We have Bloods all over Charlotte — we'll find him. It may take a few weeks, especially with his little brother getting killed, but he's going to be looking for who killed his brother," Drape spoke up.

Ant heard enough. He opened the door, pointing the AR-15 at everyone in the living room.

Everyone froze, looking at the man with the ski mask and gun. Ant shot three rounds in Body Bag's chest, who was sitting in the corner and reached for his pistol on the table. Ant then looked at the other four victims, pointing the smoking AR-15.

"Do you know who the fuck we are, nigga? What you want — money and drugs?" Nut Box asked with a mixture of fear and rage.

"Nigga, shut the fuck up. This ain't about the money and drugs." Ant slowly removed the ski mask.

Dread fell upon their hearts and defeated their nerves. This moment in their life became surreal — from the reality of facing their inevitable death.

"Ant, I swear I didn't have anything to do with that, please let me go and I promise I won't say anything," Cynthia pleaded while crying hysterically.

Ant had murder in his eyes right now.

"Sorry, bitch." He pulled the trigger, hitting Cynthia numerous times in the chest. He then turned the rifle towards

Drape and Nut Box and fired about fifteen rounds in both of them, killing them instantly.

"You see, bitch?" Ant walked towards Tiffany, who was curled up on the couch, frightened.

"This is all because of you, so I got something really special for you."

He pulled out the knife and gripped it tight. The first swing penetrated her rib cage, causing her to scream out in a high-pitched, piercing cry. He repeatedly thrust the knife — each swing a reflection of emotions: pain, sadness, anger, and hate — as tears fell from his eyes.

Ant continued to stab long after her cries were muted by death, until he was exhausted. He stepped back from the mutilated body and immediately picked up the rifle and ski mask, and ran out the back door covered in blood.

Chapter 34

Privilege woke up just the way she went to bed — alone. She got up early to prepare for the long day ahead of her. She went into the kitchen, brewed some coffee, and turned on the TV to catch the morning news.

As she drank the coffee, breaking news flashed on the screen about a house where a massacre had occurred, leaving five victims dead with no surviving witnesses. When they said the names and showed the pictures of all the victims, Privilege was instantly struck with sadness. The two girls in the photos were ex-employees at her club, and she knew both of them very well. Tears trickled down her cheeks. Even though Privilege and the two girls had departed on bad terms, she still felt a little bond with them due to their history at the club.

"Damn! What's happening to this city? Charlotte used to be such a peaceful place," Privilege spoke out loud.

The devastating news had broken her morning spirit, but she collected herself and got dressed. She usually keeps to a strict diet, but this morning she decided to make an exception and go to IHOP to treat herself to some blueberry waffles and whipped cream.

Primetime had stayed the night at Tammy's house, one of his mistresses. She was a beautiful woman, but she still couldn't compete with any of Privilege's qualities. On the other hand, Privilege was on a level far past the average bitch anyway. Now Tammy had it going on, also. She was brown-skinned with a fat ass and slim waist, and had a head game that would make any man shoot out money like a slot machine. Tammy had fucked and sucked Primetime so good all night that he decided to take her out for breakfast. They decided to go to IHOP, where both of them agreed they had the best breakfast.

Ant had stayed at the Hilton Suites last night with Kiesha. He was finally able to get a little relaxation. With four down and one to go, he felt better about being able to avenge his brother's murder. It may not bring his brother back, but he be damned if these mothafuckas were going to walk this earth while Antwan lay underneath it, he rationalized.

Kiesha had taken a lot of pressure off him last night. Not only was the sex game good, but he could talk to Kiesha about anything. They had grown up together in the same neighborhood and became very close friends over the years. Kiesha was a down-ass bitch; that's why he felt comfortable talking to her about the murders. He knew she wouldn't tell, because they had to kill a person once on a robbery gone wrong.

When they woke up, Kiesha wanted to go out to eat for breakfast. Even though Ant wanted to relax a few more hours, he decided to give in. Especially after the sex last night, how could he say no? They showered, got dressed, and left out the door.

Primetime and Tammy were sitting in IHOP, waiting for the waitress to bring them their meals. Tammy wanted Primetime to leave Privilege and be with her — that was the discussion that was taking place.

"You knew from the beginning, Tammy. I told you I'm not leaving Privilege. I never lied to you or tried to lead you on. You accepted your position willingly."

"I know, I know, sweetie, and I'm sorry, but I love you, and I was just hoping that you love me too."

"I do love you, Tammy."

"But not enough to leave that bitch," she interrupted.

"Listen, can we not discuss this anymore? I'm with you right now, and I'm here to give you my undivided attention.

When I'm with you, I'm all yours." Primetime smiled and grabbed her hand across the table.

"Yeah, until that bitch calls," Tammy said under her breath while rolling her eyes.

"If our relationship is too much for you, we can always call it off." Primetime was getting annoyed.

"Why do you always say that? You are always so quick to call it off. You must really not have any real feelings for me, talking that bullshit about you love me."

Primetime was glad when the waitress walked up to the table with their meals. He was tired of having this same conversation with Tammy. There was no way in hell he was going to give up a sirloin steak for a hamburger. He decided right there that Tammy and him were over. He understood his part for being at fault by letting Tammy get too attached, but he didn't feel guilty. *Fuck this bitch,* he thought while looking at Tammy.

When Privilege pulled into the parking lot at IHOP, the first thing she noticed was Primetime's Lexus. She felt like turning around and driving away as butterflies fluttered her stomach. She parked and composed herself, then calmly exited the car and headed to the entrance of the restaurant.

The moment she walked through the doors, she was overwhelmed by an uneasiness that trembled her nerves. She looked around the restaurant until her eyes landed on Primetime and the beautiful brown-skinned girl sitting down eating and chatting. The ache in her heart was quickly replaced by anger and jealousy from actually seeing Primetime with another woman. She bee-lined towards Primetime and his companion in a steady motion.

"I hope I'm not interrupting anything," Privilege said, folding her arms across her chest once approaching the duo.

Primetime and Tammy were completely caught off guard. Tammy almost urinated on herself, but Primetime held his composure and thought fast.

"What's up, baby? We were just discussing getting her to dance at our club," Primetime said, playing it cool.

"Is that before or after you fucked her last night?"

"It's not even like that, Privilege."

"Do you think I don't know about your two side bitches — this bitch Tammy and Jasmine? You know what though, I don't even care anymore. You can have both of those stankin' ass bitches." Privilege turned to walk away.

Ant and Kiesha pulled up in the parking lot at IHOP engaged in a conversation. Kiesha was telling Ant about her cousin that lived in Mississippi who he could go and chill with when things got too hot.

"I may take you up on that offer if shit get out of hand, but I'm not going anywhere until that nigga Primetime is in the grave," Ant said, walking into the restaurant.

He always made a quick assessment whenever he entered a building. When he looked in the back of the restaurant, he couldn't believe his eyes.

"I can't believe this nigga actually have the fucking nerve," he mumbled, flaring up with anger at Primetime's audacity.

"What are you talking about?" Kiesha turned towards Ant's penetrating gaze. Her mouth almost fell to the floor. She knew Primetime was a dead man. "Maybe you should wait until he comes out."

Her words were spoken to deaf ears as Ant walked towards Primetime.

Privilege, Primetime, nor Tammy were aware of the man flared up with anger walking towards them at a steady pace. Right when Ant approached the table, he bumped into Privilege, almost knocking her over just as she abruptly turned around.

When Primetime looked up, he was staring into the barrel of Ant's .45 automatic Glock. When he saw the face holding the weapon — the same face from the photos he had embedded in his mind — he knew his life was over. For the first time in his life, he felt inferior, incompetent, and defeated all at once. He silently ridiculed himself for underestimating his enemy. He knew damn well you can't go around killing people and not think mothafuckas aren't trying to touch you back.

He should've taken heed this morning when he saw the news about Tiffany and her brothers, but with the amount of enemies they had, he waved it off. Now look.

He took one last look into Privilege's eyes and mouthed the words, *I love you.*

"This is for Antwan, mothafucka!" Ant unloaded nine shots into Primetime's face. A closed casket will be mourned.

Tammy screamed hysterically.

"Please don't kill me!" she pleaded.

Privilege froze. She was paralyzed in the passage of time as she witnessed Primetime be murdered while staring into his eyes. The few people that were in the restaurant ran out the door upon hearing the gunshots.

Ant casually walked his way out the door and hopped in the car with Kiesha, who was already waiting with the engine running in drive.

"Revenge is now paid in full," Ant said, smiling as they drove off.

"I got them, little brother," he whispered to the wind for the angels to deliver.

Chapter 35

The news of Primetime's unexpected, cold-blooded public murder had shocked the whole city. Some were content, and others were devastated. Privilege was in a state of post-traumatic stress. She couldn't escape the gruesome images of Primetime's brain being shot out right before her eyes. Even though her love had steadily lessened for Primetime, there were still feelings involved. They had history together, and she felt like a part of her had died with him.

Her brother Ty'ron had come to the house to console her. Ty'ron always gave her comfort when she needed it the most. He was overprotective and had acted like a father figure to her ever since their father had died. He was the one who kept her strong and the one who encouraged her to go to business school. In her eyes, Ty'ron was the man who made her the woman she was today.

A week later, the funeral was held at Primetime's father's church. Many people came and showed their respect, and others came to view the body of the Eastside legend. Primetime's father knew and disapproved of Primetime's lifestyle, but the words he spoke out from the podium were contrary to that knowledge. He made it seem as if Primetime was an innocent young man taken too soon. He even had the audacity to say that his son, Ryan Rivers, Jr., was one day going to follow in his footsteps and become a minister of God.

The many people who knew Primetime knew that it was a bunch of bullshit. They even rolled their eyes and chuckled under their breath. Some just reasoned that Primetime's father was naïve to Primetime's lifestyle.

After the service and burial, Privilege went straight home to be alone and rest. She was tired of all the kisses, hugs, and fake tears coming from strangers and phony friends. She declined the offer of going to Primetime's parents' home to eat.

Curled up on the couch, Privilege's phone rang. She was tempted to ignore it and just turn it off, but decided to check the caller ID. Even though she didn't want to talk to anyone, this caller was an exception.

"Hello?" she answered.

"Sorry to hear about what happened. I hope you're holding up," Cold said.

"Yes, I'm trying to. Thank you."

"If you need anything, just holla at me and I got you. I don't want you to think that you're alone because of the circumstances. I'm here if you need someone to talk to or just someone to listen to you, okay."

"Okay, thank you." Privilege really felt Cold's sincerity.

"I hate going to funerals. Ever since my mother died, I promised myself I would never go to another funeral."

"Why is that?"

"Because when you go to a funeral, you get the fake tears, the phony hugs and kisses, and everyone telling you that they got your back with their phony promises. Then as soon as the funeral is over with, you never see or hear from them again."

"It sounds like you had a bad experience." Privilege smiled inside at the truth of his words.

"Yeah, it was. But you know what? I learned from that. That's why when I say those words to you, I mean them. So if you want, I will come and pick you up right now so you can take your mind off things."

"That sounds tempting."

"You just say the word and I got you, alright? My offer will always be on the table."

"Thanks, Cold. You are so sweet, but I have a lot of work to do around the house that's going to keep me busy for the next few weeks."

"Well, if you need any help, just let me know."

"I'm okay, Cold. Thank you."

"Alright then, I will talk to you later, Privilege."

About an hour after Privilege hung up with Cold, she reconsidered her options of going out just to get her mind out of a pity party. Being in the big house by herself was not going to keep her mind off of Primetime. She called Cold to take him up on his offer.

Cold made good on his promise and took Privilege to Uptown Charlotte, where they strolled the city.

The night went wonderful, and when they departed company, Privilege's spirit was feeling a lot better. She even took into consideration the fact that Cold had declined when she offered him to come back to her house. She was vulnerable right now, and he didn't take advantage — even though she secretly wished he would have — but she was pleased and accepted the respect.

However, she did bless him with a kiss on his lips before departing.

Chapter 36

A blurry picture of a Black male suspect walking into and out of IHOP, before and after the murder of Primetime, had been posted on the news all week, trying to be identified. Ant had left town and went to Mississippi to Kiesha's cousin's house. Kiesha, Cold, and Pree were the only selected few who knew of Ant's whereabouts, and they kept a tight lip. Cold had gotten Ant a fake ID, birth certificate, and gave him some cash to hold him over for a while. Cold stressed to Ant to stay low-key until they could come up with a plan to resolve the matter.

The following months that passed by, Cold and Privilege had begun to spend a lot of time with each other, yet Cold kept their relationship platonic. For convenience, Cold took his classes online. Privilege had introduced Cold to her brother Ty'ron and was intrigued at how quickly Cold had Ty'ron open up to him. Ty'ron wasn't much of a people person, so it was rare for Privilege to see him take a liking to someone so fast.

In Cold's perspective, he was industrializing, so he was very much aware and pragmatic of every action he approached. He had devised a plan to take over Primetime's operation, and Privilege and Ty'ron were going to play a major part in it. The more Cold communicated with Privilege, the more information he gathered about Primetime's operation. Privilege had given Cold a book with the records of Primetime's trap houses and a list of names of who he operated with. She told Cold that he'd have to put faces to most of the names and areas, but also acknowledged that most of the people could be found hanging at her club.

Cold was amazed at how thorough and professional Primetime had been — well, until Privilege informed him that she was the one who started the book. Primetime was against keeping records, fearing the fact that it was direct evidence that linked him to everything. But once she convinced him of the benefit it had in keeping his business organized, he went with it — and it paid off tremendously.

The book became a major piece that Cold used to his advantage. He had kept all the photos and reports from the surveillance he had on Primetime and his crew before Primetime's murder.

Cold, Pree, and Tricko had sat inside a room with photos taped to the walls, with names under each and the neighborhood that person operated in. The room looked similar to an FBI investigation room, the way they had everything assorted around. The three men analyzed everything. They discussed who does what, who they were going to get rid of, and who they were going to bring on board.

During the following weeks, Cold put his operation in full progress. He operated Charlotte in four different branches. Ty'ron was overseer of the Eastside, Tricko the Westside, Pree the Southside, and Damont was over the Northside. Cold had kept the surveillance team and actually made that their official position in his organization, calling them S.T.S., which stood for Street Team Surveillance.

Cold took the surveillance team to a higher level. He recruited DMV workers, people from the Social Security office, and he even opened up a bonds office. For every person that was on his payroll, a daily check was run on their names in search of any arrests, court dates, or any other legal issue that could compromise a person's integrity to his operation. His lawyers were paid handsomely in large amounts of cash, which gave them the alacrity to defend whoever Cold told them to.

Cold assigned Privilege over all the books and finances. What she did was clean the money through numerous businesses and get together the payrolls for everyone. This was the primary reason why Cold had kept their relationship platonic. The position he assigned Privilege was too valuable, and he didn't want to jeopardize what he was building because of a woman's emotions.

Cold was relentless. Everything he did was to benefit and improve his operation. What he concentrated a lot on was the surveillance team. With everything going digital, he spent a lot of money on computer hackers. He had some of them hack into police officer files and learned of their financial problems.

After surveilling, investigating, and testing the integrity of the cops, the ones he had dirt on he approached with the proposition of making money that would take little risk — which was to be his eyes and ears inside the system. The five cops agreed, which Cold anticipated they would.

Cold was aware that his organization had grown to be very well-established, but he needed a stronger foundation. He needed political connections, so after completing his courses, he registered at Johnson C. Smith University for political science. Cold coveted a power that gave him a drive beyond compare — and in his mission, the thrive was the force of success, and failure was not an option.

Chapter 37

Cold's determination and due diligence continued to progress his operation.

At Johnson C. Smith University, he met people who knew people in the right places. During his first year in college, Cold was invited to a party in Raleigh by a colleague who happened to be the niece of the Governor of North Carolina. The party was to accommodate a very prestigious guest list of political figures from all over North Carolina. Despite his excitement, Cold accepted the invitation in a calm and collected manner.

When Cold found out that Jennifer Tisdale, a colleague of his, was the Governor's niece, he took advantage of the opportunity immediately. He put S.T.S. to work right away to initiate a full personal profile on Jennifer. When he read the documents in her file, he was astounded by her repertoire. Jennifer had been kicked out of Duke University her freshman year for causing a fatal collision — leaving a man dead while she was driving under the influence of alcohol. Due to her family's political influence and a big check written by Governor Patrick Tisdale to the victim's surviving wife and kids, charges were never brought against her. But Duke University petitioned her to leave, and she transferred to Johnson C. Smith University. Other than that, Jennifer's track record was clean.

It didn't take long for Cold to manipulate his way into Jennifer's world. Cold possessed a powerful presence that attracted many women, and Jennifer was no exception — so their mutual friendship quickly turned into a sexual relationship.

Jennifer had a sex drive higher than any woman Cold knew. She was the epitome of a nymphomaniac — anything went between her sheets. Many men and women had the privilege of being there, but not many had the privilege of being invited back.

Despite her alcoholism and sexual appetite, Jennifer was a very sophisticated woman. She was outspoken and carried a presence of authority.

Growing up, Jennifer participated in gymnastics, yoga, and ballet classes. In high school, she was on the track and swim teams. She stood five-foot-five and weighed one hundred and fifteen pounds. She had blonde hair and deep blue piercing eyes. She was beautiful and demanded attention everywhere she went — and not by intention. She drove a deep sea blue C250 Coupé Mercedes-Benz convertible that complimented her eyes.

Cold enjoyed Jennifer's company but felt that she was getting a little too attached. He had no intentions of making their relationship anything serious, but he had to keep playing his cards right until he was in a better position to unlink her. Jennifer was very emotional, so when the time came, he knew he'd have to deal with the situation in a sufficient manner.

The party was taking place at the Governor's mansion. Cold looked the part of a young political figure very well. Not overdoing it, he wore a dark blue Roberto Cavalli suit with blue Stacy Adams shoes, minus the jewelry.

During Jennifer's introductions of Cold to the influential political figures, Cold articulated himself very well on his political views. He made sure to exchange and receive business cards for future references. With the affable Jennifer, Cold was being very informed about a lot of personal details. She knew enough to blackmail almost everyone at the party. Cold was impressed — he admired her shrewdness.

Before Cold and Jennifer left the party, they were asked by Governor Patrick Tisdale to stay for the rest of the weekend. Cold had made such a great impression that he immediately earned the Governor's acceptance. Governor Tisdale had been observing Cold ever since Jennifer introduced them. He knew Jennifer was intelligent, but sometimes her judgment with men was questionable. But after a few conversations with Cold, he was pleased — even astonished — by Cold's broad intelligence on political matters, which earned his respect.

The Governor was so impressed that he wanted Cold to meet his wife, Elizabeth, and daughter, Rebecca. They had been absent from the party due to business in Washington, D.C., and were set to return the next morning. More or less, the Governor wanted to show Cold off to them — especially to Rebecca, who often critiqued Jennifer's choice in men.

Cold accepted the invitation with honor, but Jennifer was skeptical about the introduction of her cousin Rebecca and Cold. Rebecca was beautiful, intelligent — and Jennifer's archenemy. Jennifer tried to talk Cold out of staying, but he insisted. He explained that this was an opportunity to better his future. After exhausting her list of excuses, Jennifer finally accepted they were going to stay — but she made it clear she wouldn't let Cold be alone with Rebecca for one second.

That night, Jennifer made love to Cold like never before — with passion and every ounce of her heart and emotions. She kissed and sucked on every part of his body until he exploded in repeated ecstasy. For the first time in her life, Jennifer Tisdale was in love.

To Cold, though, it was only a good fuck. Jennifer was just a pawn in a significant position in the rise of his dynasty.

The next day, Cold and Governor Tisdale spent hours talking about everything from political views to sports to future goals. The Governor spoke freely about his background and journey to becoming governor. He grew up a poor white kid in the Piedmont Court projects in Charlotte, North Carolina. His aim was to one day become President — or at least a Congressman. He told Cold about how, at twenty-nine, newly married with a newborn daughter (Rebecca) and fresh out of law school, he lost his mother, father, and sister in a car accident — and was left to raise his niece, Jennifer.

Cold was impressed and gained a newfound respect for the Governor — or Pat, as he preferred to be called.

Elizabeth and Rebecca arrived later that evening and were easily lured by Cold's charisma. Rebecca was mind-blowingly gorgeous, sophisticated, and refined — but Cold wasn't besotted by her beauty. What caught him was the competitive tension between Rebecca and Jennifer. It was thrillingly sexy — it magnetized a desire to fuck them both while they competed between the sheets to see who could fuck him better.

Cold was self-controlled and strategic. He manipulated the women by slyly comparing and challenging them on everything — focusing with precision on their flaws. By the end of the night, it became a sexual contest . . . and by morning, Cold had fucked Rebecca and Jennifer into a comatose sleep.

Chapter 38

In Beaumont Federal Penitentiary, Benny Rivers was serving a thirty-year sentence under the R.I.C.O. Act. When he got locked up, his nephew Primetime was just getting his feet wet in the game and was making a name for himself quickly, so Benny—well, Uncle Benny, which is what he was called—decided to school Primetime and put him at the head of his operation.

Primetime eventually got the big head and started running things his own way. Uncle Benny just played the background and eventually fell out of the loop on the streets.

Uncle Benny sat in his cell, listening intently to JoJo on the other end of the cell phone.

"The kid that killed your nephew is still AWOL, but we still got our ears to the streets. I gathered some more information about why shit happened, and this shit gets deep."

"Will you just get to the fucking point of this call since you're not telling me that the killer of my nephew is dead?" Uncle Benny exclaimed, angrily interrupting JoJo.

"Okay! Here's the story. Primetime got into some beef with this kid named Cold that ran the westside. Blood was shed on both sides. Primetime had gotten the identity of one of Cold's soldiers and decided to kidnap the guy's little brother and kill him. Long story short, the guy sees Primetime in IHOP and, well, you know. Anyway, we did get some information on the female that was with the guy in IHOP, and we're trying to locate her now."

"So what type of info do you have on this nigga Cold?"

"This nigga is major. And after Primetime was killed, his operation has become stronger. He even recruited a lot of our people that worked the streets."

"So why am I just now hearing about this shit?" Uncle Benny exclaimed angrily. "Listen to me very carefully," he continued, speaking through gritted teeth. "I want that nigga who killed Primetime found and killed, and I want that nigga Cold's operation dismantled."

"Listen, Uncle Benny," JoJo interrupted. "This is not a fucking easy task you're asking. We've been out here on these streets for almost a year just to get this far. We don't have the manpower to go up against this nigga right now."

Uncle Benny thought over JoJo's words.

"That means we need to get inside of his operation and attack from there. You said that he recruited some of our men, so find out who—and see who is still willing to be loyal to us."

"You know, I did hear that Primetime's girlfriend, Privilege, has been doing some business with Cold. I don't know how personal it is between them, but we can start with her."

"Bitches ain't shit, sleeping in the enemy's bed," Uncle Benny mumbled. "Go with that angle, but still send all we have from every angle, because we don't know how deep this nigga has gotten in that bitch's head."

"Alright. Bet that up. I'm out."

Chapter 39

While Cold was attending his stay at the governor's mansion in Raleigh, Pree, Gina, and Tim drove to Florida as usual to pick up fifty kilos of cocaine from Marco. Everything was set up according to how they always met up. This time, Pree felt a little uneasy about things. Marco had brought with him a few extra men that Pree had never seen before, which heightened Pree's apprehension about the situation.

"Why did you bring these extra men?" Pree asked.

"I'm preparing them for when I won't be able to be here. Did Cold not tell you?" Marco replied.

"As a matter of fact, he didn't," Pree said curtly.

"Shall we postpone business until you speak with Cold?" Marco asked.

Everything in Pree kept telling him something wasn't right, because Cold would have informed him of any changes.

"That won't be necessary. We'll continue with our business," Tim spoke up, interrupting the brief pause. He then turned to Gina. "Go get the money out of the car."

During the exchange, Pree's eyes constantly flickered around. His street senses were on high alert. In his peripheral vision, he saw sudden movement, but when he turned around, it was too late. One of Marco's men shot Tim in the back of the head. Another took aim at Gina and let bullets rip into her chest. Both died instantly.

Pree turned, and the gun was already waiting — aimed at his skull. The guy was in close proximity, so in one motion Pree swung at the gun, knocking it out of the guy's hand, punched him in the face, then took off running behind one of the parked cars. He pulled out the two Glocks from his waist and shot over the trunk of the car.

Everyone shot and dodged bullets. There were six men against one, and Pree was in their territory. He thought fast. The odds were against him, but he was not trying to die. He needed to make every bullet count. Taking careful aim while peeping over the hood, he fired two shots and hit one man in the head. A rapid burst of gunfire erupted, nearly shredding the car Pree was shielding behind. He heard them moving in on him. He crawled away from the demolished car, got up, and sprinted away, firing a widespread of shots to clear a path.

Pree was familiar with this part of Florida because here— or close by—was where they always did the exchange. Pree didn't stop running until he knew he had lost them and was clear of any more danger.

Pree figured that if Marco was trying to kill him, then Cold had to be behind it all. But then again . . . why would Cold want him dead and go through this amount of trouble to kill him, Gina, and his Uncle Tim?

Shit didn't make sense.

He never crossed Cold in any way, and to his knowledge, Marco didn't need the money badly enough to try and rob or betray Cold—and they were blood. Or did he?

Pree's mind was racing with conflicted thoughts, and right now, he couldn't trust anybody. And one thing for sure . . . someone was going to answer for this.

Pree didn't know who to call but one person.

"What up?" Ant answered.

"What up, baby boy. This cuzo. Listen up! I'm in some deep shit. We need to meet up and talk. I'm on my way out there and I'll call you when I get there, a'ight?"

"Where are you at? Do you need me to come and get you?" Ant was alarmed.

"Nah, you good, but shit is real. Don't tell anyone I'm coming or that you talked to me. I mean no one, brah. And lay low and watch your position until I get there."

"Okay, brah."

After hanging up with Ant, Pree called for a cab to take him to rent a car. Once everything was signed with the fake credentials, Pree jumped straight on the highway and exited Florida.

Pree was in Alabama when he got pulled over by state troopers for speeding. After he gave the troopers his North Carolina driver's license and the rental documents, the officers started verbally harassing him. They wanted to know why he had a North Carolina license leaving Florida and was now in Alabama.

When Pree brusquely told them it was none of their fucking business and that he needed to go, the troopers didn't take lightly to the disrespect from a young Black man from out of town.

What began as a routine traffic stop became a catastrophe within minutes. The officers roughly yanked Pree out of the car, and that's when the struggle began. Pree managed to withdraw his gun from his waist and shoot both troopers in the head. Immediately, he jumped back in the rental and took off, leaving the dead bodies—and witnesses—behind.

Pree drove about two miles before exiting the freeway. He didn't know where he was but knew he had to get rid of the rental and find another ride.

He drove aimlessly around town, making sure he wasn't being followed. He tried to remember the street names— Albert Lane, Moore Drive, Davis Street—repeating them in his head.

Pree's instincts told him to call Cold. He needed answers. He was now in more shit than he could handle alone, and soon there would be a nationwide manhunt. His identity would be exposed once they traced the tag to the rental car center. The info was fake, but his picture was real, and they had already photocopied his ID.

Pree parked behind an abandoned warehouse to conceal the rental. He had no choice but to call Cold—not knowing anyone else who could help.

He called.

And for the second time in his life, he prayed.

Cold picked up on the fourth ring.

"Hello?"

Pree sat silent for a moment before speaking.

"Who is this?" Cold questions.

"It's me. Pree."

"What up? Is everything alright?"

Pree tried to recognize anything in Cold's voice that might convince him Cold was involved.

"Nah, man. Everything is fucked up. Shit is real bad."

The first thought that crossed Cold's mind was that they had been hit by the feds.

"So what happened? Where are you at?"

Pree hesitated before responding. When he spoke, his tone had a dangerous stillness.

"I need to know, Cold . . . did you have something to do with it?"

"Do with what, Pree?" Cold responded, voice just as quiet and cold.

There was another short pause.

"It was a setup. Tim and Gina are dead."

"What the fuck you mean Tim and Gina are dead?" Cold was now on his feet. The words pierced his heart like a sword.

"Marco set us up and killed them. He tried to kill me too, but I got away."

Cold was at a loss for words. He couldn't believe what he just heard. It couldn't be true. Marco had too much going for himself—and he was blood.

"Where are you at, Pree?"

"The shit gets worse, Cold. I had to kill two state troopers, and right now I'm in Alabama ducking from the law."

"Pree, I don't know what the fuck is going on, but I promise you I had nothing to do with that. I don't want you to say anything else over the phone. I got you, Pree. Just stay put, and I'm going to call you back and send someone to come get you."

Both men disconnected the call without another word.

Cold immediately began making phone calls.

The first one was Marco.

But Cold got no answer.

Chapter 40

Marco was in the basement of his house, pacing back and forth while lost in thought. He was furious at the men that sat before him, and his thoughts were relentless. What was supposed to be an easy hit had turned into a disaster because these idiots were incompetent. Every last one of them disgusted him, and he wanted to kill all of them right now.

The plan was as simple as the ABCs. All they had to do was kill Pree, Gina, and Tim, take the money, and tell Cold that they were set up and robbed by one of his most trusted soldiers. Marco was even going to sacrifice two of his own men by killing them as part of the setup, so the loss of casualties wouldn't just be on Cold's end. But with Pree still alive and on the loose, the whole plan had twisted. They had searched the whole city looking for Pree, with no luck.

It all began about two months ago, when Marco wanted to formulate his own operation but lacked the finances. He had devised a plan and went over it again and again, testing it, probing and searching for any flaws until he felt optimistic enough to carry it out.

Marco was tired of being the middleman. With the amount of money Cold was spending, all he needed was one hit to add to what he already had saved up, then he could buy his own weight and supply Cold. But with the plan now in disarray, Marco had not devised a plan B — and now there was only one solution: war.

Marco came out of his reverie, listening to the men speak that sat before him.

"I don't know how in the fuck did that nigga get away!"

"At least we got the money."

"Fuck that nigga. He won't come back here, and if he do
. . ."

Marco was fed up. When he interrupted, his words were spoken slowly and vibrated a cold chill throughout the whole room.

"This nigga we just robbed is not your corner hustler. We just robbed a nigga for close to a million dollars and killed two of his people — and one of them happened to be his fucking uncle. Y'all think a nigga not coming back to answer for that shit?"

He paused, letting his words sink in.

"Shit is about to get real. I mean, it's about to be a fucking blood bath — and half of y'all niggas are not going to survive. So I suggest y'all walk sideways, sleep with both eyes open, keep your finger on the trigger, and get the fuck out of the country."

The silence that followed enveloped the room with apprehension.

"I'm not running any fucking where," Jermaine interrupted the silence.

"So what the fuck are you going to do?" Marco asked with sarcasm.

"Is it possible we can get to him before he get to us?" Jermaine asked.

"You sound stupid right now. That'd mean we gotta go on his turf and go to war, without telling how many soldiers."

"We can set up a trap by using the element of surprise. Don't you know where he is staying?"

Marco waited to respond, cogitating the idea. These idiots couldn't set up a mouse trap, he thought, flashing back to the botched hit that had landed them in this mess.

Right now, his options — and time — were limited. He was going to have to plan this very carefully.

"Listen, to follow through with this, we have no room for any more mistakes, and we must act ASAP. So if all y'all are with it, then I have a plan." He paused, giving each man eye contact to assure that they understood and were in. "I guess that means everyone's in?"

"We'll meet back here tomorrow night, and I'll go over everything with y'all. Bring a few things to travel with."

And with that, everyone departed.

Chapter 41

Early the next morning, Cold had caught the first flight back to Charlotte. He had sent Tricko to Alabama to pick up Pree. He still couldn't comprehend what was going on. All night he had tried to reach Marco but to no avail.

Back in Charlotte, Cold had made arrangements with his hitmen and surveillance team to head out to Florida. He had waited for Tricko and Pree to arrive so he could get the whole story from Pree.

Sitting in the confinements of Cold's abode, Cold listened intently to Pree while he gave a verbatim account of the incidents that took place in Florida and Alabama.

"This shit doesn't make sense. I don't know what the fuck is going on or why Marco had plans on killing us," Pree concluded angrily.

"I don't fucking understand this shit. That's my fucking blood. If he had any problems or needed anything, he knew I had his back one hundred percent," Cold proclaimed angrily.

Cold was interrupted by David, the captain of the surveillance team. "Excuse me, but I have Valentino on the phone."

Valentino Sanchez was Mario's connect in Florida. Cold reached out to Valentino because he needed answers.

"Hello, Valentino, my name is Cold and I would like to discuss a situation with you about Marco."

"Yes, Cold, I know exactly who you are. Was there a problem with the exchange?" he asked.

"Yes, but I'd rather not discuss it over the phone. I would like to fly out there tonight and meet up with you in the morning, if it's convenient for you?" Cold asked.

"For you to contact me and actually want to meet up with me in person, it has to be a very urgent matter. How about I come to you, Cold. I can use the travel," Valentino more so stated than asked.

"Sure, just give me a call upon your arrival and I will have a driver meet you at the airport."

"That won't be necessary, but thanks for the offer. I have a means of transportation, but I will call you upon my arrival. I will see you later, Cold," Valentino said. Then the call was disconnected.

Cold had his most trusted men sitting in the house waiting for his orders. "Listen up! Valentino Sanchez operates one of the major cartels on the East Coast, so this is going to be a very delicate meeting. I don't know what Marco's agenda was or what he's told Valentino as of yet or if Valentino is involved also. So from the time Valentino exits his private jet, I want surveillance and snipers on his ass. And David," Cold turned.

"What's up?" David asked.

"What I need you to do is trace Marco's phone and maybe we can find his whereabouts. I also want you to call all of our connections we have in Florida, Georgia, and South Carolina and put an alert out for Marco. I do know he operates business in those states as well."

"Got you, boss!" David immediately jumped on the phone.

"And Shawn," Cold turned to the captain over the hitmen. "I need you to get soldiers prepared to stand guard around the clock. We may need to travel if things don't go right tomorrow."

"I'm on it, boss!" Shawn said.

"Pree, I truly apologize for the actions of my cousin and I promise you he will not go unpunished."

"Well, I want to be the punisher of his fate," Pree spoke in a menacing tone while locking eyes with Cold.

"That, I assure you, will be granted."

Their meeting was abruptly interrupted when Privilege walked into the room. "Excuse me, Cold, may I speak with you privately?" she asked.

"Sure!" Cold led Privilege out of the room into another room. "What's on your mind?" he asked. He shut the door behind them.

"There's something I've been meaning to tell you."

"And that is?" he asked.

"Primetime has an uncle that's incarcerated in the Feds. He was actually the one that was behind Primetime and his operation — well, until Primetime shunned him out."

"And you are just now telling me this because?" he asked.

"Well, with Primetime gone, I didn't think Uncle Benny would come back into the picture. I overheard some guys at my club talking about Uncle Benny. Everyone calls Benny 'Uncle Benny.' Anyway, they were saying that Uncle Benny is trying to rebuild his operation and was searching for recruits."

"I've heard of Uncle Benny, but I didn't know he was Primetime's uncle. Didn't he get thirty years or so?" Cold asked.

"Yeah, but Cold, we don't need to take this light because if Uncle Benny is trying to rebuild his operation, that means he's looking for who killed Primetime, and if he thinks or hears that you had some type of involvement, then he's going to come at you. So please be careful."

Cold had partially informed Privilege of the Ant situation, so she was aware of the connection.

"Privilege," Cold looked into her eyes with a solemn expression.

"Yes?" she asked.

"Where do your loyalty stand?" he asked.

"Cold, you shouldn't have to ask me that."

"I asked you that because I know that you have been a part of their family for a long time and this is the time that you have to decide because I need to know that you're on my side."

"Cold, I've always been on your side since the day I met you, but you must n't see that. I will die for you and will kill for you, but you have so much focus on your operation that you fail to notice that. And what else you fail to notice is how much I'm in love with you," Privilege stopped speaking and allowed the tears to fall from her eyes.

"Do you mean that?" he asked.

"Every word!" she replied.

Seeing the sincerity, Cold slowly pulled Privilege into his arms and began to kiss her tears away. He planted soft kisses on her lips and slowly unbuttoned her blouse. He tossed the blouse on the floor and unfastened her bra and tossed it on the floor as well. He massaged her breasts and kissed her neck. The sensation was tingling every nerve in Privilege's body. He led a trail of kisses down her neck to her breasts and continued down until he reached her navel and began pulling her pants off.

The sight of Privilege's flawless naked body aroused Cold even more. He picked her up and carried her over to the bed and laid her down softly. Stepping back, he stripped his clothes off, not once taking his gaze off Privilege, who laid there waiting hungrily for his touch. Cold climbed between her legs and kissed her passionately. He used his hands to explore her body. He took one breast at a time and sucked and nibbled on both of them lightly, giving each one an equal amount of attention until both nipples stood hard and lascivious. He continued to glide his wet tongue down her stomach and between her thighs and kissed around her pussy lips, teasing with each touch. Soft moans escaped while she rotated her hips, anticipating and yearning for his tongue to make love to her pussy.

Cold took two fingers, spread open her pussy, and stuck his tongue inside and licked in circular motions. Privilege was wetter than ever; this was the moment she'd been waiting on for so long. She was in a state of euphoria. Cold softened his tongue and concentrated on her clitoris, licking it fast and steady, up and down, and from side to side. Privilege began to shake uncontrollably while her pussy juices flooded from the climax of her sexual excitement.

Cold came up and inserted his dick inside her wet and throbbing pussy. He began with slow, long, and hard deep strokes. He made love to Privilege passionately. He switched her positions and shifted strokes from side to side and around, and he thrusted fast and harder. Her body constantly convulsed with multiple orgasms that she had yearned for.

Tears came down Privilege's eyes at the realization of being in love; she was in utopia. Caught in the rhythm, Cold began to explode; unable to pull out, he released every drop of his cum inside her. Exhausted, he rolled off of her and moments later she was cuddled in his arms.

"Cold," Privilege whispered.

"Yes," he replied.

"What does this mean between us?" she asked.

"It means that you are my better half, in which you always were. I guess you didn't notice that," Cold said.

Privilege smiled blushfully with excitement. She rolled over and gave Cold the same treatment that he had just put on her with every ounce of her heart into it. They made love continuously through the night until they both drifted off into a blissful sleep.

Chapter 42

The dawn was cracked with a restless Cold, who shitted, shaved, and showered to prepare for the events that waited ahead of the day's agenda. He exited the room quietly to avoid disturbing Privilege in her sleep.

In the study, David was at the computer typing away.

"So what do we have?" Cold startled David.

"Oh, ah, we have located Marco by GPS'ing his phone, and from the route he's on, it looks like he is heading our way right now." David clicked a few keys that pulled up a map. "He is now in Georgia, so he should be here in about four hours or so. I took the initiative of having the surveillance and sniper team set up post around the South Carolina and North Carolina borderline to get a trail on him once he enters the state. I don't know how many cars will be joining him, because I doubt he's coming alone, so I ordered five cars to watch him. I also put a team on guard at the airport, as you wished. And one more thing . . ." David clicked a few more keys until the screen showed the CNN breaking news.

A photo of Pree's face was posted on the corner of the screen as the news anchor spoke.

"Police are in search of this suspect for the murders of two state troopers during a routine traffic stop on the interstate in Alabama."

The screen switched to the video from the state trooper's car.

"As you can see on the video footage, the suspect was yanked out of the car by the state troopers, in which a struggle took place. The suspect then pulled out a firearm and shot both troopers at point-blank range in the face and then fled the scene. We've just received further information from authorities in Riviera, Florida. They believe the suspect was also involved in a triple homicide prior to the murders of the state troopers. Authorities linked the crimes from the license plates of the cars left at the scene through the rental car service. If you have any information on the whereabouts of this man, please call your local authorities. The suspect is considered armed and dangerous."

David clicked the screen off.

"Hey, Cold, we're going to have to hide Pree immediately until we come up with a plan, because right now, he's going to bring a lot of heat to the operation, which is going to put us all at risk."

"I know, David, and right now I've come up with two suggestions."

At that moment, Pree entered the room looking exhausted and stressed.

"What up, Pree? You're right on time," Cold said.

"What up?" Pree asked.

"This is where we stand. Right now you are the number one most wanted man in America. The whole country is looking for you, so you're limited with options. First, we have to get you out of the country, and second, plastic surgery. Unless you have a better plan?"

"I was just starting to like this handsome face," Pree half-joked, and no one laughed or smiled.

"Pree, unfortunately your fate has been twisted in which you can't escape, but I promise you that I will do everything in my power so that you won't see the inside of a prison again. But you're going to have to follow my lead and trust me."

"Cold, you're the only person I trust, and I trust you with my life. Just tell me what I need to do."

"Right now you're safe here until I can make arrangements. You are willing to get plastic surgery, right?"

"I don't give a fuck if I look like Freddy Krueger, as long as I don't have to go back to prison."

Their conversation was interrupted by Privilege, who opened the door and stuck her head into the room.

"Excuse me, gentlemen, but Cold, can I speak with you for a second?"

"Sure."

"Y'all give me a second." Cold stepped into the hallway. "What up?"

"I'm about to head home, and I'm going to see if I can find out some more information about what Uncle Benny is planning."

"Okay, but be careful." Cold then gave Privilege a passionate kiss.

"I'll call you later." Privilege then left.

Chapter 43

Boom! Boom! Boom!

"Who the fuck is it?" Kiesha yelled at the top of her lungs while getting out of bed.

Boom! Boom! Boom!

"Stop banging on my damn door this early in the fucking morning!" Kiesha continued to yell on her way to the door. "This better be the fucking police banging on my goddamn door."

She yanked the door open.

Pow! The punch sent her tumbling backward into the house on her back.

Four armed men quickly rushed into the house and shut the door behind them. Two of the men snatched Kiesha up off the floor and covered her mouth while one pointed a 9mm at her head.

"Is there anyone else in the house?" JoJo asked.

Kiesha shook her head no.

"Bitch, you better not be lying or they're dead," JoJo said.

Two of the men began searching the two-bedroom house for any unwanted surprises. They looked in closets and under beds until they were sure the house was empty.

In the living room, Kiesha was being duct-taped to a chair. She was a little shaken up but managed to keep her composure. She thought they were just there to rob her and be on about their business. Hell, she'd been robbed before. She had five thousand dollars and a pound of kush stashed that she always kept ready for the stick-up kids.

"Y'all can have the money and the weed. Just hurry up and get the fuck out of my house," Kiesha exclaimed.

Whack!

"Bitch, shut the fuck up. Where in the fuck is that nigga Ant?" JoJo said through gritted teeth after slapping her.

Tears came down Kiesha's face from the sting of the slap. With the mention of Ant's name, Kiesha knew her life was about to end. She should've followed Ant's advice and went with him, she thought.

"I don't know," she muttered.

Whack!

"Bitch, stop fucking lying to me. I'm going to ask you one more time, and if you don't give me the answer that I'm looking for . . ."

JoJo paused.

One of the other men pulled out a mini blowtorch and sparked the flame.

Kiesha's eyes lit up with fear.

"I'm telling you the truth! I swear I haven't seen him in almost a year!"

JoJo grabbed Kiesha's face with one hand.

"Kiesha, if anyone would know where Ant is at, that would be you. So what I'm going to do first is burn off your fingers. Now if that don't get me my answer, I'm going to burn your ass to a slow and painful death. Tape her mouth shut and hold this bitch still," he ordered the men.

He grabbed her wrist and turned the flame on the torch up.

Kiesha struggled. She tried to twist and turn but accomplished nothing. JoJo torched her fingers one at a time on one hand. The pain was excruciating. Kiesha passed out more than once. JoJo stopped and poured a bottle of cold water on her fingers, causing the flesh to sizzle, leaving an unpleasant scent of burnt flesh. One of the men removed the tape from over her mouth.

"Now do you know where Ant is at?" JoJo asked with a sinister smile.

The pain was overbearing. Kiesha had urinated and defecated on herself. She could not go through another round of that much pain. She prayed and hoped that Ant would forgive her.

"He's . . . in . . . Mississippi. At my cousin's house. Just please don't . . . hurt my cousin. The address is 464 Nelson Street, Jackson, Mississippi," Kiesha managed to stutter through the tears and pain.

"Now that wasn't so hard, was it?" JoJo smiled, then shot her once in the head. "Let's get the fuck out of here."

They all exited the house calmly and locked the door behind them.

Chapter 44

Privilege arrived at her house feeling invigorated. Cold was beyond compare to anyone in her life. He replenished the meaning in her life that was once lost along the way in despair and loneliness. Exiting her car in blissful thoughts, Privilege was oblivious to the intruder that shadowed her to the front door.

"Oh my God!" she yelped, startled by the intruder. "What are you doing here?"

"I just came by to check on you since I haven't seen you since the funeral," JoJo said. "So are you going to let me in?"

"Oh, ah, sure." Privilege hesitated, feeling skeptical about the pop-up visit. "Would you like something to drink?" she asked once they were fully in the house.

She led JoJo into the kitchen so she could get in accessible possession of the 9mm that was kept in the counter drawer.

"Sure!"

"So what brings you here?" Privilege gave him the drink.

JoJo took a sip and cleared his throat.

"I'm going to cut straight to the point, Privilege. The reason why I'm here is because I need to know about that guy Cold. We know the guy Ant — that killed Primetime — was working for Cold. Yeah, it's sad that Primetime's murder was a vendetta, but we also know there was a deep beef between Primetime and Cold over territorial reasons. Which leaves us to ponder if it was actually a hit that was ordered by Cold."

"We must mean Uncle Benny sent you?" The silence was enough to confirm her suspicion. "Well, I can tell you that

Cold had absolutely no involvement with Primetime's murder."

"And how can you be so sure of that?"

"Because I know Cold, and he wouldn't have killed Primetime impulsively like that," Privilege replied sharply.

"How well do you know Cold?"

"Well enough."

JoJo paused for a moment and stared into her eyes before asking his next question.

"Does Cold have your heart or mind?"

"What matter is that to you?"

"It's like this, Privilege — you've been with our family for a long time, and Uncle Benny still love you like you are his own niece. And he's willing to forgive you for going to the enemy's side, especially with you being vulnerable due to witnessing Primetime's sudden death."

"So what does Uncle Benny want of me?"

"We need to get inside of Cold's operation."

"And if I don't agree?"

There was a long pause with some intense eye contact before JoJo broke the silence.

"Privilege, we're not asking you to pull a trigger and put a bullet in his head. We're just asking you to get us close to him."

"Well, isn't that like I'm pulling the trigger? Because I seriously doubt that y'all want to set up a joint venture."

Seeing that he wasn't getting anywhere, yet hiding his frustration, JoJo got up and prepared to depart.

"Listen, Privilege, just think about what I said. For everyone's best interest, let's not break Uncle Benny's heart. He truly loves you."

JoJo headed toward the door.

Once JoJo's back was turned, Privilege retrieved the 9mm from the counter drawer and walked behind him with the gun tucked behind her back.

"JoJo!" Privilege called out while standing on the porch.

Halfway down the driveway, JoJo turned around to acknowledge her.

"Cold has my heart and my mind. And for Uncle Benny's best interest, he should concentrate on doing his time and not on these streets. What he's trying to go up against is something he's not prepared for. Cold tried to spare Primetime, but Primetime caused his own death through his recklessness. He killed an innocent boy that had a future. I may not know everything about these streets, but some lines you and I know shouldn't be crossed."

"Your words are spoken wisely, but you ride with family whether they're wrong or right."

And with that, JoJo walked to his car and drove away.

Chapter 45

Valentino had arrived at Charlotte Douglas Airport in his G5 jetliner with five armed bodyguards. He stepped out of the G5 in a five-thousand-dollar Armani suit. He adjusted his tie and took a glance around at the bright blue sky through a pair of twelve-hundred-dollar Ray-Ban sunglasses. He felt like the world was his as he descended the jet's steps.

Awaiting at the platform was a Mercedes-Benz limousine, with the chauffeur holding the back door open. Valentino and two of his bodyguards got into the limousine. The other bodyguards quickly hopped into the awaiting Cadillac Escalade that was parked directly behind the limousine, and they followed Valentino in close proximity.

"Where is our destination?" the chauffeur asked through the speakerphone.

"Take me Uptown to the Omni Suites so I can refresh," Valentino answered. He then picked up the phone and called Cold.

"Hello?" Cold answered.

"Hello, Cold. This is Valentino calling to inform you of my arrival. What time is our rendezvous?"

"Well, if it's convenient for you, I would like to begin as soon as possible because time is of the essence."

"Will one hour be convenient enough?"

"That will be perfect," Cold relayed. He then gave his address and hung up.

At first, when Valentino was reached and notified that Cold wanted to speak with him, he was skeptical, with many conflicting thoughts.

After their brief conversation and learning the subject would be Marco and the transaction, his curiosity was aroused. He wanted to call Marco and get an idea of what was going on but decided against it. Besides, the last time Marco and he had spoken, it was said that the transaction had gone successfully. His instinct was telling him that Marco wasn't completely honest with him.

Business with Cold had been prosperous for his empire, so if it took getting Marco out of the way to keep his business arrangement going with Cold, then so be it. Laying aside his thoughts, Valentino took a shot of tequila out of the limousine's minibar and gulped it down.

Arriving at the Uptown Omni Suites, Valentino went upstairs to freshen up and prepare for the day's agenda that patiently awaited.

Chapter 46

The surveillance team had located Marco's exact whereabouts coming up on I-85 North and began their inconspicuous pursuit. About five miles into their pursuit, Marco exited off the interstate for a pit stop at a convenience store. That's where the surveillance team was able to pinpoint three other cars coupled with men accompanying Marco. The surveillance team watched as the entourage pumped gas and conversed with one another. Ten minutes later, Marco and his entourage got back into their cars and hopped back on the interstate.

Tricko, who was leading the surveillance, radioed in to Cold.

"We're about ten miles from our destination. It's an entourage coupled in four cars. Marco's leading the pack in a black Lincoln Town Car."

"Okay, is everyone in position?"

"Yes!" many voices radioed back.

Oblivious to their tails, Marco was discussing with Jermaine the plan he had formulated to get Cold.

"We're going to Cold's baby mother Andreka's house and make that bitch call him over there."

"So how are we gonna do that without him bringing an army of soldiers with him?"

"He'll probably come alone to his baby mother's house. We just gotta make that bitch convince that nigga she need to see him without him suspecting anything."

"And what if she warns him that we're there?"

"Her ass will be real convincing with a pistol to her kid's head. Hell, that nigga'll jump off a mountain when it come to them kids and bitches of his."

"You think that nigga keep money stashed at her house?"

"He probably does, but we'll find that out once we get there. Just remember though, we gon' make it look like a murder-suicide."

"I don't think this nigga gonna see this coming."

"We still can't underestimate this nigga — that's why we in this fucked up situation now."

Traffic had been light the majority of the ride, but up ahead traffic had slowed down and gotten congested. From the looks of it, it was caused by a car accident. Marco gave no attention to the van riding beside him on the passenger side.

"This nigga gotta be stupid," Jermaine said, referring to the guy on the motorcycle riding beside them.

That caused Marco to focus his attention on the motorist.

"Yeah, these niggas in Charlotte don't know how to ride bikes. Ain't no way in hell I'm cruising bumper to bumper on a bike and on a freeway."

Marco and Jermaine ducked in their seats at the same time upon hearing the rapid, abrupt gunfire around them. The three cars that were aligned behind them — Marco's entourage — were being shredded with bullets until all the passengers were slumped over and lifeless. Stuck in the middle of traffic, Jermaine couldn't pull away.

Two armed men with ski masks jumped out the van's side doors that had been riding alongside Marco and Jermaine and aimed AR-15s at their heads. The guy on the motorcycle pulled out a .45 automatic and shot Jermaine in the head, blowing brain spatter out all over Marco.

The passenger door was yanked open, and Marco was snatched out and quickly thrown into the van. The van sped away on the gutter of the interstate and exited off the ramp.

The ambush happened so fast and so efficiently that the assailants managed to escape with a clean getaway, leaving everyone in traffic in a state of shock.

In the van, Marco's arms were being handcuffed behind him. No one in the van spoke until Trick broke the silence to radio Cold.

"We got him, boss. So far it's a clean getaway."

"Okay. Bring him to me."

Chapter 47

Valentino arrived at Cold's house ten minutes ahead of time, refreshed and prepared. He only had two bodyguards accompany him inside the house. The other three bodyguards waited in close proximity to the house.

"Welcome to my home," Cold greeted Valentino at the door with his hands extended.

"Thank you very much. It's a pleasure to finally meet you in person, Cold." Valentino firmly shook Cold's hand.

"Come on in. Would you like a drink?" Cold led Valentino into the den to have a seat.

"Tequila with no ice."

Cold went to the minibar and poured himself and Valentino a shot of tequila. He handed Valentino the drink and took a seat directly across from him.

"I want to skip past the small talk because, as I said, time is of the essence. The situation I have with Marco is that he killed two of my people on the last delivery and took the money. One of my men managed to escape." Cold nodded to Pree, who was standing a few feet away. "Was Marco in any type of bind with you that would have caused him to commit these actions?"

"Cold, I'm surprised to hear this, and no, Marco wasn't in any bind with me. I'm just as perplexed as you are. I would have given Marco anything he asked for."

"Well, there's something going on, and I've given Marco nothing but loyalty."

"Do you need me to call Marco?"

"That won't be necessary. As a matter of fact, he will be arriving here any minute."

As on cue, Cold was interrupted by Pree.

"Excuse me, Cold, but they've arrived."

"Let's go and meet our guests of honor." Cold stood up and ushered Valentino to follow.

The van pulled up to Cold's house and drove around to the back. Marco was taken out of the van and led through the back door, where Cold, Pree, and Valentino were waiting.

Pow!

Pree immediately punched Marco in the face, causing blood to squirt from his nose.

"Hold up!" Cold grabbed Pree. "Take him downstairs to the basement."

Pree grabbed Marco with aggressive force and dragged him toward the basement door. The basement had twenty-seven steps descending. Pree opened the door and kicked Marco down the steps. Fortunately for Marco, he only broke a shoulder bone. When Pree reached the bottom of the steps, he snatched Marco up off the floor and dragged him to a chair that was sitting in the middle of the room on plastic.

Pow! Pop! Whack!

Blow after blow connected. Marco's face had swollen and bled profusely.

"Enough!" Cold calmly grabbed Pree and pulled him back. "I need to ask this nigga some questions." He positioned himself in front of Marco. "Why, Marco?" Cold was hurt and angry.

"Greed!" Marco answered honestly.

"But I would have given you anything you wanted." Cold's anger continued to rise. "Your greed allowed you to betray me. Whose idea was this?"

"It was all my idea. I'm tired of being the fucking middleman, eating the crumbs between you and Valentino. I'm the only one taking all the risk while you two mothafuckas enjoy the fruits of my labor. I put this connection together. Without me, neither one of y'all's operations would've grown to the extent that they are. But how do y'all show me thanks? By not doing a mothafucking thing for me." Marco spoke with fury.

"If you wanted a piece of territory, I would have given that to you," Valentino cut in.

"Then why didn't you? I told you I could handle more responsibilities!" Marco screamed.

"You should have been clear about your wishes. Your role in my operation was one of the most powerful. I never had one problem out of your deliveries. That's why I allowed you to handle things on your own terms. You were very important to me. I trusted you. You should have communicated with us." Valentino finished speaking and stepped aside.

"Marco, you are my blood, but you betrayed me for greed, so I can't have mercy on you. But I'll give you a merciful death," Cold said.

"Our DNA ain't even from the same bloodline." Marco said with a sinister grin.

"What's that supposed to mean?"

"One day you'll figure it out. Just too bad you can't ask your whore-ass mother." Marco laughed dramatically.

Pow!

Cold punched Marco in the face so hard that Marco went flying backward and flipped out of the chair. Two guys quickly went to sit Marco back up in the chair.

"Fuck all y'all!" Marco spat.

"Nah, fuck you." Pree pulled out a 9mm and shot Marco in the temple one time. They all watched as Marco's body slumped over.

Pree, Tricko, and the rest of the guys began wrapping Marco's body up in the plastic that was laid out on the floor while Cold and Valentino went back upstairs.

"Before you go, I would like to discuss future business with you," Cold said to Valentino once they were back in the den. "I hope business between us can continue. My business is expanding a little further around the surrounding cities, and if our business continues, I would like to begin purchasing a hundred kilos a month. I'm still willing to take full risk of coming to you and picking up the product, and I would like to negotiate a reasonable price."

"Cold, I would love to continue doing business with you. I like the way you operate, and I see that your establishment is well put together. How does eight thousand dollars a kilo sound, with you taking full risk of picking up the product?"

"That sounds wonderful. Thank you, Valentino. Another thing — to avoid the same mistake, I will be opening up a mechanic shop out there in Riviera, Florida, so we can have a place to exchange the money and product. That will lessen the risk on both of our ends. Now I have one more issue I would like to know if you can help me with."

"Sure. What's the problem?"

"My friend Pree is one of the FBI's most wanted persons. I need him out of the country ASAP."

"That can be arranged. Is there a certain country you have in mind?"

"I do know that Brazil doesn't have an extradition treaty with the U.S."

"I can arrange that. I also have a few connections I can hook Pree up with that will welcome his stay. Has he thought about plastic surgery? I do know a doctor that I can call."

"That will be perfect, and I will compensate for all expenses."

"That won't be necessary. Just have Pree ready tonight when I call."

They both shook hands, and Valentino departed with his bodyguards.

Chapter 48

Ant was devastated and heartbroken when he received the news of Kiesha's murder. He swore to himself that once he was back in a position to move, he would avenge her murder.

After talking to Pree, he had been updated on all the events that had taken place since he'd been gone. It was a misfortune for Pree, but he trusted that Cold was going to take care of him. Ant admired Cold because through all the trials and tribulations, Cold had told him that there were lawyers working on his cases and to continue to stay low — but Ant couldn't resist the life on the streets, so every now and then he'd slang a few ounces here and there.

Ant was enjoying Tonya's company a lot, despite her having three kids. Things between them started off as a mutual arrangement, but after a few weeks, some blunts and drinks, he couldn't keep his dick out of her. Besides, it was convenient with no strings attached. Tonya reminded him so much of Kiesha — just a little more ratchet.

Tonya had introduced Ant to a few guys around the neighborhood, but one in particular Ant bonded with more, because the guy was originally from Charlotte. Priceless was sharp and quick on his feet, but a hothead. Priceless played the streets real hard. Ant took a liking to him because he was respected and feared, and Priceless reminded him so much of himself.

Hanging with Priceless is what got Ant moving through the hood without any altercations. Ant didn't need money, but the streets were addictive, and he played the streets for the thrill.

Ant was sitting on the porch smoking a blunt when Priceless pulled up in his blue Chevy Caprice on twenty-six-inch rims.

"Ant, come here and let me holla at you," Priceless yelled out the window.

Ant got up and walked to the car and hopped in the passenger seat.

"What up, my nigga?" he dapped up Priceless.

"Check this out, right? I've been watching this nigga for a while on the other side of town, and he is making some major gwap. I know he's sitting on at least a hundred grand, plus a few bricks. So what's up — you wanna go on this lick with me?" Priceless grabbed the blunt from Ant.

"Do you have everything laid out?"

"Hell yeah! Like I said, I've been watching that nigga's every move," Priceless said, holding the weed smoke in his lungs.

"So what's the layout?" Ant grabbed the blunt back.

"There's five niggas that hang together, but one of them is officially the boss — he got the gwap. I followed the nigga to his crib, and he got two kids and a girl that live with him. All we gotta do is go to the house, tie up his bitch and kids, and wait for him to come home. You feeling that, my nigga?"

"When you tryna do this?"

"I'm doing it tonight. I need that gwap like ASAP. But if you are not ready, I'll catch you on the next one."

"Have you ever killed someone?" Ant turned and looked Priceless in his eyes.

"Yeah, you can say that," Priceless responded nonchalantly, not completely giving Ant eye contact.

Ant was a little skeptical. "A'ight. What time are we doing this?"

"Tonight is Wednesday, so he'll be home early, before 9:00 p.m. We can get there about eight o'clock and wait on the nigga."

"A'ight, well come back around seven and get me."

"I'll hit you up when I'm on my way." Priceless dapped Ant up before he got out, then pulled off.

Ant had Priceless drive around the block a few times to scope out the neighborhood for all possible escape routes.

"Why in the fuck do we gotta keep driving around the fucking block?" Priceless was getting irritated.

"Because, nigga — if shit go wrong, I need to know how to get the fuck outta here."

"We got this shit. Ain't shit going wrong."

They finally parked the car around the corner and walked to the house. The laughter of kids could be heard coming from inside. Ant ducked off to the side while Priceless rang the doorbell. For a moment, Ant felt a queasiness grip his stomach, but it quickly vanished.

"Who is it?" a pleasant voice of a young girl asked from behind the door.

"I'm a friend of Tony's and I was supposed to meet him here," Priceless responded.

Upon the mention of her uncle's name, the naïve sixteen-year-old girl opened the door with a warm smile. "Well, he's not here yet, but he should be here at any moment. Charlene's in the kitchen; just wait here and I'll go get her."

The girl turned around, but before she could run off, Priceless grabbed her and put his hand over her mouth, quickly overpowering her. His dick had stiffened a little from being pressed against the young girl's behind. She struggled, trying to get free. Ant came in behind Priceless and shut the door quietly with his gun drawn.

"Stop moving and listen . . . unless you want to die," Ant whispered to the young girl. "We don't want to hurt anyone, but we will if you act stupid. Do you understand?"

The girl had stopped struggling and nodded with tears falling from her eyes. Ant turned and began to move in the direction in the house where the voices of the kids were heard.

"Missy, who is that at the door?" Tony's girlfriend, Charlene, yelled out from the kitchen.

Ant came around the corner to the kitchen where he heard Charlene's voice with his pistol pointed at her head. "Bitch, don't fucking move."

"Ahh!" Charlene yelped with fear. "Please, I have kids in the house."

"If you do what the fuck I say, then nobody gets hurt. Now move!" Ant shoved Charlene into the living room where the kids' voices were heard.

Charlene quickly ran to the kids and grabbed them into her arms. Priceless came around the corner with Missy and pushed her over to where Charlene and the kids were curled up on the floor.

"Where's the fucking money?" Priceless asked.

"It's in my purse upstairs," Charlene answered.

"Nah, we're talking about the big stash. We know who the fuck's house this is," Priceless snapped.

At that moment, they heard the engine of a car pull into the driveway.

"If anybody makes one fucking noise, I swear I'm going to start off blasting the kids first," Ant said through gritted teeth. "Go meet the nigga at the door," he told Priceless.

Priceless took off to the front and stood behind the door. When the door opened, Tony and another guy came into the house deep in conversation. As soon as Tony went to close the door, Priceless came from behind the door with his pistol drawn.

"Y'all make any fucking move and I'm going to blow your fucking heads off. Now before anyone decides to do something stupid — Tony, your girl and kids are in the next room with a gun pointed at them right now."

The words of his kids having a gun pointed at their heads stopped Tony from making any sudden move.

"What do you want?" Tony asked.

"You know what the fuck we want: money and drugs. Now walk y'all ass in the other room," Priceless said while keeping enough distance behind them.

When they got into the living room, Tony's heart dropped upon seeing his girlfriend with his kids and niece balled up upon the floor, frightened in tears.

"The money's upstairs in the safe. There's about two hundred and fifty grand; y'all can have that shit, just let my family go. I don't keep drugs in my house. The money is all I have, I swear. I'll take you upstairs," Tony said in defeat.

"Nah, nigga, you ain't taking me anywhere. You come here," Priceless pointed to Missy.

Missy grabbed onto her aunt until Priceless walked over and snatched her up.

"What's the fucking code? And if anybody does anything stupid while I'm up there, I'm going to kill this little bitch," Priceless said.

Tony relayed the code to the safe and Priceless dragged Missy upstairs to the room.

"Open it!" Priceless demands.

Missy hovered down with shaking hands and was failing to open the safe through the tears and nervousness. Priceless watched as Missy struggled to open the safe. He became aroused as he admired her little petite round ass and her perky titties bounced every time she sniffled.

"Hurry the fuck up!" Priceless yelled.

Missy finally managed to get the safe open. Stacks of cash were filled in the safe. Priceless quickly grabbed a pillow and pulled off the pillowcase.

"Put it in here," Priceless threw the pillowcase at Missy.

After she had all the money in the pillowcase, Priceless grabbed her off the floor, threw her on the bed, and began ripping her clothes off. Missy screamed and struggled to get him off of her, but she was powerless. He penetrated her forcefully, ripping into her virgin pussy. Missy screamed and cried from the unbearable pain. He jammed his twelve-inch dick into her, stroke after stroke, ignoring her cries.

Downstairs, Ant was infuriated while listening to Priceless rape the young girl, but there was nothing he could do. He was downstairs with five hostages that were not tied up.

"What kind of sick mothafuckas are y'all?" Charlene yelled.

"Just shut the fuck up," Ant screamed.

Minutes later, Missy came running downstairs naked and bleeding from between her legs and crying hysterically. Priceless came trailing behind with the pillowcase.

"Why in the fuck did you do that stupid ass shit, nigga?" Ant yelled at Priceless.

"I got the money, nigga, so let's go," Priceless ignored Ant's question with an attitude.

"I didn't sign up for this shit," Ant scolded.

Ant saw the movement in his peripheral vision, turned, and fired twice into the chest of the guy that had come in with Tony. The guy had pulled out a gun but wasn't fast enough to let out a single shot before both bullets penetrated and killed him instantly.

Priceless had jumped from the abrupt shots and a single shot fired out of his gun. The bullet hit one of the little kids in the head and killed him instantly.

"Ahhhh!" Charlene let out a piercing shrill.

For a moment, everyone stood frozen in shock.

"Shut the fuck up!" Priceless yelled at Charlene. "I said shut the fuck up!" he yelled again at Charlene, who continued to scream hysterically while holding her dead son.

Bang! Priceless shot Charlene straight in the head to shut her up. Tony quickly wrapped Missy and his other child in his arms, trying to protect them.

"Let's go!" Ant shouted.

"Nah, nigga, we can't leave any witnesses," Priceless said.

Even though Ant wanted to object, he knew Priceless was right. They had just killed a kid, two adults, raped a minor, and committed a robbery. That was a death sentence by lethal injection.

"Hurry the fuck up and don't kill the baby — hell, what the fuck can he say?" Ant grabbed the pillowcase off the floor.

"Yeah, a'ight," Priceless said with a smirk. He walked over to the three and pointed his gun and fired a shot in all three of their heads. "Oh, my bad; the gun slipped," he said sarcastically and walked past Ant to exit the house.

Chapter 49

"So she chose to walk the gun line with the enemy," Uncle Benny stated rhetorically after hearing JoJo relay the encounter that took place with Privilege.

"What's the plan, boss? Do you want me to take her out?" JoJo inquired.

"No, not yet. What I want you to do is tell her to tell Cold that I'm willing to compromise to prevent a bloodshed. I will allow him to continue to operate on the eastside for twenty percent of the profits every month. And that will be our treaty for the bloodshed of my nephew."

"What does he gain from this?"

"Resources and soldiers."

"I hear he's very resourceful, and I don't think he's lacking soldiers."

"I'm not talking about street soldiers. I'm talking about government soldiers. Now what's the news on Ant?"

"He's in Jackson, Mississippi. It's a pretty tough neighborhood, but we're going to make our move soon."

JoJo blew out smoke from his cigarette as he watched Ant and Priceless come back around the corner, hop back in their car, and pull off.

"Okay, just keep me updated. I got to get off this jack." Uncle Benny hung up.

JoJo waited a few seconds before he ordered the driver to follow Ant and Priceless so they could keep an unnoticeable distance.

JoJo had been tailing Ant ever since Priceless had picked him up from Tonya's house. When they reached this neighborhood, Ant and Priceless had driven around the block so many times that JoJo thought they had blown their tail. JoJo was about to pull away when he suddenly realized that Ant and Priceless were actually scoping out the neighborhood and were completely oblivious to their tails. They had finally parked and got out and walked around the corner. JoJo had staked out a couple of blocks from their car and just waited until they came out.

Chapter 50

The ride had started off quiet between Ant and Priceless. The sideways glances carried a murderous tension in the air. Their trust had been contorted into shattered pieces, which left both men puzzled in their own thoughts.

"What the fuck was that about?" Ant asked, fracturing the silence.

"Sex, money, and murder, mothafucka," Priceless responded aggressively.

"Nah, nigga, that's rape, prison, and death, you stupid mothafucka."

"What the fuck are you tripping about? We got the money, and there's no witnesses."

"You don't need a fucking witness when you just left your DNA in a dead girl's body, you stupid mothafucka."

"Man, it takes like thirty years for them to trace DNA."

"So you think?"

"Fuck!" Priceless yelled and simultaneously banged the steering wheel. "We have to go back and burn the house down."

He made a sharp U-turn.

Arriving back around the corner of the house, Priceless jumped out of the car and began making his way toward it, then stopped. He turned around when he realized Ant was still sitting in the car.

"Nigga, come on and help me," he yelled in a high whisper, waving Ant to come on.

193

"Nigga, you're on your own," Ant yelled out the window and leaned back.

Priceless waved Ant off and made his way back around to the house. When he entered, the stench of blood and feces attacked his nose. He moved around the house in search of anything to set ablaze. Unable to find a flammable chemical, he grabbed a sheet from upstairs, wrapped Missy's body in it, and set the sheet on fire. Once the fire kicked in, he threw couch pillows and other objects that were easy to catch fire.

Satisfied with the rising flames, Priceless escaped, retracing his steps back to the car, and hopped in with his gun clutched across his lap.

"All evidence and witnesses are destroyed . . . well, besides one."

Priceless quickly extended the gun at Ant's head and pulled the trigger, blowing Ant's brains out. He grabbed the pillowcase with the money, hopped out of the stolen car, and began walking down the street in the darkness of the night.

Less than thirty yards away, a black Cadillac Escalade pulled alongside Priceless with the passenger window rolled down.

"I come in peace," JoJo yelled out the window to Priceless, who had brandished his pistol, anticipating an ambush.

"Who the fuck are you?" Priceless took a step back and stopped.

"An enemy of my enemy is a friend of mine. That nigga you just killed ain't who you think he is. In less than a week, you'll be dead. Hop in and let's talk. Besides, walking ain't a good way to escape a murder scene."

JoJo unlocked the back door.

"How do I know y'all niggas ain't trying to set me up?" Priceless tightened his clutch on the pillowcase.

"Nigga, if I wanted you dead or that pillowcase, we wouldn't be having this conversation. Now get the fuck in, or I'm out," JoJo said, losing his patience.

Hearing the sirens getting closer, Priceless calculated his options before taking one more look around. Outnumbered three to one, he hopped in the back seat and clutched the pistol across his lap. The Escalade pulled off and disappeared into the night.

"I'm from Charlotte, North Carolina, and I go by JoJo. I'm part of a team in Charlotte that I'd like you to be a part of. Right now, we're in the process of rebuilding, so I'm recruiting new soldiers that's hard and heartless. We're in the middle of a territory war."

"What's in it for me?" Priceless asked.

"We're connected in the streets, from drugs to the law in our pockets. You follow my lead, and I promise you'll be king on the streets of Charlotte."

Priceless contemplated the offer and took it into deep consideration. He wouldn't mind going back to the city he was born in and becoming king of the streets of the Queen City. His inside smile quickly faded when the realization of why he had left in the first place surfaced in his mind.

"What do you say? Because how I see it, your options are limited, and I'm afraid to even ask what went on in that house, but I'm willing to bet it's more than one body."

"I have a situation that happened in Charlotte about ten years ago. If you could take care of that, then I'm in."

"Say no more." JoJo smirked, anticipating the wrath and prosperity he was about to create.

Chapter 51

Growing up, Priceless, his younger sister, and mother were victims of his father's physical and verbal abuse from his drunken rages. Over the years, Priceless constantly begged his mother to leave his father, but she would always make excuses.

"It's just his way of showing his love. He's been through a lot, he can't help it. He's going to change, he just needs time, baby," his mother would say, but the change never came.

At the age of fourteen, Priceless developed into his own man. The physical abuse had stopped on him and his sister, but the verbal abuse stayed consistent. The physical abuse on his mother was still there, but it was hidden. Although they didn't see the fights, the black eyes and busted lips always appeared.

One night, Priceless had come home late. The house was in a wreck; he ran straight upstairs to his sister's room. His mother was badly beaten and holding his sister, who was crying. He didn't see any physical abuse on his sister; that was a moment of relief, short-lived.

"What happened?" Priceless asked, seeing the pain in his ten-year-old sister's eyes.

"What happened?" he yelled again after getting no response the first time.

"Da . . . ddd . . . dy raped me!" his sister said between sobs.

Priceless's temperature flared to a hundred degrees. "Where's that mothafucka at?" he screamed and raced around the house.

His mother jumped up and went after him. "He's not here, baby, but please don't do anything stupid."

"Don't do anything stupid!" Priceless repeated with disgust.

Just then, his father came shambling through the door in his usual drunken state. Priceless attacked him immediately, throwing blow after blow in a fit of rage. They tumbled and flipped around the house, breaking everything they touched that wasn't already broken. His mother screamed for them to stop while his little sister looked on in terror. Finally, his mother was able to pull them apart.

"That's your father!" his mother yelled, then bent down to caress her husband.

Priceless couldn't take it no more; he ran to his room and came back with a .38 Special revolver and pointed it down at his parents. The tears escaped his eyes rapidly and blurred his vision. The first shot he fired went straight into his father's brain, killing him instantly.

"Noooo!" his mother shrilled.

"You a stupid bitch!" Priceless whispered before pulling the trigger and sending her soul to be with her husband.

When he turned around and looked at his little sister, the pain was unbearable. The thought of his little sister living through this was something he couldn't imagine.

"I love you always," he told her.

Her eyes were blank, like her soul had already escaped. Priceless pointed the gun at her and pulled the trigger. She didn't even blink when the bullet pierced her heart. That was the last time Priceless shed a tear and the night his heart became cold. He ran out of the house and never looked back.

Chapter 52

Sitting in the study, Cold waited patiently for Privilege to arrive while mentally acknowledging his current circumstances. His operation was reaching heights far quicker than he could have imagined. Valentino had connected him with Marco's old clientele in Georgia and South Carolina. With the addition of the three other cities in North Carolina that he recently acquired, his operation expanded within weeks. At the pace he was going, in a month he had to purchase two hundred kilos.

Dealing two hundred kilos and dealing on other territories, Cold had to move and live accordingly. He didn't want to fall into the same mistakes as so many others he learned about. He limited interactions with the business deals and kept security around the clock.

"The blood never stopped shedding around the life of a gangsta," Cold remembered his Uncle Tim once told him.

Cold had received the news of Ant's murder and was perplexed by the events that surrounded his murder of a slain family that he had partook in then turned victim. Cold had sent people out to Mississippi to get the news expounded to clear his conscience of that iniquity.

His thoughts were interrupted by the doorbell. Privilege arrived looking as sexy as always, but by her vexed facial expression, Cold immediately picked up that there was a bigger significance to this visit.

"What's going on?" he asked with concern.

"JoJo came by and saw me today and said that Uncle Benny wanted to offer you a proposition," Privilege said.

"And that proposition is?" Cold asked.

"Uncle Benny wants to make a peace treaty with you for the blood of Primetime, if you will agree to his terms," she explained.

"Which are?" he asked.

"He wants twenty percent of the profits that you make on the Eastside for you to continue to do business over there. He will provide you with inside sources in the CMPD and more soldiers on the streets as a part of the agreement," Privilege replied.

"And if I decline?" he asked.

"He didn't say, but I fear that he's not going to walk away accepting no for an answer. When JoJo came by my house, he had this guy with him that really gave me the creeps. I don't know—I just don't feel right about this guy," she answered.

"I'll put security around you, and if it will make you comfortable, you can stay here with me, because I will be damned if I give Uncle Benny twenty percent of anything," Cold stated.

"No, I don't need to stay here, but Cold, please be careful because Uncle Benny is not Primetime," she warned.

"Don't worry, I won't underestimate my enemy again," he said.

"So anyway, I can stay the night," Privilege converted flirtatiously and rubbed a hand down Cold's chest and palmed his dick.

"You know what happens when you wake up a sleeping monster, don't you?" Cold asked, using his fingers to tilt her chin up.

"Hmmm!" Privilege moaned and allowed Cold to plant a soft kiss on her lips.

The kiss was passionate; they undressed and explored each other's body. Privilege turned around and bent over. Cold admired her smooth ass cheeks before he slowly inserted his dick inside her wet vagina. He took long and slow strokes while squeezing her waist.

"Mmmm, it feels so good," Privilege moaned as his strokes got faster and harder. "Yeah, baby, that's how I . . . li . . . ke . . . it," she stuttered but threw her ass back matching each stroke. "Oh . . . oh . . . oh . . . " she continued to scream the harder he pounded.

Cold pulled out of her before ejaculating and laid on the floor. Privilege climbed on top and inserted his dick inside of her and grinded her hips in circular motions.

"Your pussy is so good, baby," Cold whispered. "Go faster, baby . . . yeah, that's what I'm talking about . . . ride this dick, girl!"

The more Cold talked, the faster and harder Privilege rode him until her body started convulsing. Seeing her orgasm, Cold pumped and grinded his hips under her with short, fast, and hard thrusts until he released every drop of cum.

Exhausted, they both laid there caught up in ecstasy.

Chapter 53

"What's the news?" Uncle Benny asked from the cell phone.

"Your offer was declined," JoJo said.

"Well, did you get the men together?"

"Yes, I have the soldiers ready, but I was thinking we should hit him where it hurts."

"I told you I don't want you touching Privilege."

"I'm not talking about Privilege. I know where both of his baby mothers and grandmother live. Maybe we should hit him there?"

"No, JoJo, that's too personal. And besides, we don't have the manpower to go up against the wrath he can probably bring upon us, so let's keep this on the streets for now."

"So killing your nephew isn't personal enough?" JoJo was annoyed that Uncle Benny wouldn't even consider his strategy.

"When you choose these streets, you're risking your life for death or prison. There's only a few that actually make it out, and Primetime knew the consequences. That boy chose this life—didn't nobody force him to do anything. That boy came from a good fucking home, so don't bring that personal shit to me. When you let business get too personal, you're doomed in this game, because that's when your emotions are going to affect your logical thinking, and that's when your enemy will conquer. Use your fucking head, JoJo," Uncle Benny screamed angrily through the phone.

"Maybe we need this to get personal. It may just cause him to make a mistake."

"From what I've been learning about this kid, he's not an emotional character. He's young, ambitious, intelligent, and calculated. He's a dangerous kid. And if you don't follow my lead, we're going to fail. Trust me, JoJo."

In JoJo's mind, Uncle Benny was getting soft. All this talk about this nigga Cold being intelligent, calculated, and dangerous was a bunch of bullshit. Those were words that a coward would speak. Hell, *he* was intelligent, calculated, and very dangerous. If Uncle Benny would've listened to him in the first place, they wouldn't be in this situation. But no— Uncle Benny wanted his young and dumb-ass nephew to run the streets for him.

JoJo was tired of being Uncle Benny's do-boy, and if it wasn't for Uncle Benny's resources and drug connections, he would've branched off and created his own legacy. Uncle Benny may have saved him from going to prison on numerous occasions, but considering the amount of work that he had put in for him . . . his debt had been paid in full.

"So what's the plan?" JoJo asked, with a subtle annoyance.

"First, we take our side of town back!"

Chapter 54

After declining Uncle Benny's terms, Cold prepared and strategized for the anticipation of his traphouses being attacked. He had snipers in the shadows of all the traphouses, not knowing which would be hit. It was logical that Uncle Benny would attack from that angle, considering the terms were over territory. Cold didn't take Uncle Benny as an impulsive man like Primetime was, but his patience and strategy of war had yet to be discovered.

Cold did some research on Uncle Benny and learned that Uncle Benny had a well-put-together organization going for years on the eastside of Charlotte. Uncle Benny's reign ended when a kid was murdered in a dice game by one of his crew members—who also happened to be the brother of another crew member. Matt, feeling betrayed after Uncle Benny refused to let him avenge his brother's murder, walked into the federal building on his own accord and told the FBI agents the whole layout of Uncle Benny's organization.

A forty-man indictment for conspiracy to traffic drugs and commit murder was issued on the whole crew. That cost Uncle Benny thirty years in a federal prison. He would've received a life sentence, but he took a plea agreement. A year later, Matt was found dead in a Florida home with his head and tongue chopped off. All that happened over seven years ago.

Cold didn't find out too much about JoJo or how much he was in charge of making decisions for Uncle Benny. Privilege asked him if he would be willing to have a sit-down with JoJo to compromise so a war would be prevented, and he agreed.

Cold was now waiting patiently in his new uptown restaurant for JoJo to arrive.

JoJo walked into the restaurant with Priceless and two more goons on his side. A waitress escorted them to the table where Cold and Privilege were waiting. They stood up upon their arrival.

Privilege made the introductions, and Cold and JoJo shook hands, then took a seat.

Eying Priceless, Privilege had that same uncomfortable feeling flutter through her stomach.

"Let's cut straight to the point. First, I'm not about to give Uncle Benny twenty percent of anything I've earned. But I'm willing to give y'all the eastside back if y'all are willing to buy your product from only me," Cold said.

Cold's appearance was nothing like what JoJo had imagined. Here he was, talking to a kid that looked no older than eighteen years old, telling him how he would give them back their streets—under *his* terms. Immediately, JoJo disdained Cold.

"Quite frankly, we don't need you as a connect. I came here to ask you politely to move out, because one way or another, we will reclaim what's ours. Now I know you think because you took out Primetime that those streets were up for grabs, but that's not the case. So our last offer is that you give us fifteen percent and the traphouses in Hampshire Hills, Dinglewood, and Milton Road."

"Let's get one thing straight. I didn't order Primetime's murder. His arrogance and stupidity got him killed. But you guys got your revenge." Cold paused and eyed Priceless for a second. "Since it looks like we're not going to come to any agreement, I say this meeting is over." Cold stood up.

The tension in the restaurant was thick. Cold and JoJo stared each other in the eyes with murderous thoughts. Not one broke eye contact or blinked until Privilege cleared her throat and began to speak.

"Well, I guess y'all should give each other some time to come up with an agreement that will be suitable for both parties before someone gets hurt. JoJo, could you just please run the idea past Uncle Benny?"

Without a word, JoJo and his crew backed out of the restaurant and hopped in their cars and drove away.

Chapter 55

"Join us because you can't beat us," Uncle Benny said out loud, deciphering the message Cold was sending.

"I say we hit him from all angles at once—starting with the traphouses on the east side, his grandmother, and kids' mothers. With that type of attack, we're guaranteed to unbalance him emotionally and weaken his operation," JoJo said.

"So you want to start killing women and children?"

"We don't have to kill the kids. I just want to send him the message that he can be touched . . . Listen to me, Uncle Benny—let me take back control of our streets my way."

There was a brief silence that allowed each man to collect his thoughts. JoJo's patience had run its course. With or without Uncle Benny's approval, he was going to begin making his own moves.

Uncle Benny knew in his heart that he wasn't going to be able to keep a hold on JoJo much longer. There was a beast inside of JoJo that was dying to be set free, and Uncle Benny feared that beast. He feared the chaos it would cause—not only around JoJo, but the destruction it would also bring upon himself.

"I've been knowing you your whole life. I practically raised you, JoJo," Uncle Benny began calmly. "But I see that you have become your own man. I've tried to guide and teach you so you would be smarter than me. Even though you weren't my son, I made a promise to your mother before she died that I would always protect you. But I can no longer control you or teach you. There are things in life you're going to have to experience on your own, and I hope your actions don't bring about your death before it's too late."

"I'm not you, Uncle Benny, and I'm nothing like you. Your mistakes came from your heart. You tried to rule the streets with your heart. I'm going to rule these streets with fear . . ."

"Do you understand that concept? Putting fear in people doesn't always mean through violence. You have to make people fear what your mind is capable of," Uncle Benny interrupted.

"People fear God because of the wrath he can bring upon the world—and in history, he had to show that wrath to be feared," JoJo interjected.

"Dr. Martin Luther King Jr. was feared because of the power he had over minds," Uncle Benny punctuated.

"Well, the power over the minds in the streets can only be conquered through the fear of violence. We're not in the life of finding Jehovah. The Almighty we're chasing is green. The power we're chasing is achieved through fear, and the respect is gained through blood. This is the way I'm prepared to go," JoJo exhaled deeply.

"Then so be it, JoJo." Uncle Benny hung up.

Chapter 56

Cold had gathered the kids and was spending the day at his grandmother's house, enjoying her home cooking and splashes in the pool with the kids. He had only one bodyguard to accompany him, who posed as a friend so as not to worry his grandmother. She would have a million questions of concern if her house was shielded with armed men.

It was a beautiful day of laughter and joy that was much needed in Cold's solemn life. Cold felt normal again in these hours of escape from his reality. He had ordered not to be contacted unless there was a life-or-death situation. Today, his priorities were the kids and grandmother, and seeing the smiles on their faces as they played gleefully around the yard made his life so much more meaningful.

"So how are you, baby?" Cold's grandmother asked as she sat down beside him at the picnic table.

"I'm doing fine, Grandma. But how are you doing?"

"Getting old," she chuckled.

"No, you're getting better."

His grandmother's expression became serious.

"I'm so proud of you, Peter. You have grown into a wonderful man. There's something I need to tell you about your father."

"I'd rather not talk about him."

"I don't know any other way to explain this to you, but you have the right to know. It's time that you know the truth before I die . . ." She paused for a second. "Your father is not who you think he is. Your father's name is Vinny Castano. He's part of the Italian mafia in Boston, Massachusetts. He had an affair with your mother and got her pregnant. When he found out your mother was pregnant, he threatened to kill her if she had the baby. So your mother came back home with me. He never came after her, but your mother lived in fear for many years. That's why she concealed you. She met Freddie—as you know, your father—and he fell hard for your mother. They got married, and he accepted you as his own. But eventually, he took your mother down with the drugs, and after he left, she ran to the streets."

Cold was taken by surprise. He sat there in a daze, lost in thoughts. For so long, he'd been hating this man for abandoning him and his mother. For so long, his identity had been a lie. But deep in the core of his heart, he couldn't hate his mother or grandmother for hiding the truth. He looked at his grandmother, who was in tears.

"I'm sorry I didn't tell you the truth much sooner, baby."

"It's okay, Grandma. I've made it this far without the coward. I think I can continue to manage without him."

His grandmother put back on a solemn expression and looked Cold in his eyes.

"Always remember this, Peter—prosperity comes from wisdom through a discerning mind, and a fool is a victim of his own pride. Pain is inevitable. It's how you deal with that pain that determines the man you will become." With that, she kissed Cold on the cheek and got up to join her grandkids.

On the other side of town, JoJo and Priceless' morning began with the implementation of JoJo's plot against Cold. JoJo had his new recruits ready and prepared to carry out the attacks. There were five eight-man crews that were set to attack Cold's traphouses all over the eastside of Charlotte simultaneously at sunset.

JoJo planned to annihilate Cold's whole operation with one blow. Decapitating the head and dismembering the body was the mission statement to his strategy of war. At the same time, he wanted to send a message across Charlotte. He also wanted to prove to Uncle Benny his capability of ruling the streets. He wanted to prove that his method would set the foundation for them to reign for many years.

Uncle Benny watched JoJo grow up being a fucking screw-up, but JoJo always had the heart of a lion. When he was young, yes, he was reckless and rambunctious and didn't always think things through. That's why Uncle Benny didn't trust him to run the streets. But he was older now and mature, and after being in Uncle Benny's shadow for so long, he felt that by far he had mastered the game—and his next move would justify it.

It was his turn to rule, and by all means, he was not about to fail. His patience and well-thought-out plan, once accomplished, would prove to Uncle Benny that he was born to be the king of Charlotte.

Chapter 57

Andrea and Andreka's relationship with each other was still in the developing stage. They were past the peaceful congregation, considering the circumstances of their acquaintance—of them having a physical altercation. They both had grown to accept the fact that either one would be out of the picture of Cold's life.

When Cold called and told them that he wanted the kids for the day, they decided that they would hook up and spend some time with each other. They agreed to meet up at South Park Mall to do some shopping and get to know one another. They explored designer store after designer store, swiping their credit cards, indulging themselves in the finest brands. They purchased hats, purses, belts, and clothes for all occasions.

After hours of shopping, they were hungry and exhausted, so they made their way to the food court and decided on having Chinese food.

"I can't believe that I'm actually sitting here having a good time with you," Andreka spoke from her heart.

"I know, right! The last time we were this close to each other, bitch, you pulled my weave out!" Andrea laughed at the memory.

"I know, and I'm sorry."

"You don't have to be sorry, because Cold played the both of us, and if that nigga dick wasn't so good, I would have went AWOL."

"And his money," Andreka added, and gave a high five.

211

The more they communicated, the more they found in common with each other and began creating a bond. Observing from the outside, one would have thought that they were best friends or even sisters.

They finished their meals and wrapped up their conversation with plans of ending the night drunk in a club. They got up to leave and were approached by two guys who offered to help them with their bags. The guys didn't come off as being broke or up to something, and their energy was pleasant. They were well groomed, and their attire consisted of the finest brands.

"Sure!" both girls responded while blushing and led the way to their cars.

Their conversations were pleasant and flirtatious along the way. The guys were complete gentlemen; they helped put their bags in the trunks of their cars and politely held the doors open for them to get in their cars, as the ladies were parked two car spaces away from each other. They continued to converse and exchange numbers through the windows.

A black SUV pulled up behind them and stopped as if waiting on a parking space. The two men eyed each other. They looked around the parking lot for anyone that would be focused on them. Once they were clear of no attention, they gave each other a nod. At that instant, they both extracted pistols with silencers and shot both women in the head before a scream could even escape their tonsils.

The men quickly retreated, hopped in the awaiting SUV, and left the scene without any notice.

Chapter 58

The morning quickly exhausted into evening. The darkened sky was accompanied by a full moon. The moment had arrived where fate would be determined. Priceless and two goons hopped out of the SUV around the corner from Cold's grandmother's house. They made their way to the back of the house by crossing through the neighbor's backyards. Luckily, they didn't cross a yard with a dog, but if so, they had silencers to silence the bitches.

Priceless positioned himself at the back door with his goons on either side. One was strapped with an AK-47, while Priceless and the other goon brandished Glocks. When Priceless looked through the window on the back door, he saw Cold and his grandmother in the kitchen, washing dishes and talking with one another.

"I have Cold and his grandmother in the kitchen. They're no threat," Priceless whispered into the micro radio that was strapped around his head.

"Keep an eye on them, we're moving in the front," JoJo radioed back as they hopped out of the SUV one house down from Cold's grandmother's.

One goon stayed in the SUV as the getaway driver, while JoJo and two other goons walked straight up to the front door. One goon had an AK-47 with a navy suppressor attached. He positioned himself, aiming the AK-47 at the locks on the door, waiting on JoJo to give the signal to fire. The other goon watched the streets.

"Are you ready?" JoJo whispered to Priceless on the radio.

"Just say go!" Priceless switched positions with the other goon who had the AK-47, which also had a navy suppressor attached, and was now aiming at the back door.

"Go!" JoJo yelped into the radio and his goon.

Splat! Splat! Splat! Boom! Boom! The back and front doors abruptly exploded and busted open, with masked men coming in through either door, guns extracted and pointing.

Two shots were inserted into the head of Cold's bodyguard, who was sitting in the living room with the kids. The kids screamed in terror, not fully understanding what was happening.

In the kitchen, Cold took off running to the living room to his kids and was met by the butt of JoJo's gun, knocking him down. The kids quickly ran to their daddy and cried in fear.

"Get this nigga up!" JoJo screamed.

His goons forcefully yanked Cold up off the floor and threw him on the couch. Priceless and the other two goons came into the living room with Cold's grandmother and pushed her onto the couch beside Cold.

Cold's heart didn't register fear; death he was ready for, but his heart ached for his kids and grandmother. He hoped his kids were too young to remember this.

"I'm not about to plead for my life. I just ask that you take me in the other room and kill me. I don't need my kids to witness this."

"You don't make the fucking rules, nigga," JoJo said as he removed his mask. "I tried to compromise with you, but your life wasn't worth fifteen percent to you, so now you have to face the consequences of your actions."

"Nigga, I just told you I'm not begging for shit, so kill me and get the fuck out," Cold said with a calm fury.

"It's not going to be that simple." JoJo nodded to Priceless.

Priceless aimed the Glock at Cold's grandmother and fired two shots into her chest. The kids screamed and clutched their father tighter. The rage in Cold's eyes was murderous, yet he was helpless.

"That's just the beginning of my show," JoJo said with a sinister smile.

At that moment, JoJo's goons began snatching the kids from Cold. Cold tried to fight them, but he was easily overpowered by the goons, who began pistol-whipping him.

"Get your hands off my fucking kids!" Cold yelled while struggling against the restraints from the goons.

"Don't worry, I don't kill kids." JoJo smiled after getting the emotional reaction from Cold.

Cold relaxed. "Just do what you came to do to me. I don't care if you torture me, just lock my kids in the room."

JoJo nodded to his goons to take the kids in the other room, but they were stopped by Priceless.

"What the fuck you doing?"

"What the fuck do it look like I'm doing? We need to go ahead and kill this nigga and get the fuck out of here. I don't leave witnesses behind."

"Those are fucking babies . . . they can't identify anybody." JoJo looked at Priceless like he was crazy.

"Yeah, whatever." Priceless turned around and abruptly snatched one of the kids from the goon and fired a single shot in his head.

As the kid's body dropped, everyone stood in shock. Time froze in a dimension of a tormented reality. Cold's adrenaline and rage gave him a strength that only a father's love could rouse. He threw one goon off him and punched the other one in the face, then jumped up and charged at Priceless, but multiple bullets pierced his back and legs. Cold dropped to the floor just meters away from Priceless.

Cold was still alive, but numb to the bullets. Tears streamed down his face. The pain he was experiencing in his heart ached hard while he watched helplessly as Priceless executed his kids one by one and dropped them on the floor.

Priceless then stood over Cold and fired three more bullets, one in his face and two in his chest, sending Cold into a darkened oblivion.

The seven-man crew escaped. JoJo was furious at Priceless, but his heart had too much fear to reprimand him.

On the other side of town, the attacks on Cold's traphouses were devastating. The streets had lit up like it was World War Three; bullets had flown and bodies had dropped. Casualties had ravaged both sides. Their sneak attacks on the traphouses had been an ambush, but they had refused to retreat, and JoJo's goons were able to penetrate with their powerful weaponry. The attacks lasted a long ten to fifteen minutes before sirens were heard coming in the distance. The traphouses were dismantled, and triumph was accomplished for JoJo and the goons, and the goons that made it out alive were able to escape.

Chapter 59

A downcast of sorrow fell upon the night while nature erupted in a fuss. Rain battered from the sky and booms of thunder rattled the earth as lightning cracked sparks. Inside the house was an emotional quietness as the forensic techs gleaned the scene for evidence.

In thirty years, Detective Roundhouse had never witnessed such a gruesome scene. A cold chill shivered through his nerves as he looked at the dead bodies of the kids.

"What would make someone commit such an atrocious act?" Detective Wilson asked.

"I don't know, but whoever did this is a cold son of a bitch. We need to figure out who these people are and what they were into," Detective Roundhouse responded.

The lead forensic tech, Allison, approached the detective.

"Can you give us a walkthrough of the scene?" he asked Allison.

"Yes. We found casings from an AK-47 on both the front and back porch, which answers the question of what was used for the forced entry. I believe the perpetrators entered the house simultaneously from the front and back door and caught the victims completely by surprise," Allison said.

"If they used AK-47's to shoot off the doors, then that means they had silencers, because none of the neighbors reported hearing gunshots," Detective Roundhouse said.

"We got identification off the two adult male victims, and the owner of the house we believe is the elderly victim on the couch. She fit the description from what the neighbors described. We haven't positively identified the kids, but the neighbors reported that they believe the kids were the elderly woman's great-grandchildren and that Peter Franklin was their father, who is one of the victims."

"This was either an act of revenge or the perpetrators wanted something of high value. Whatever the case, I will begin by finding out what the father was into."

Allison gave Detective Roundhouse a piece of paper with the victims' names.

"Which one is Peter?" Detective Roundhouse asked.

"That one right there." Allison pointed to the body on the floor.

Detective Roundhouse walked over to the body of Cold and squatted down.

"What the fuck were you into?" he asked, thinking aloud.

When he stood up, Cold's head jerked up, then quickly relaxed. He bent back down and felt for a pulse. There was a slight pulse that was hard to detect, but it was there.

"Get the fucking ambulance here now! We have one that's still alive!" he screamed.

Chapter 60

Privilege was emotionally beaten. Cold was in a coma, struggling for his life. Every day for the past months, Privilege stayed at the hospital praying for Cold. Every day she would massage his muscles and whisper in his ear.

"Please come back to us, we need you," Privilege whispered in his ear. She took his hand and rubbed it across her stomach and lay snuggled up against Cold while still holding his hand. She was drifting off to sleep when his hand slightly gripped hers. She quickly rose up and looked into his opened eyes. A cold shiver flooded throughout her body, but was gone in an instant.

"Oh my God, Cold, I love you so much." She kissed him repeatedly while tears streamed down her face. She tried to get him to say something. The blankness in his eyes was like his mind was trapped in another world. Not receiving a response, she buzzed for the doctor.

"How are you, Mr. Franklin?" the doctor asked while he flashed a light in Cold's eyes upon his arrival. "If you can hear me, blink." Cold complied.

"Blink if you feel this." The doctor tapped Cold's toes with a pen.

Privilege held her breath. The moment felt like an eternity, and when Cold blinked, she exhaled a sign of relief. After the doctor finished with his tests and questions and was about to depart, Privilege stopped him.

"Can you not update the public or anyone about his current condition considering the circumstances?"

"Sure. Now I will not update anyone in the public of his current condition, but I will have to notify the authorities."

"Well, can you just give us some time before you do?"

"I'll give you until the end of my shift."

"Thank you so much!" Privilege followed the doctor into the hallway. After the doctor walked off, she turned to Tricko, who was standing guard at the door with three other armed men.

"I need to speak with you, Tricko."

She walked back into the room.

Cold was now back, sleeping peacefully.

"What's up?" Tricko asked after closing the door behind him and walked over to Cold.

"He's out of the coma!" Privilege held back her tears.

Tricko stood there and looked at Cold. A single tear escaped his—eye, which he quickly wiped away.

"Welcome back, boss man."

"We need to keep this between us. I don't want anyone to know that he's out of the coma until we get him out of the hospital."

"Valentino's in town, and he wants to see him."

"Okay, but no one else."

Tricko nodded and got on the cell phone.

"What's up, Valentino? He's resting right now, but he's back with us. Alright, see you in a few."

Tricko hung up.

"Valentino's on his way. He can help us get Cold out of the hospital."

"Okay! Thank you, Tricko, for being here."

"You don't have to thank me. Cold's my family," Tricko said.

Tricko walked back into the hallway.

Chapter 61

The past month in Charlotte was a bloody war zone. The lives of many men were sacrificed for the gain of money, power, and respect. It was a cold wrath that shattered the souls throughout the whole city. JoJo and Priceless continued to ravage Cold's traphouses on all sides of town. They were merciless to their adversaries. They inflicted brutal deaths of decapitation and castration on those who refused to oblige under their reign.

Then it became time to replenish the neighborhoods with their product. The product wasn't as good as Cold's customers were used to, but it was good enough. JoJo knew it was going to take time before things completely came together as planned. Every day was a process, and within a month, things had begun to reform and the demand increased.

JoJo and Priceless had heard that Cold had survived, but also that he was a vegetable and was being hidden out of town. Cold's whole team had been destroyed, or they went underground. However, they were no longer a threat to them.

They moved around the city with confidence and with newfound respect. In clubs, they were always VIP without paying for anything. The women flaunted themselves, and the dope boys wanted to be a part of their team. The jealousy and envy stayed discreet.

As the months passed by, the money, power, and respect continued to increase on the streets for the duo, but Priceless' actions were getting bolder, or rather, reckless. One night in a club, Priceless invited a couple to join him and his crew in the VIP section. The girl was young and sexy, with the body of a goddess. She was accompanied by her naïve boyfriend, who was eager to be in the presence of such respected men.

After about an hour in the VIP section, the girl was unsettled. Priceless had attached himself to her like she was his possession. Her boyfriend was too busy getting drunk to even take notice. When the club was getting ready to close, Priceless invited the couple to an after-party. The girl declined, but her boyfriend insisted that they go, and eventually she gave in.

The after-party consisted of Priceless and three of his goons in a house in the Hidden Valley housing development. The blunts were being passed, and the bottles were being tipped. The girl was sitting on the couch between Priceless and her boyfriend. She had declined every time Priceless tried to pass her the blunt or offer her something to drink.

The weed and alcohol had kicked in, and Priceless got straight bold. He put his hand between the girl's thighs and stuck it straight up her skirt.

"I'm ready to go!" she jumped up and yelled to her boyfriend.

"Baby, just chill. We'll leave in a little bit," the boyfriend said.

"Yeah, just chill." Priceless stood up, then palmed her ass.

"Stop fucking touching me!" she yelled.

"Aye, chill, man. That's my girl." The boyfriend jumped up.

"Nigga, fuck you!" Priceless punched the kid in his face. His goons jumped up and began pummeling the kid.

"Please, stop!" the girl yelled in tears.

"Bitch, shut the fuck up!" Priceless slapped her, and she went flying backward and fell on the floor. He bent down and ripped her clothes off. The more she struggled, the more blows he threw to her face until she lay there still. Without lubricating, he penetrated her, ripping right into her vagina.

She screamed out in pain with tears falling from her eyes. "Please, stop!" she cried out.

Priceless pounded her with no remorse until he climaxed all inside of her. The other three goons all took turns viciously raping her while her boyfriend lay helplessly on the floor, brutally beaten.

After the men were finished, Priceless threw cold water on the couple.

"I shouldn't have to tell y'all the consequences for going to the law, so I'm going to give y'all five minutes to get the strength and get the fuck out of here, or I'm going to dead both of y'all mothafuckas," he said.

The girl was the first one to get up. She struggled to help her boyfriend get up and walk out, and eventually they made it to their car. She drove away with a cold pain and left her soul behind.

Chapter 62

Cold was housed in Colombia, South America, at one of Valentino's mansions. He was rapidly rehabilitating mentally and physically. Every day was a struggle as he tried to block out the vivid images of the gruesome murders of his family. Many nights during the first month out of the hospital, he was awakened from nightmares in a cold sweat.

It was painful for Privilege to watch Cold mourn in silence, but she refused to leave his side, so she silently mourned with him. His reticence and lack of emotion were piercing her heart. When she revealed to him that she was pregnant, he had only acknowledged her with a kiss on the cheek.

As the months passed by, his physical therapy became intense. His walking became more balanced and steadier, but he still walked with a slight limp. Cold read and researched the Internet obsessively. He was materializing something that only a broken man could understand and a madman could implement. His revenge for the blood that was spilled, not only of his family but of his soldiers as well, was going to be merciless.

He grew dreads and a thick beard to change his description. After seven months, Cold quietly returned to the United States and inconspicuously began to rebuild his operation. He upgraded his surveillance team with the latest technology of microcameras, listening devices, and GPS systems.

JoJo and Priceless were easily located, considering how flamboyant they were, and Cold documented their every move. In a matter of weeks, Cold had their cars, houses, girlfriends' houses, and even their club and other businesses wired with devices. The way JoJo and Priceless moved around the city, Cold could have taken them out with snipers, but that would have been too easy. Cold wanted them to endure pain inflicted by his hands, and patience was his virtue.

In his grandfather's graveyard, Cold had built an underground dungeon to carry out the most grotesque, imaginative fate he had fantasized for them. Their days were numbered, and the war had just begun.

Chapter 63

Privilege was in excruciating pain while giving birth to a baby boy. She pushed and pushed as the doctor pulled the baby out. The quietness that followed sent the doctors and nurses into a medical frenzy. The baby was dead and blue.

"Why is our baby not crying? What's wrong?" Privilege began to panic.

Cold watched in anger as the doctors and nurses performed medical treatment on his only child that had a chance of existing. He refused to pray because he had already made a vow that he would walk through the gates of hell for the revenge of his family, so there was no need for him to call on God. He would endure the pain and accept the consequences of his actions because he would never break again.

"He's dead!" he answered Privilege.

"No, please bring my baby to life!" Privilege cried out to the doctors.

Moments felt like an eternity. A light cry interrupted Cold's thoughts as he watched his son wiggle his legs and arms, exploding into life.

"Allegiance," Cold whispered, just audible enough for Privilege to hear.

"Allegiance Franklin," Privilege said to Cold.

Cold looked into her eyes and realized how much Privilege loved him. He had been inconsiderate toward Privilege when she had been standing by his side every step of the way. Words he never thought would ever escape his mouth came out without any regrets.

"Will you marry me?"

Privilege was speechless. Tears of joy escaped her eyes, and the only thing she did was shake her head up and down.

"Yes! Yes! Yes! I love you so much, Cold," Privilege managed to utter through a cracked voice from her overwhelming emotions.

Cold broke out into a smile that had been hidden beneath a body caged in pain for so long. He bent over and passionately kissed Privilege.

"Excuse me," the doctor—who had been sewing Privileges back up—interrupted.

"Oh, we're sorry," Privilege said after breaking free from Cold's lips.

"When can we see our son?" she immediately asked.

"The doctor took him to perform some tests, so once they're through, your son will be brought back to you immediately," the doctor said, finishing up.

"Thank you so much, doctor," Privilege said, feeling exhausted and drained.

"Go to sleep and I'll wake you up when they bring him back," Cold said.

Hours later, when Privilege awoke, she was alone in the room, feeling sluggish. She paged for the nurse and wondered where in the hell Cold had gone off to.

The nurse entered the room as if she had been disturbed by something very important.

"What is it?" she asked offensively and boldly.

Privilege's patience was usually short when it came to other females, but today she was not in the mood to put this one in her place.

"Can you just tell me where my baby is?"

"How in the hell am I supposed to know? I just got here. Shouldn't your baby be where they keep all the other babies?" the nurse said.

"Listen here!" Privilege began calmly and looked at the nurse's name tag. "Christina, can you just get me some medication and find out where my baby is, please?"

When the nurse left, Privilege picked up her cell phone and dialed Cold's number. After a few rings, it went to voicemail.

The nurse returned with the same irritable attitude she left with.

"Here's your medication, and I don't know where your baby is."

Privilege's patience had run its course.

"Bitch, you need to find out where in the hell my baby is before I turn this—"

She was interrupted by the door opening, with Cold walking in and holding their baby boy. He stopped and looked at both women and could feel that he had interrupted something intense.

"Bitch! There's your baby," the nurse said and walked out.

"What was that about?" Cold asked as he handed Privilege their son.

"PMS! Oh my God. He's so beautiful." Privilege's attitude changed. "So what did they say about the tests?"

"He's healthy!"

The nurse came back into the room, and Privilege looked at her with disgust.

"Did you kidnap your baby?" she asked Cold.

Cold looked from the nurse to Privilege, who was looking astonished.

"You stole our baby?" Privilege asked.

"Technically, I didn't steal or kidnap our baby."

"See, that's the problem with black folks. I need to take him back to the nursery," Christina said irritably.

"Hold up, could you just give us a second?" Cold asked.

"No, because I'm not about to lose my job. The nurse in the nursery will bring him back."

Cold looked at the nurse's name tag and took a good look at her face.

"Christina, was your brother named Chris?"

Christina looked at Cold's face and sensed a familiarity but couldn't quite put a name to it.

"Why?" she asked.

"I see you don't recognize me, but I'm Cold."

She recognized Cold immediately. She gasped, and tears escaped her eyes.

"Oh my God! Cold, I thought you were dead. I heard what happened to you. I'm so sorry. You look so different with your dreads and beard, and you have gold teeth. It's been so long. How have you been?" she vented and gave him a hug.

"I've been okay. How are you?" Cold saw the painful expression and knew things weren't going well for her. "How about you take our son back to the nursery and come back," he said after she paused upon his question.

She nodded and held back her tears, then took Allegiance back to the nursery. She returned with her emotions a little more collected, but the pain in her eyes could not be hidden. Cold got up and allowed her to take a seat on the sofa while he sat on the edge of the bed next to Privilege.

"This is my fiancée, Privilege. Privilege, this is Christina, a good friend from the past," Cold said. The women nodded to each other in acknowledgment.

"So what's been up, Christina?"

Christina inhaled and exhaled a deep breath.

"I don't know where to begin, but first I would like to apologize to you, Privilege, for how I acted earlier. It's just that I've been going through so much these past six months."

She was unable to control her emotions any longer, and tears fell freely down her cheeks. She straightened up and cleared her throat, then continued.

"About six months ago, my boyfriend and I went to this club, and we started hanging out with some guys. They asked us to go to an after-party with them. I swear I didn't want to go because I had this funny feeling about these guys, and I knew about their reputation. Anyway, my boyfriend kept insisting that we go with them, so I eventually gave in. They took us to this house in Hidden Valley, and . . ."

She broke down crying uncontrollably.

"It's okay. Just take your time," Cold said as he got up and sat beside her on the arm of the sofa, rubbing her back to console her.

She finally regained control of herself and continued.

"Anyway, when we got in the house, things got bad quickly. They beat up my boyfriend real bad, and when I tried to stop them, they beat and raped me. Then a few weeks ago, my boyfriend committed suicide right in front of me because I threw it in his face that he couldn't protect me, and I told him that I wanted to leave him. I didn't mean it. It's all my fault."

She began crying again.

"It's not your fault, so don't you blame yourself for his actions," Cold encouraged. "Do you know any of those guys' names?"

"The main guy was named Priceless. The other three, I didn't get their names, but I'll never forget any of their faces," Christina said with a menacing look.

When Christina mentioned Priceless' name, Privilege and Cold locked eyes for a split second.

"Listen, Christina, I don't want you to worry about them anymore. I'm sorry that I abandoned you in the first place, but everything's going to be okay now. I promise you that they will get what's coming to them," Cold assured her.

"Thank you, Cold," Christina said.

"Now can you go and get my baby boy before I have to go and kidnap him again?"

"Okay," Christina said with a smile as she got up.

Chapter 64

Mellow-T and his crew had put together a neighborhood cookout at the Little Rock Apartments on West Boulevard. The sun was shining and the faces were smiling. The music was blasting and the blunts were being passed. Free beers and liquor were being distributed at the bar. They had games and prizes for the kids and bingo for the adults. The grill flamed with hot dogs and juicy burgers, while fish and chicken crackled in the deep fryer, seasoned Southern-style.

Mellow-T and his crew were known for busting their guns, but now they were establishing themselves in the game for getting money. So today they decided to give back to the community. West Boulevard was now Mellow-T's and his crew's, and he protected the boundaries with a *meet your maker* policy if anyone crossed those boundaries with the wrong intentions. Today, it looked as if that policy may have to be put into effect.

Mellow-T and his crew were walking through the parking lot when they noticed four guys standing outside a black SUV looking out of place. As they approached the guys, anxiety fluttered through Mellow-T instantly upon recognizing Priceless and his goons.

Mellow-T stayed cool. "So what brings you and your goons over here?"

His crew formed a circle around Priceless and his goons.

"Don't worry, I didn't come to bury niggas today," Priceless said arrogantly, looking around at Mellow-T and his crew with a sinister grin.

"So what do you want? Because I know you didn't come to play bingo."

Priceless inhaled a long drag from his cigarette, flicked it away, and dramatically exhaled the smoke slowly. "It's like this, little nigga. You have two options. One, you can start buying your product from me, or two, you can work for me. Oh, I almost forgot—there's also option number three."

Priceless pointed his middle and index finger at Mellow-T's head like it was a pistol. "Pow!" he said with his mouth like he fired a gun.

Mellow-T and his crew drew their guns instantly on Priceless and his goons, and they didn't even try to reach for their weapons.

"Well, I chose option three, nigga. And the only reason why I'm not going to shoot your ass in the face right now is because of all these kids out here. So get the fuck out of my neighborhood before I change my mind."

Priceless took out another cigarette and fired it up. He glared Mellow-T in his eyes with a sinister grin, then turned away to get in the SUV—but then he stopped and turned to look back at Mellow-T.

"You see, that's the difference between you and me."

With that, he and his goons hopped in the SUV and drove off.

"We should have killed those niggas," one of Mellow-T's crew members said.

"Don't worry. We'll have our chance. They'll be back, trust me. We just have to be prepared for them," Mellow-T said as he walked away.

Chapter 65

The past week had been a tornado of misfortune for JoJo. On Monday, his club had burned down due to a faulty electrical circuit wiring. On Wednesday, the pipes in his house burst, flooding the whole house and damaging the twenty-five-thousand-dollar carpet and over fifty thousand dollars' worth of furniture.

Then there was Priceless. Priceless was a liability. JoJo thought Priceless would have calmed down now that they were making money beyond measure, but no; Priceless was more arrogant and reckless beyond measure, and he was untamable. Their resources in the CMPD were also complaining about Priceless' behavior, informing him that Priceless was getting beyond their control to protect. JoJo really needed to sit Priceless down and have a serious talk with him, but damn if it's not one thing, then it's another.

His brand-new BMW X5 was having a computer chip malfunction. JoJo was impatiently waiting at the BMW dealership to receive another car. He verbally expressed his disapproval to the sales manager, who in return continued to apologize for the company's unfortunate service.

"Sir, your car is ready," the sales manager said, handing JoJo the keys.

JoJo hopped in the BMW X5 that was a replica to the last BMW. He exited the BMW car lot onto Independence Boulevard and headed to one of his lady's houses. He needed to release some of the tension that was built up. He called, and Mimi answered on the first ring.

"Hey, baby!" Mimi answered.

"You got that pussy washed for daddy?" JoJo asked.

"It's always washed for you, daddy, but I can get in the tub and soak it until you get here if you want me to?" Mimi said seductively.

"Yeah, do that," JoJo said.

"Okay, daddy, I'll see you in a little bit," Mimi said before she hung up.

When JoJo arrived at Mimi's house, she was in the tub as promised, sucking on a seven-inch dildo while seductively rubbing on her breasts.

"Umm," Mimi moaned as JoJo stood over her and watched the show.

She dropped the dildo in the tub, stood up, and unbuckled JoJo's belt. She undressed him, pulled him into the tub, and ushered him to sit down. She stood with her pussy right in his face. He rubbed his hands slowly up the back of her thighs and squeezed her ass cheeks in circular motions. She put one leg on the edge of the tub and spread them apart. JoJo tilted his chin up to position his mouth on her clean-shaved pussy. His tongue dived inside her pussy greedily, from up and down and in circular motions.

"Umm, baby, it feels so good!" Mimi moaned, grabbing the back of his head.

He stuck a finger in her asshole and pumped slowly in and out while still hungrily feasting on her pussy. She rotated her hips to the rhythm of his tongue and finger. "Oh, JoJo, please don't stop," she screamed.

He feasted on her pussy until her legs wobbled and her body convulsed. She slowly bent down, inserted his dick inside of her pussy, and bounced up and down. JoJo tried to suck on her titties, but the harder and faster she bounced, it kept her titties slipping out of his mouth.

"I love this dick, JoJo. Oh my God . . . it's sooo . . . good!" Mimi screamed.

JoJo grabbed her waist and helped her bounce harder and faster on his dick. The water splashed and flopped everywhere. He felt the tingling sensation flutter through his groin and stopped her. They stood up and Mimi bent over. JoJo inserted his dick back inside of her wet pussy with ease. He grabbed her waist and pounded hard, slow strokes.

"Oh . . . oh . . . oh!" Mimi moaned with each stroke.

The strokes got faster and the screaming got louder. This time, when the tingling sensation fluttered, JoJo let his semen erupt all inside of her, jolting with each squirt.

They showered and continued their sexathon for the next few hours all over the house until they were both exhausted.

Chapter 66

Mellow-T and his crew were nicknamed *4715*. They went by that because every time they killed or robbed someone, they used an AK-47 or an AR-15 assault rifle. Hence how West Boulevard got the cognomen *Chopper Boulevard*. His crew had started off with five members; now there were fifteen members, and each one had at least one murder under their belts.

The day had fallen to night. Mellow-T and his crew were spread out around Little Rock Apartments in the darkened shadows. They anticipated the infamous Priceless to return with his goons. Priceless' reputation perceived him, and only a fool will take light of a threat from such a monster. Mellow-T's anxiety was building; every organ, muscle, and nerve told his intuition Priceless was out there lurking.

An hour past midnight, Mellow-T's patience had run its course, and he began to call his crew out of the shadows. The butterflies came in his stomach before he saw sparks. The silent night exploded from everywhere around the apartments. Mellow-T and many of his crew members were able to duck for cover and get in a position to return fire.

Mellow-T peeped around the car he was taking cover behind, searching each area he saw the shooting coming from. His mind was in search of one target. He knew that arrogant mothafucka was out there lurking, and he was going to die finding him.

He let out a few rounds from the AR-15 and took off in a sprint around the building. Bullets shot past, hitting the bricks on the building. He continued to run all the way around the building until he came to the other side. He peeped around the corner and zoomed in on the faces behind the opposing weapons. And there, behind one of his goons, Priceless stood leaning against the corner of one of the buildings, calmly smoking a cigarette, observing the chaos.

The best way for Mellow-T to get close to Priceless was to run two buildings down and come back up on the opposite side; then he could creep up on Priceless. He took off in a sprint and made his way back up on the opposite side. He peeped around the corner, and Priceless was still standing arrogantly in the same position. Priceless' goon was behind a car, shooting in the direction of his crew.

Mellow-T aimed the AR-15 at Priceless, and as soon as he was about to pull the trigger, Priceless turned his head and saw him. Priceless ducked and took off running, escaping each bullet that was meant for his head. Mellow-T sprinted from behind the building in pursuit. He fired two shots into Priceless' goon, exploding his back wide open. Sirens could be heard in the distance. Mellow-T continued chasing and firing shots at Priceless, exploding everything besides his intended target. Priceless began returning shots while weaving and ducking between cars and buildings.

The AR-15 clicked, signifying it was empty of ammunition. Mellow-T dropped the weapon and pulled out two Glock 22 .40 calibers. He saw Priceless run from behind a parked car. He took careful aim and fired numerous rounds. Priceless dropped to the ground but quickly got back up and shambled into the woods. Mellow-T ducked behind a car when the police came racing into the apartments. He ended his pursuit and faded into the darkness of the apartments.

Priceless scrambled through the woods. He had been hit twice: once in the upper back and once in the rib cage. He came out of the woods on West Boulevard, staggering, trying to keep his balance, but his oxygen was low. He finally made it to Al's Corner Store, which was closed. He took a deep breath and watched the world spin before fainting on the sidewalk.

Chapter 67

JoJo woke up feeling relaxed. He looked at a sleeping Mimi and admired her beauty for just a second. He eased out of the bed with the intention of not waking her up, in which he accomplished. He got dressed, left the house, and got in his ride. It was a little past one a.m., so traffic was very scarce.

Sitting at the red light on Sharon Amity Road and Monroe Road, JoJo's car suddenly shut off. He tried to crank it back up, but to no avail. He reached for the door handle, but he was locked in.

"What the fuck is going on?" JoJo spoke out loud while continuously hitting the switch for the locks.

A car pulled up beside him and stopped. When he looked into the window, his heart dropped. There, scowling at him, was a man with dreads and a thick beard, but a face he'll never forget. Cold glared with a menacing look that only the devil could emulate. Suddenly, the vents of JoJo's car hissed, and the cabin filled with a thick cloud of Sevoflurane gas.

Cold's face was the last thing JoJo remembered before going unconscious.

A van pulled up beside JoJo's BMW, and the side door opened. Two men hopped out with gas masks on and hit a button on a remote that bypassed the BMW's security system.They pulled JoJo out, threw him in the van, and tied him up. One of the guys hopped in the BMW. He rolled the windows down and they all drove away from the scene. The kidnapping took less than sixty seconds.

JoJo was awakened by a splash of cold water in his face. He found himself tied to a table, naked and spread eagle. The room was dark with the exception of a bright light that was shining directly above him. The air was moist and cold with a stench of rusty metal and wet dirt. When his vision cleared and he was able to focus, the adrenaline of fear recaptured his nerves when his eyes rested upon Cold. Cold stood over him with an empty cup. Knowing he was about to die, his pride wouldn't let him go out like a coward.

"JooooJoooo," Cold slowly stretched his name out while looking into his eyes.

"Do what the fuck you want, but I'm not about to beg you for my life like a bitch," JoJo proclaimed.

"Oh yeah, you're going to beg me like a bitch. You're going to beg me to hurry up and kill you. Matter of fact, the first thing I'm going to do is chop off your dick and watch you scream like the bitch that I'm about to make you," Cold said, leaning closer to his face.

JoJo squirmed a little when Cold mentioned chopping off his dick. "That's some homo shit. Gangstas don't play with niggas' dicks," he tried to use reverse psychology.

"Well, the acts that I'm about to commit on you aren't gangsta at all. They are rather . . . psychotic and downright sick that only a madman can commit. But guess what, JoJo?" Cold paused for a thrill.

"I am that fucking madman," Cold said as he put on a plastic bodysuit, a mask, and gloves.

He rolled a small cart out beside the table JoJo was laying on. The cart carried an electric drill, an electric saw, two rusty knives, and a syringe. Cold picked up one of the rusty knives.

JoJo began twisting wildly against the restraints, cursing and ranting.

Cold lifted the mask from over his face. "Now JoJo, it sounds to me like you're begging," he smirked a sinister smile, then pulled the mask back over his face.

"Fuck you, Cold," JoJo continued to curse and rant.

Cold grabbed JoJo's dick and proceeded to roughly cut it with the rusty knife. JoJo's screams were a piercing shrill, but it was music to Cold's ears. Once finished, Cold threw JoJo's dick in his face.

"As promised!" Cold grabbed the syringe off the cart and held it up. "You see this, JoJo? This is a straight shot of Epinephrine. It's going to keep your heart pumping and your brain wide awake so you don't have the luxury of passing out from the pain. I can't do this unless you're here with me." He found a vein in JoJo's arm and slammed the adrenaline into his bloodstream.

He picked up the drill and pressed the bit against JoJo's kneecap and pulled the trigger. The falsetto of JoJo's screams was the sweetest sound of revenge served cold, or rather served bloody and painful.

Cold was able to keep JoJo alive for thirty minutes through excruciating pain before sawing his body into pieces.

Chapter 68

Christina was in the hallway reading a chart when the paramedics busted through the door. They had a victim with gunshot wounds laying on the gurney. When Christina saw who it was on the gurney, she immediately followed them to the intensive care unit. They lifted Priceless onto another gurney and proceeded to hook tubes to him to begin surgery. The doctors and nurses were screaming orders back and forth. Everyone was moving in an experienced rhythm, desperately trying to keep him alive.

Christina hopped into the rhythm, doing the bare minimum while silently observing and awaiting the outcome. Secretly, she prayed that he'll die, but after a few hours of surgery, her prayer was denied. After the surgery, Priceless was released from ICU and put into a room where he was still passed out from the anesthesia. Christina used that time to go to the hospital's pharmacy. She searched for two specific vials: Succinylcholine and Potassium Chloride. She found them and slipped them into her pockets. She picked up a box of syringes and aspirin, signed for them, and headed back to Priceless' room.

When she got back to the hallway, an orderly from the hospital's kitchen was about to enter Priceless' room with a food cart. Christina hurried and stopped her.

"I'll take it from here," Christina told the orderly and grabbed the cart.

Priceless was just waking up and was sluggish from the aftereffect of the anesthesia. His vision was clearing up, but it was still a little blurry. He turned his head, focusing on where he was at. A nurse was entering the room with her back turned, pulling in a food cart. His memory instantly came back to the shootout he had with Mellow-T and his crew. He also remembered Mellow-T chasing and shooting him. Mellow-T was his first appointment when he got out of the hospital, he promised himself.

The nurse still had her back turned to him, but he could see that she had fixed up a syringe. She turned around and injected the Succinylcholine into the IV line and walked into the bathroom. The drug took effect with terrifying speed. His muscles seized, locking his body into a frozen state; he was now paralyzed, unable to even twitch a finger, but he was still able to move his eyes and speak with a strained, shallow breath.

"Excuse me, nurse!" Priceless managed to yell out, his voice sounding thin as his diaphragm began to tighten

"Just a second, Mr. Priceless," Christina yelled from the bathroom, purposely using his nickname.

She came out of the bathroom and stood over Priceless and tilted her head to the side. "Is there a problem?" she searched his face for any sign of recognition.

"What was that you gave me?" Priceless asked, showing no sign of recognition or even acknowledging that she had called him by his nickname.

Ignoring his question, she asked, "So you don't remember me, do you?"

He focused hard on her face but couldn't quite place the event of their encounter. "You must be a groupie bitch I fucked and didn't call back. So now what, you're trying to get revenge?" Priceless arrogantly stated and asked.

Christina wanted to explode, wishing she could give him a much more painful death, but she kept calm. "Well, you did fuck me unconsenually along with three of your friends, and beat me and my boyfriend half to death."

Priceless' eyes lit up in recognition. "Oh yeah, I remember you. Don't act like you didn't like that shit. So what, you want some money?"

"Oh no, sweetie," she climbed on top and straddled him. She leaned down close to his face. "I want my face to be the last face you see before you die and go to hell," she whispered seductively and kissed him on his lips.

Her left hand held the second syringe, filled with the Potassium Chloride. She lifted her face inches from his and stuck the needle directly into his jugular, squeezing the lethal liquid into his bloodstream to stop his heart mid-beat.

"Listen to me!" she demanded. "Because in thirty seconds you'll be dead, so tell my boyfriend I delivered you to him."

They stared into each other's eyes until she felt Priceless' chest deflate from loss of breath. She got up, grabbed all the evidence, and calmly walked out the room. When she got a few rooms down the hallway, she took off the latex gloves, threw them in the garbage can along with the syringe and empty bottles that contained the substance. She walked to the elevator, hopped on, and exited the hospital.

Christina sat in her car and cried; the reality of what she did had settled in. She picked up her phone and called Cold.

"What up?" Cold answered on the third ring looking at the caller ID. He silently listened to the soft crying and heavy breathing for a second before he spoke again. "What's the matter, Christina?" he patiently asked.

"I killed him," Christina managed to say between sobs.

"Who?" he asked.

"Priceless."

There was a moment of silence before Cold responded. "Where are you now?"

"I'm still at the hospital."

"Go home and get some rest, and I'll come by to see you tonight," Cold said and disconnected the call.

Chapter 69

Cold had finished boxing up the pieces of JoJo's body in numerous boxes to be delivered to all of JoJo's traphouses. He wanted his message to be interpreted clearly and the impact to be highly effective. His next move had taken some precise and delicate planning, and if accomplished, will gain much respect from gangstas across the nation.

After the boxes were loaded up on the fabricated UPS trucks, Cold went to Christina's house. It was late, but he wanted to make sure that she had covered her tracks.

Christina opened the door wearing a gray silk bathrobe, partially exposing an enticing amount of cleavage. It gripped her figure, leaving little to the imagination. It was short to mid-thigh, baring her caramel legs. She had an innocent beauty about herself. Her hair was in a ponytail and her eyes were puffy from crying.

They sat on the couch and Cold listened to her tell him verbatim the events that took place. He held her head buried in his chest when she cried again after completing the story.

"Oh, I'm so sorry, Cold," Christina broke his embrace.

"It's okay. This is what I'm here for," he said.

"No, I mean for being so rude. Here I invite you into my home and I don't even ask you how your day was or offer you something to drink."

"It's okay; my day was satisfying, but I'll take a glass of water, thank you," Cold replied.

"Okay!"

When Christina stood up, her bathrobe rose up just enough to expose her red panties. She slightly looked away, adjusting the bathrobe, and caught Cold admiring her ass. Flustered, Cold quickly turned his head because that was not the door he wanted to open. She smiled and walked off and returned with the glass of water. She handed it to Cold and sat back down a little closer to him.

"Listen, I didn't mean to be inappropriate or send you the wrong message."

"I understand, Cold. You have a fiancée at home and it's your duty to be loyal to her. I don't want to come between you and Privilege, but I'll always be here for you," she said.

"Thank you, Christina."

"You should stay and let me twist up your dreads," she suggested as she rubbed her hand in his dreads.

"Okay, you can do that," Cold went against his better judgment. "Let me take a shower so I can wash my hair."

She got up and gave him a towel and washrag and showed him to the bathroom. He got out of the shower and came out of the bathroom with just the towel wrapped around his waist.

"Christina!"

"What's up, Cold?" Christina walked in the hallway. She paused, admiring his chiseled body. A tingling sensation shot between her legs. *This was going to be hard*, she thought.

"Um, um!" Cold cleared his throat, breaking her thoughts.

"Oh ah, what's up?" Christina regained focus.

"Can you go to my car and get my bag of clothes?" he asked.

"Yeah, I'll go get them," she said.

She went to his car and grabbed the bag. When she returned, Cold was sitting on the couch with the towel still wrapped around his waist. Christina could no longer resist. She dropped the bag on the floor and walked over to Cold, undoing the tie on her bathrobe, and let it fall to the floor. She was left with nothing but a pair of red panties on. Cold swallowed hard, looking at her flawless body. His dick instantly hardened. She straddled his lap and planted kisses on his neck.

"We shouldn't be doing this," Cold stuttered, unable to fully resist.

She planted a trail of kisses down his neck, chest, and lower body. She positioned herself on the floor between his legs, opened the towel, and grabbed his dick. She wrapped her lips around it while looking up into his eyes. She sucked it in and out of her mouth.

"We can't do this," Cold grabbed her head, stopping her.

She stood up, and when he tried to stand up, she pushed him back down and took off her panties and threw them on the floor. Cold's dick was now rock-hard. This time when she straddled him, she inserted his dick inside her wet pussy real slow.

"Damn, girl. Why are you doing this to me?" Cold whispered without bothering to resist anymore.

"Because I know you want it just as much as I want it. That's why we can't stop," Christina whispered back into his ear while grinding her hips up and down. "Ooohh, Cold, your dick feels so good inside me," she moaned.

Cold knew she was right. The more she grinded and moaned in his ear, the more he got turned on and began to participate. He rubbed her back. She grinded her hips harder and faster. He palmed her ass, squeezing each cheek firmly, trying to keep a grip. He picked her up and turned her around on the couch and delivered hard and faster strokes. Christina's juices were flowing heavily. With each stroke he took, their bodies made a loud wet clapping sound.

He pulled out of her, bent her over the couch, and inserted himself back inside of her wet pussy and delivered the same hard and fast strokes, not missing a beat. He pounded her like a madman. He grabbed her ponytail with one hand and wrapped his other hand around her throat. Each hard thrust he took, he pulled her ponytail and choked her harder.

Christina was loving every minute of it. The pain gave her an adrenaline rush that increased the intensity of her orgasm. It felt like she had three orgasms at one time—in her mind, throughout her body, and the nerves in her pussy. Her body jerked and squirmed. Cold felt himself coming; he thrusted, choked, and pulled harder until every drop of his semen burst inside of her. He pulled out and laid beside her, breathing heavily.

"We shouldn't have done this." Cold was now feeling ashamed of his disloyalty to Privilege. What really made him disappointed in himself was the fact that he hadn't had sex with Privilege ever since the murder of his family. Privilege was the only one that was there supporting and lifting him back up, and not only that, he had committed himself to her by proposing to her.

"Don't worry, I'll keep us a secret," Christina said flirtatiously while taking her foot and rubbing across Cold's limp dick.

He moved her foot, got up, and got dressed. "There's no 'us,' Christina, so let's get that clear. I made a mistake. We can't do this anymore. This was only a one-time thing. Are we clear?" he asked.

"It's clear, Cold, but I don't think this was a mistake and I promise you that I'll play my position," she replied.

Cold looked at her innocent beauty and knew that he wasn't going to be able to stay away from her, and he knew that she knew it too. He grabbed his bag and left out the door.

Chapter 70

Doc had been housed at Beaumont Federal Penitentiary, serving a life sentence. For the past two years, he'd been working in the prison's kitchen. A former associate from his past had reached out to him with a proposition. He was paid a hundred grand to deliver a box to Uncle Benny's cell with strict instructions not to open it. The package was supposed to come on the dairy food truck delivered to the kitchen. He was given the distinction mark that will be on the box.

Doc's heart was beating fast and the anxiety made him jittery as he watched the dairy truck back into the dock. He knew something big was going on because a hundred grand to deliver a box to a nigga in prison meant that your life was on the line.

Doc and the other kitchen workers began unloading the boxes onto the cart. The correctional officer marked the boxes off the chart as they were unloaded. Doc noticed one of the other inmates carrying a Blue Bunny dairy box with a small, hand-drawn black crescent moon inked into the corner. The corrections officer marked the box off the chart without giving it a second glance.

They finished unloading the truck and began pushing the carts to the kitchen's freezer. Doc walked beside the cart with the marked box. When they bent the corner in the kitchen, Doc snatched the box off the cart and threw it in a garbage can he had set up against the wall. Another inmate bent the corner going the opposite way and grabbed the garbage can. He took it to the front of the kitchen and set it aside.

After stocking the freezer, Doc made his way back to the front of the kitchen. He told the corrections officer that he needed to go to the block for a minute and that he'll be right back.

The box had been picked up by another inmate with a big push garbage can. That garbage can was used for Wheeling around the yard to pick up the trash from all the units. Doc noticed that the guy on trash detail was picking up trash in front of Uncle Benny's unit, so he hurried down the walkway. He reached Uncle Benny's unit and grabbed the box out of the garbage can and headed inside.

It was still early, so most of the inmates were in school, work, or on the recreation yard. Uncle Benny was on the recreation yard and his cellmate was in school. Doc lifted his coat over his head to avoid being seen by the camera. He went straight upstairs to Uncle Benny's cell. The instructions were to just leave the box on the bed, so that's what he did. He left back out and went straight back to work.

At 10 o'clock a.m., they called yard recall, which meant all inmates were to report back to their assigned units and prepare for count and chow. Uncle Benny came off the rec-yard in a deep conversation with a few homeboys from Charlotte. He departed from them and went upstairs to his cell. He opened the door and noticed the box on his bed, just a little bigger than a shoebox. He stopped and looked around the block for any suspicious stares before he went into the cell. He stared at the box, wondering if it was some type of mistake. His cellmate came into the cell and interrupted his thoughts.

"So what do you have there?" his cellmate asked.

"I don't know. It was here when I came in," Uncle Benny said.

"So open it up," Uncle Benny's cellmate urged.

Uncle Benny picked up the box and gave it a little shake. The box was cold and the contents were heavy and solid. He sat it back down and peeled the tape off and opened the top.

A strong stench came out the box and a letter was on top of some crumbled-up newspapers. He read the letter that consisted of three words:

A Cold World!

He dropped the letter and reached into the box and removed the newspaper. JoJo's decomposing head was looking up at him. Uncle Benny turned and ran to the toilet in the cell and began vomiting.

"What the fuck was that about?" Uncle Benny's cellmate asked and went to look in the box. Instantly he jumped back upon seeing the decomposing head. "Man, you got some serious fucking enemies," he yelled.

Uncle Benny just stared at him with a look of defeat.

To be continued…

Coming Soon

Money And Dead Homies 2
A Cold Bitch!

Lock Down Publications and Ca$h Presents
Assisted Publishing Packages

Due to an increase in the price of services we have increased our prices. The prices below reflect the price increase as of 11/1/24.

BASIC PACKAGE	UPGRADED PACKAGE
$699	$1000
Editing	Typing
Cover Design	Editing
Formatting	Cover Design
	Formatting
	Upload eBooks to Amazon
	Upload Paperback to Amazon
ADVANCE PACKAGE	**LDP SUPREME PACKAGE**
$1,400	$1,700
Typing	Typing
Editing (line editing/content)	Editing (line editing/content)
Cover Design	Cover Design
Formatting	Formatting
Copyright Registration	Copyright Registration
Proofreading	Proofreading
Upload eBooks to Amazon	Set up Amazon Account
Upload Paperback to Amazon	Upload eBooks to Amazon
	Upload Paperback to Amazon
	Advertise on LDP's Amazon and Facebook Page

***

Other services available upon request.
Additional charges may apply

Lock Down Publications
P.O. Box 944
Stockbridge, GA 30281-9998
Phone: 470 303-9761
Email: lockdownpublications@gmail.com

251

Submission Guideline

Submit the first three chapters of your completed manuscript to ldpsubmissions@gmail.com. In the subject line add **Your Book's Title**. The manuscript must be in a Word Doc file and sent as an attachment. Document should be in Times New Roman, double spaced, and in size 12 font. Also, provide your synopsis and full contact information. If sending multiple submissions, they must each be in a separate email.

Have a story but no way to send it electronically? You can still submit to LDP/Ca$h Presents. Send in the first three chapters, written or typed, of your completed manuscript to:

LDP: Submissions Dept
P.O. Box 944
Stockbridge, GA 30281-9998

DO NOT send original manuscript. Must be a duplicate. Provide your synopsis and a cover letter containing your full contact information.

Thanks for considering LDP and Ca$h Presents.

NEW RELEASES

BLOODLINE OF A SAVAGE 1-3
THESE VICIOUS STREETS 1-3
RELENTLESS GOON 1-3
BY PRINCE A. TAUHID

THE BUTTERFLY MAFIA 1-3
BY FUMIYA PAYNE

A THUG'S STREET PRINCESS 1&2
BY MEESHA

CITY OF SMOKE 3
BY MOLOTTI

GET IT IN SLUGS 1 &2
BY B. STALL

STANDING ON HER BUSINESS 1&2
BY DG SANTANA

STEPPERS 1,2&3
THE REAL BADDIES OF CHI-RAQ
BY KING RIO

THE LANE 1&2
BY KEN-KEN SPENCE

THUG OF SPADES 1&2
LOVE IN THE TRENCHES 2
CORNER BOYS
BY COREY ROBINSON

TIL DEATH 3
BY ARYANNA

DERRICK L. SUMMERS

THE BIRTH OF A GANGSTER 4
BY DELMONT PLAYER

PRODUCT OF THE STREETS 1-3
BY DEMOND "MONEY" ANDERSON

NO TIME FOR ERROR
BY KEESE

MONEY HUNGRY DEMONS 1-2
BY TRANAY ADAMS

HUB CITY MENACE 1-3
BY J. WHITE

A THUGGISH PASSION 1&2
LAND OF DA HOOLIGANZ 1-4
KILLAZ ON STANDBY 1&2
BY IRA B.

FO'EVA ROLLIN 1&2
BY ASSA RAYMOND BAKER

THE LEVEL UP 1&3
BY LUXURY KING

Coming Soon from Lock Down Publications/Ca$h Presents

IF YOU CROSS ME ONCE 6
ANGEL V
By Anthony Fields

A THUGS STREET PRINCESS 3
By Meesha

CORNER BOYS 2
By Corey Robinson

THA TAKEOVER
By Keith Chandler

BETRAYAL OF A G 2
By Ray Vinci

SAVAGE FAMILY EMPIRE 1&2
SOULLESS GOON 1,2&3
THE DIRTY SIDE OF MONEY 1,2&3
By Prince

FOR MY ENEMY'S SAKE
AMBITIONS OF A SLIDER
FRESH OFF DA PORCH
By IRA B.

BY THE TRUCKLOAD 1-4
TIPPIN' THE SCALES 1-3
BAD BITCHES WIT GUNZ 3
PROBLEM SOLVED 2
By Christopher "Diesel" Hornezes

DERRICK L. SUMMERS

Available Now

RESTRAINING ORDER 1 & 2
By **CA$H & Coffee**

LOVE KNOWS NO BOUNDARIES 1-3
By **Coffee**

RAISED AS A GOON I, II, III & IV
BRED BY THE SLUMS I, II, III
BLAST FOR ME I & II
ROTTEN TO THE CORE I II III
A BRONX TALE I, II, III
DUFFLE BAG CARTEL I II III IV V VI
HEARTLESS GOON I II III IV V
A SAVAGE DOPEBOY I II
DRUG LORDS I II III
CUTTHROAT MAFIA I II
KING OF THE TRENCHES
By **Ghost**

LAY IT DOWN I & II
LAST OF A DYING BREED I II
BLOOD STAINS OF A SHOTTA I & II III
By **Jamaica**

LOYAL TO THE GAME I II III
LIFE OF SIN I, II III
By **TJ & Jelissa**

IF LOVING HIM IS WRONG…I & II
LOVE ME EVEN WHEN IT HURTS I II III
By **Jelissa**

PUSH IT TO THE LIMIT
By **Bre' Hayes**

MONEY AND DEAD HOMIES

BLOODY COMMAS I & II
SKI MASK CARTEL I, II & III
KING OF NEW YORK I II, III IV V
RISE TO POWER I II III
COKE KINGS I II III IV V
BORN HEARTLESS I II III IV
KING OF THE TRAP I II
By **T.J. Edwards**

WHEN THE STREETS CLAP BACK I & II III
THE HEART OF A SAVAGE I II III IV
MONEY MAFIA I II
LOYAL TO THE SOIL I II III
By **Jibril Williams**

A DISTINGUISHED THUG STOLE MY HEART I II & III
LOVE SHOULDN'T HURT I II III IV
RENEGADE BOYS 1-4
PAID IN KARMA 1-3
SAVAGE STORMS 1-3
AN UNFORESEEN LOVE 1-3
BABY, I'M WINTERTIME COLD 1-3
A THUG'S STREET PRINCESS 1&2
By **Meesha**

A GANGSTER'S CODE 1-3
A GANGSTER'S SYN 1-3
THE SAVAGE LIFE 1-3
CHAINED TO THE STREETS 1-3
BLOOD ON THE MONEY 1-3
A GANGSTA'S PAIN 1-3
BEAUTIFUL LIES AND UGLY TRUTHS
CHURCH IN THESE STREETS
By **J-Blunt**

CUM FOR ME 1-8
An LDP Erotica Collaboration

257

DERRICK L. SUMMERS

BLOOD OF A BOSS 1-5
SHADOWS OF THE GAME
TRAP BASTARD
By **Askari**

THE STREETS BLEED MURDER 1-3
THE HEART OF A GANGSTA 1-3
By **Jerry Jackson**

WHEN A GOOD GIRL GOES BAD
By **Adrienne**

THE COST OF LOYALTY 1-3
By **Kweli**

BRIDE OF A HUSTLA 1-3
THE FETTI GIRLS 1-3
CORRUPTED BY A GANGSTA 1-4
BLINDED BY HIS LOVE
THE PRICE YOU PAY FOR LOVE 1-3
DOPE GIRL MAGIC 1-3
By **Destiny Skai**

A KINGPIN'S AMBITION
A KINGPIN'S AMBITION II
I MURDER FOR THE DOUGH
By **Ambitious**

TRUE SAVAGE 1-7
DOPE BOY MAGIC 1-3
MIDNIGHT CARTEL 1-3
CITY OF KINGZ 1&2
NIGHTMARE ON SILENT AVE
THE PLUG OF LIL MEXICO 1&2
CLASSIC CITY
By **Chris Green**

MONEY AND DEAD HOMIES

DERRICK L. SUMMERS

LOVE & CHASIN' PAPER
By **Qay Crockett**

TO DIE IN VAIN
SINS OF A HUSTLA
By **ASAD**

BROOKLYN HUSTLAZ
By **Boogsy Morina**

BROOKLYN ON LOCK 1 & 2
By **Sonovia**

GANGSTA CITY
By **Teddy Duke**

A DRUG KING AND HIS DIAMOND 1-3
A DOPEMAN'S RICHES
HER MAN, MINE'S TOO 1&2
CASH MONEY HO'S
THE WIFEY I USED TO BE 1&2
PRETTY GIRLS DO NASTY THINGS
By **Nicole Goosby**

LIPSTICK KILLAH 1-3
CRIME OF PASSION 1-3
FRIEND OR FOE 1-3
By **Mimi**

TRAPHOUSE KING 1-3
KINGPIN KILLAZ 1-3
STREET KINGS 1&2
PAID IN BLOOD 1&2
CARTEL KILLAZ 1-3
DOPE GODS 1&2
By **Hood Rich**

THE STREETS ARE CALLING
By **Duquie Wilson**

MONEY AND DEAD HOMIES

STEADY MOBBN' 1-3
THE STREETS STAINED MY SOUL 1-3
By **Marcellus Allen**

WHO SHOT YA 1-3
SON OF A DOPE FIEND 1-4
HEAVEN GOT A GHETTO 1&2
SKI MASK MONEY 1&2
By **Renta**

GORILLAZ IN THE BAY 1-4
TEARS OF A GANGSTA 1/&2
3X KRAZY 1&2
STRAIGHT BEAST MODE 1&2
By **DE'KARI**

TRIGGADALE 1-3
MURDA WAS THE CASE 1-3
By **Elijah R. Freeman**

SLAUGHTER GANG 1-3
RUTHLESS HEART 1-3
By **Willie Slaughter**

GOD BLESS THE TRAPPERS 1-3
THESE SCANDALOUS STREETS 1-3
FEAR MY GANGSTA 1-5
THESE STREETS DON'T LOVE NOBODY 1-2
BURY ME A G 1-5
A GANGSTA'S EMPIRE 1-4
THE DOPEMAN'S BODYGAURD 1&2
THE REALEST KILLAZ 1-3
THE LAST OF THE OGS 1-3
By **Tranay Adams**

MARRIED TO A BOSS 1-3
By **Destiny Skai & Chris Green**

DERRICK L. SUMMERS

KINGZ OF THE GAME 1-7
CRIME BOSS 1-4
By **Playa Ray**

FUK SHYT
By **Blakk Diamond**

DON'T F#CK WITH MY HEART 1&2
By **Linnea**

ADDICTED TO THE DRAMA 1-3
IN THE ARM OF HIS BOSS
By **Jamila**

LOYALTY AIN'T PROMISED 1&2
By **Keith Williams**

YAYO 1-4
A SHOOTER'S AMBITION 1&2
BRED IN THE GAME
By **S. Allen**

TRAP GOD 1-3
RICH $AVAGE 1-3
MONEY IN THE GRAVE 1-3
CARTEL MONEY 1&2
By **Martell Troublesome Bolden**

FOREVER GANGSTA 1&2
GLOCKS ON SATIN SHEETS 1&2
By **Adrian Dulan**

TOE TAGZ 1-4
LEVELS TO THIS SHYT 1&2
IT'S JUST ME AND YOU
By **Ah'Million**

MONEY AND DEAD HOMIES

KINGPIN DREAMS 1-3
RAN OFF ON DA PLUG
By **Paper Boi Rari**

THE STREETS MADE ME 1-3
By **Larry D. Wright**

CONFESSIONS OF A GANGSTA 1-4
CONFESSIONS OF A JACKBOY 1-3
CONFESSIONS OF A HITMAN
CONFESSIONS OF A DOPE BOY
By **Nicholas Lock**

I'M NOTHING WITHOUT HIS LOVE
SINS OF A THUG
TO THE THUG I LOVED BEFORE
A GANGSTA SAVED XMAS
IN A HUSTLER I TRUST
By **Monet Dragun**

QUIET MONEY 1-3
THUG LIFE 1-3
EXTENDED CLIP 1&2
A GANGSTA'S PARADISE
By **Trai'Quan**

CAUGHT UP IN THE LIFE 1-3
THE STREETS NEVER LET GO 1-3
By **Robert Baptiste**

NEW TO THE GAME 1-3
MONEY, MURDER & MEMORIES 1-3
By **Malik D. Rice**

CREAM 2-3
THE STREETS WILL TALK
By **Yolanda Moore**

DERRICK L. SUMMERS

THE STREETS WILL NEVER CLOSE 1-3
By **K'ajji**

LIFE OF A SAVAGE 1-4
A GANGSTA'S QUR'AN 1-4
MURDA SEASON 1-3
GANGLAND CARTEL 1-3
CHI'RAQ GANGSTAS 1-4
KILLERS ON ELM STREET 1-3
JACK BOYZ N DA BRONX 1-3
A DOPEBOY'S DREAM 1-3
JACK BOYS VS DOPE BOYS 1-3
COKE GIRLZ
COKE BOYS
SOSA GANG 1&2
BRONX SAVAGES
BODYMORE KINGPINS
BLOOD OF A GOON
By **Romell Tukes**

CONCRETE KILLA 1-3
VICIOUS LOYALTY 1-3
BLOODY MONEY BAGS
By **Kingpen**

THE ULTIMATE SACRIFICE 1-6
KHADIFI
IF YOU CROSS ME ONCE 1-3
ANGEL 1-4
IN THE BLINK OF AN EYE
By **Anthony Fields**

THE LIFE OF A HOOD STAR
By **Ca$h & Rashia Wilson**

NIGHTMARES OF A HUSTLA 1-3
BLOOD AND GAMES 1&2
By **King Dream**

MONEY AND DEAD HOMIES

GHOST MOB
By **Stilloan Robinson**

HARD AND RUTHLESS 1&2
MOB TOWN 251
THE BILLIONAIRE BENTLEYS 1-3
REAL G'S MOVE IN SILENCE
By **Von Diesel**

MOB TIES 1-7
SOUL OF A HUSTLER, HEART OF A KILLER 1-3
GORILLAZ IN THE TRENCHES
OOPS CRY TOO 1&2
THE DAUGHTER OF A CARTEL BOSS
By **SayNoMore**

BODYMORE MURDERLAND 1-3
THE BIRTH OF A GANGSTER 1-4
By **Delmont Player**

FOR THE LOVE OF A BOSS 1&2
By **C. D. Blue**

KILLA KOUNTY 1-5
TENDER
By **Khufu**

MOBBED UP 1-4
THE BRICK MAN 1-5
THE COCAINE PRINCESS 1-10
STEPPERS 1-3
SUPER GREMLIN 1-4
A GANGSTA'S SON
By **King Rio**

MONEY GAME 1&2
By **Smoove Dolla**

DERRICK L. SUMMERS

A GANGSTA'S KARMA 1-5
By **FLAME**

KING OF THE TRENCHES 1-3
By **GHOST & TRANAY ADAMS**

BAD BITCHES WIT GUNZ 1&2
PROBLEM SOLVED
By "Christopher Diesel" Hornezes

QUEEN OF THE ZOO 1&2
By **Black Migo**

GRIMEY WAYS 1-3
BETRAYAL OF A G
By **Ray Vinci**

XMAS WITH AN ATL SHOOTER
By **Ca$h & Destiny Skai**

KING KILLA 1&2
By **Vincent "Vitto" Holloway**

BETRAYAL OF A THUG 1&2
By **Fre$h**

COUNTDOWN OF A KILLA 1&2
SEX, MURDER AND GOD 1&2
GUNS DOWN, BOTTOMS UP 1&2
By Lo-Life

THE MURDER QUEENS 1-7
By **Michael Gallon**

FOR THE LOVE OF BLOOD 1-4
By **Jamel Mitchell**

MONEY AND DEAD HOMIES

HOOD CONSIGLIERE 1&2
NO TIME FOR ERROR
By **Keese**

PROTÉGÉ OF A LEGEND 1,2&3
LOVE IN THE TRENCHES 1&2
By **Corey Robinson**

THE PLUG'S RUTHLESS DAUGHTER 1&2
By **Tony Daniels**

BORN IN THE GRAVE 1-3
CRIME PAYS
By **Self Made Tay**

MOAN IN MY MOUTH
By **XTASY**

TORN BETWEEN A GANGSTER AND A GENTLEMAN
By **J-BLUNT & Miss Kim**

LOYALTY IS EVERYTHING 1-3
CITY OF SMOKE 1-3
By **Molotti**

HERE TODAY GONE TOMORROW 1&2
By **Fly Rock**

WOMEN LIE MEN LIE 1-4
FIFTY SHADES OF SNOW 1-3
STACK BEFORE YOU SPLURGE
GIRLS FALL LIKE DOMINOES
NAÏVE TO THE STREETS
By **ROY MILLIGAN**

PILLOW PRINCESS
By **S. Hawkins**

DERRICK L. SUMMERS

THE BUTTERFLY MAFIA 1-3
SALUTE MY SAVAGERY 1&2
By **Fumiya Payne**

THE LANE 1&2
By Ken-Ken Spence

THE PUSSY TRAP 1-5
By **Nene Capri**

DIRTY DNA
By **Blaque**

SANCTIFIED AND HORNY
by **XTASY**

BOOKS BY LDP'S CEO, CA$H

TRUST IN NO MAN
TRUST IN NO MAN 2
TRUST IN NO MAN 3
BONDED BY BLOOD
SHORTY GOT A THUG
THUGS CRY
THUGS CRY 2
THUGS CRY 3
TRUST NO BITCH
TRUST NO BITCH 2
TRUST NO BITCH 3
TIL MY CASKET DROPS
RESTRAINING ORDER
RESTRAINING ORDER 2
IN LOVE WITH A CONVICT
LIFE OF A HOOD STAR
XMAS WITH AN ATL SHOOTER